ttyl

ttfn

bff

The Infinite Moment of Us

Shine

Bliss

Rhymes with Witches

Luv Ya Bunches

Violet in Bloom

Oopsy Daisy

Awesome Blossom

Eleven

Twelve

Thirteen

Thirteen Plus One

Peace, Love, and Baby Ducks

Let It Snow: Three Holiday Romances
(with John Green and Maureen Johnson)

How to Be Bad (with E. Lockhart and Sarah Mylnowski)

LAUREN MYRACLE

l8r, g8r

AMULET BOOKS · NEW YORK

Library of Congress Cataloging-in-Publication Data
Myracle, Lauren, 1969–
L8r, g8r / Lauren Myracle. — [10th anniversary edition]
pages cm — (The Internet girls)
"Originally published in hardcover in 2007 by Amulet Books,
an imprint of ABRAMS."
Summary: Throughout their senior year in high school, Zoe, Maddie, and Angela continue to share "instant messages" with one another about their day-to-day experiences as they consider college, sex, the importance of prom, and the inevitable end of their inseparable trio.
ISBN 978-1-4197-1143-5 (pbk.)
[1. Instant messaging—Fiction. 2. Friendship—Fiction. 3. Interpersonal relations—Fiction. 4. High schools—Fiction. 5. Schools—Fiction.] I. Title. II. Title: Later, gator.
PZ7.M9955Laad 2014
[Fic]—dc23
2013038414

56515504
06/15

Printed and bound in U.S.A.
10 9 8 7 6 5 4 3 2 1

ABRAMS

THE ART OF BOOKS SINCE 1949

115 West 18th Street
New York, NY 10011
www.abramsbooks.com

For all the real live Zoes, Maddies,
and Angelas out there,
Never stop loving your buds!

zoegirl: maddie!!! i'm so excited, i can't sit still! i can't believe i'm going to see doug in 2 hrs!

mad maddie: i hear ya—even i'm kinda excited to c the guy. i wonder if he's changed?

zoegirl: do you *ever* check his instagram? he's gotten tanner. his hair is longer. he is even more handsome than he used to be, which seems impossible.

mad maddie: deeper changes. like, changes on the inside.

zoegirl: it's been SIX ENTIRE MONTHS. *6 months* of no doug!

zoegirl: aye-yai-yai—what if he doesn't like me anymore?

mad maddie: oh, please. doug is doug is doug, and no semester at sea is gonna change that.

mad maddie: anywayz, haven't you guys been skyping every single day?

zoegirl: that's true, but it's still different from being with someone in person.

zoegirl: what i liked even more than skyping—maybe— were the snail mail letters he sent. well, snail mail postcards, mainly, from all the different places they docked. sooo romantic.

mad maddie: speaking of romantic, what's doug gonna say when angela and i show up at the airport with you?

zoegirl: er . . . hi, maddie? hi, angela?

mad maddie: he's not gonna be pissed?

zoegirl: why would he be pissed?

mad maddie: that it's not just the 2 of you

zoegirl: course not. 1st of all, his parents are going to be there. and 2nd of all, i'm way too nervous to go by myself.

zoegirl:	i have to have my maddie and my angela—he knows that!
mad maddie:	how's he gonna feel, waltzing back to school in the middle of our senior yr? is that gonna be weird for him?
zoegirl:	PAST the middle of the year. i was *supposed* to have him back at the beginning of the semester.
mad maddie:	i'm still reeling from the unfairness of that, btw. let's pretend i was the lucky 1 who jaunted off to Sea the World. would the administrators let ME take an extra month off to travel with my parents? i don't think so.
zoegirl:	but you don't have straight As like doug—no offense.
mad maddie:	none taken. i'm proud of my Bs. 👍
zoegirl:	doug's mom called it "cultural enrichment." that's the excuse she gave the school. but i say he's seen enough of the world. now he needs to see ME!
mad maddie:	ah yes, now it's time for him to be enriched in OTHER ways, nudge-nudge, wink-wink.
zoegirl:	maddie!!!
zoegirl:	i'm just glad we're going to be together again. i mean, he had a great time, and i'm proud of him for doing it, but he's definitely ready to be home.
mad maddie:	god, and i am definitely ready to NOT.
mad maddie:	seriously, if i could graduate tomorrow, i would. i'd be like, hasta la vista, baby! g-bye, atlanta— hello, santa cruz!
zoegirl:	*if* you get in. which you will. i hate that you want to go so far away, though.
mad maddie:	blame angela. if we hadn't gone to california with her over the summer . . .
zoegirl:	too ironic. she escapes california to move back

to atlanta, and now all you wanna do is escape
atlanta and move to california.

mad maddie: **U.C.S.C., here i come. go, banana slugs!**

zoegirl: is that honestly their mascot?

mad maddie: **it honestly is their mascot. it's 1 of the many cool
things about them—their whole who-gives-a-
damn attitude about typical college stuff like rah-
rah football teams. that and the fact that they're
3,000 miles away, heh heh heh.**

zoegirl: oh, wow

zoegirl: maddie . . . i just realized something

mad maddie: **what?**

zoegirl: things really are changing, aren't they? we're
seniors, we're going to graduate in 3 months,
we're all going to go our separate ways . . .

mad maddie: **and this comes as a surprise?**

zoegirl: no . . . i just don't know if i'm ready

mad maddie: **i sure as hell am**

mad maddie: **repeat after me: change is good**

zoegirl: omg—no *way* did you just say that!

zoegirl: if angela were here, she'd be rolling on the
ground.

mad maddie: **pardon me, but all i said was that change is good.
why is that funny?**

zoegirl: oh, mads. aren't you the one who was outraged
when they switched brands of soap in the girls'
bathroom?

mad maddie: **the old kind was better! it smelled like lavender!**

zoegirl: and you have a fit if you can't start the day with
your pop-tart and dr pepper. i thought you were
going to stage a riot that day the drink machine
was out!

mad maddie: **i'm a growing girl. i need my caffeine.**

zoegirl: and every time facebook changes its layout,

	you swear you're going to shut down yr fb page forever
mad maddie:	your point?
zoegirl:	my point is that you *hate* change
mad maddie:	no i don't
zoegirl:	yeah, you do
zoegirl:	it's cute
mad maddie:	i thought we were talking about marching off into the big bad world, not what kind of soap comes out when you squirt the thingie in the bathroom. and all I was saying is that we can't stay in high school forever, even if we wanted to.
zoegirl:	i know that. but it still feels huge.
mad maddie:	anywayz, no reason to get worked up about it now. there'll be plenty of time for weeping and gnashing of the teeth before it's over.
zoegirl:	i already gnash my teeth—that's why i wear a mouth guard at nite. my dentist says it's the curse of being an overachiever.
mad maddie:	an overachiever? YOU?
zoegirl:	haha
zoegirl:	hey, can i tell you something stupid that's totally not worth dealing with, but at the same time i'm kind of disturbed by?
mad maddie:	shoot
zoegirl:	it has to do with jana. still wanna hear?
mad maddie:	oh god. not THE J-WORD.
zoegirl:	you and jana have a past. i'm just trying to be sensitive.
mad maddie:	you might have to excuse me while i retch, but other than that, go ahead.
zoegirl:	well, right before i left school today, i ran into terri. now, normally we wouldn't have even exchanged hellos, because of the fact she's

jana's best friend. but terri had been crying—
her eyes were red and her face was all puffy—
and i would have been a complete jerk to not say
anything.

mad maddie: **if i'd seen terri and she'd been crying, i wouldn't**
have said anything.

zoegirl: yes you would've

mad maddie: **and if the situation were reversed, i wouldn't**
want HER to say anything, either.

zoegirl: well, i am a good human, so i said, "um . . . terri?
you ok?" which made her burst into tears all over
again.

mad maddie: **c? that is why you should leave crying ppl alone.**

zoegirl: she was *horrified* to be falling apart like that
in front of me, i could tell. she kept saying, "i'm
fine, i'm fine," but she obviously wasn't. so i took
her to the girls' room and gave her a wet paper
towel to press against her eyes, and we ended up
sitting down below the sinks and talking.

mad maddie: **so what was wrong? or rather, what terrible and**
awful thing had jana done to her?

zoegirl: they'd gotten into a yelling match over terri's
hair, if you can believe it. you know how it's now
the same shade as jana's? jana had cussed terri
out for being a clone, and i guess she took it too
far and said some really nasty things.

mad maddie: **jana takes everything too far. she always has, but**
this year even more so.

mad maddie: **she should go thru life armed with an apology**
and a complimentary bag of peanuts.

zoegirl: well, i felt bad for terri, even tho she's not my
favorite person. i hate it when i fight with you or
angela.

mad maddie: **what r u talking about? we don't fight.**

zoegirl: so i said something like, "she shouldn't treat you that way," and terri said, "she treats *everybody* that way." i said she better stop or she won't have any friends left, and terri snorted. she was like, "poor little jana, alone in a corner. just her and her teddy bear." 🐻

mad maddie: HA

zoegirl: that's what *i* said. because it's such an oxymoron, the image of jana—mistress of death and destruction—clutching a teddy bear.

mad maddie: ooo, nice use of the word "oxymoron." i KNEW i should have taken that SAT prep course.

zoegirl: but terri goes, "for real, jana has this mangy old teddy bear that smells like spit. she takes it with her everywhere."

mad maddie: ???

mad maddie: i've never seen jana with a teddy bear

zoegirl: she leaves it in her car. that's what terri says. which is entirely possible. have you seen all the crap in the back of jana's station wagon?

mad maddie: it's a mobile junk heap. it's disgusting.

zoegirl: according to terri, jana's dad gave her the teddy bear when she was little, and she's unhealthily attached to it.

zoegirl: its name is Boo Boo Bear.

mad maddie: Boo Boo Bear???

mad maddie: omfg, i am loving this so much. Boo Boo Bear!

zoegirl: terri was like, "i can't believe i'm telling you— jana would *die*."

mad maddie: heh heh heh, jana whitaker is unhealthily attached to Boo Boo Bear. suddenly the world is a MUCH brighter place!!!

zoegirl: er . . . not necessarily. because 2 seconds later, jana herself stormed into the bathroom. "*there* you are," she says to terri, all fuming. "you're not even going to let me apologize?"

zoegirl: then she noticed me, and her jaw dropped. she was like, "what are YOU doing here?"

mad maddie: plz, it's a public bathroom. does she think it's her private office?

zoegirl: my heart got all poundy, because—as you know—i'm a wimp, although jana had already switched to ignoring me. she said to terri, "get up, we're leaving."

mad maddie: ok, that is the perfect example of the evilness of jana. she's bossy and she's mean.

zoegirl: but amazingly, terri didn't obey. she said, "you can't treat me like dirt and then expect me to be your slave."

zoegirl: "terri, get up," jana said, still very pointedly not looking at me. "we can talk about your 'issues' later."

mad maddie: oh god

zoegirl: so terri goes, "*my* issues? you're the one with issues! keep acting the way you're acting, and you won't have any friends left!"

mad maddie: which is exactly what YOU said!

zoegirl: i know! and for some reason that made me get all stupidly brave, and under my breath i said, "no one but Boo Boo Bear."

mad maddie: holy shit! u da BOMB!

zoegirl: i shouldn't have, though! it was totally unlike me!

mad maddie: that's what's so great!

mad maddie: did jana hear?

zoegirl: she whipped her head toward me and was like, "WHAT did you say?" and terri goes, "she SAID no one but Boo Boo Bear."

mad maddie: gee, thx, terri

zoegirl:	jana was speechless. i've never in my life seen her speechless, but for that single moment she was. big splotches of color bloomed on her cheeks. it was freaky.
mad maddie:	cuz she IS a freak
zoegirl:	then she pulled herself together and said to me, "you've got nerve, sticking your nose up. not all of us live in a perfect plastic bubble, you know."
mad maddie:	exsqueeze me? what is that supposed to mean?!
zoegirl:	she was trying to make me feel like a spoiled little baby, in comparison to her, the jaded and worldly jana.
mad maddie:	who has a teddy bear.
zoegirl:	her tone said 1 thing—see how cool and detached i am? i couldn't care less that you know about my stupid bear—but her eyes said something else entirely. she looked like she wanted to kill me. i'm not kidding.
mad maddie:	well, duh. if anyone had to be there for that lovely moment, i'm sure you were the last person she'd pick. you or me or angela, that is.
zoegirl:	that thought crossed my mind, but i tried to tell myself, "no, you're being silly."
mad maddie:	except yr not. we have what jana doesn't have—actual true friends who lift each other up instead of tear each other down—and it's like a knife inside her heart.
mad maddie:	think of it like this: jana's a dragon (SO not a stretch) and terri exposed her secret piece of weakness. so now jana's screwed twice: 1st cuz u know about Boo Boo Bear, and 2nd cuz u know how easily terri would betray her.
zoegirl:	jana the dragon. i just hope she doesn't flame me.
mad maddie:	if she does, she'll have ME to deal with.

mad maddie: now isn't it time to pick up your long-lost boyfriend? it's 5:15.

zoegirl: it is? EEEEEK! IT IS!!!!!

zoegirl: go pick up angela from her aunt's house and then swing by here. i'll be the 1 gnawing my fingernails to the quick!

mad maddie: i'm heading out the door. l8r, g8r!

Tues, Feb 7, 5:17 PM E.S.T.

SnowAngel: mads, i'm not going to the airport after all, k?

mad maddie: angela! i was JUST about to come get you, and now i'm staring at you dumbfounded.

mad maddie: of course yr coming. zoe's expecting you!

SnowAngel: but c, doug's HER boyfriend, right? why does she need us to go with her to the airport?

mad maddie: uh, cuz she's zoe?

mad maddie: and cuz she hasn't seen the guy for a whole semester. more, if you add the time we spent in california over summer break. we got back, and she saw him for . . . what? a grand total of 1 week before he took off in his sailor suit to "Sea the World"?

SnowAngel: r we doing that again? making fun of the name?

mad maddie: yes, cuz it demands to be made fun of!

mad maddie: seriously, who goes to "Sea the World" during the 1st semester of their senior yr? senior yr is a time for madcap partying, not for sailing about the globe and stuffing yourself with culture.

SnowAngel: *coughs* on a party boat under jet blue skies, surrounded by girls in bikinis . . .

mad maddie: like i said. what was he thinking?

SnowAngel: i watched an episode of "girls" last nite where there was a guy from the navy, and he was hot in his sailor suit.

mad maddie: i don't think doug would be hot in a sailor suit.

SnowAngel:	well . . . no
SnowAngel:	but hot or not, i'm not going to be there to see him. it's not that i don't WANT to, it's just that
mad maddie:	yesssssssss?
SnowAngel:	i have a flesh-eating virus. i DO!
SnowAngel:	i have a virus and it is attacking my nose and i am DISFIGURED. 😡 don't you dare laff!
mad maddie:	angela, i saw you at school and you were fine
SnowAngel:	but it was beginning. i could feel it
mad maddie:	uh huh. and how did you suddenly get this flesh-eating virus?
mad maddie:	does it by any chance have to do with the fact that we're talking about doug?
SnowAngel:	what? NO!
mad maddie:	r you sure? cuz i know you, angela. don't think i've forgotten your whole "doug will be my starter husband" spiel.
SnowAngel:	maddie, that was LAST YEAR, way before doug and zoe even started dating.
SnowAngel:	anyway, did you happen to forget the one small fact that i'm going out with logan now???
mad maddie:	ohhhh, right. logan.
SnowAngel:	*puts hands on hips* why do you say it that way?
mad maddie:	what way?
SnowAngel:	u know what way
mad maddie:	and YOU know why. so drop it.
mad maddie:	i think it's interesting that you develop a flesh-eating virus on the very day yr supposed to c doug, that's all.
SnowAngel:	you think i'm making it up? i'm not making it up, maddie. if you insist on being technical, it's a staph infection. it's all nasty under my nose—and even up INSIDE my nose so that it looks very booger-ish and vile—and i'm NOT going out in public like this!

mad maddie:	**wait a sec—i'm having a flashback**
mad maddie:	**didn't this same staph infection thing happen last year?**
SnowAngel:	yes *sniff, sniff*
SnowAngel:	it happens every year when i get a bad cold, and now i'll have to go on antibiotics and it'll take a week to clear up and until then everyone will think i've got a huge booger oozing out of my right nostril. they'll call me booger girl! that's what it'll say in the senior section of the yearbook. angela silver: booger girl!
mad maddie:	**god, yr vain**
SnowAngel:	yr calling me VAIN?!!! *pops a blood vessel*
SnowAngel:	of COURSE i'm vain. i've been vain my entire life!
mad maddie:	**so suck it up and come with us to the airport!**
SnowAngel:	yr not grasping the full disgusting-ness of this. it's an OPEN SORE under my nostril. it's bubbly and slimy with neosporin, and it's growing even as we speak.
SnowAngel:	it PULSES, maddie
mad maddie:	**what is it with you and things that pulse?**
SnowAngel:	???
mad maddie:	**oh, angela, don't even! 1) your staph infection pulses. 2) you can't bear to touch your wrist cuz the vein there pulses. and 3), dear god, we certainly can't forget your neck.**
mad maddie:	**"woe is me. i can feel my blood pulsing thru my pillow! it jams up wrong against my carotid artery!"**
SnowAngel:	WELL IT DOES
mad maddie:	**then get a new one. you've been complaining about it for frickin ever!**
SnowAngel:	*adopts a wounded expression* i have had a series of unfortunate pillows, thank you very much. aunt sadie is a sweetie, but her pillows r crap. that's the only bad thing about living with her.

mad maddie: that and the fact that she burns every single thing she tries to cook.

SnowAngel: well, true

mad maddie: and she's a shopaholic.

SnowAngel: TINY shopaholic. small insignificant problem.

mad maddie: yr parents have no idea what they've gotten you into, do they?

SnowAngel: my parents think that aunt sadie is taking very good care of me, which she is!

SnowAngel: anyway, shouldn't you be driving to the airport right now?

mad maddie: yeah, guess i better go. u really don't wanna come?

SnowAngel: it's not that i DON'T—it's that i CAN'T.

mad maddie: all right. but remind me to tell you about the latest jana drama, involving an ill-fated stuffed animal named Boo Boo Bear.

SnowAngel: Boo Boo Bear? oh no, plz tell me jana didn't steal some poor kid's teddy bear!

mad maddie: jana didn't steal Boo Boo Bear. she OWNS Boo Boo Bear.

SnowAngel: what??? explain!

mad maddie: sorry, no time

SnowAngel: maddie! you CANNOT throw that out there and leave me hanging!

mad maddie: call me, babe. gotta run!

Tues, Feb 7, 6:11 PM E.S.T.

mad maddie: have u ever noticed how much airports are like shopping malls? i cld buy noise reducing headphones! caramel apples! an i 🖤 atlanta shirt with OR without babydoll sleeves!

SnowAngel: babydoll sleeves, for sure

mad maddie: yeah, that's gonna happen

mad maddie: also, so many peeps with signs that say things like, "welcome back, troops!" it's odd, but sweet. i asked a guard if today was some special day for the military, and he said no, that EVERY SINGLE DAY ppl come to the waiting area to support the armed forces. it made me a little teary.

SnowAngel: you? really???

mad maddie: not cuz i believe in the war. i'm a lover, not a fighter! but there's something slightly amazing about all this outpouring of support.

SnowAngel: where's zo?

mad maddie: angling for the closest spot she can get to the place where passengers come out of security. she looks like she's going to piddle her pants.

SnowAngel: aw, cute. what a warm welcome that wld be. a "warm" welcome??? get it???

mad maddie: hilarity, hilarity. hey-hey, new group of peeps coming off escalator. bye!

Tues, Feb 7, 11:01 PM E.S.T.

zoegirl: oh, angela, i am so in love!

SnowAngel: hey, zo. sorry about not making it to the airport.

zoegirl: that's ok. i mean, i'm sorry 2, but no big deal.

zoegirl: doug says "hi," btw

SnowAngel: aw, "hi" to him 2

SnowAngel: so did you fall into a passionate embrace the instant you saw him?

zoegirl: well, his parents were there, so more like a really big hug. but omg, it felt *amazing*! it was like my whole body just opened up against his. like, ahhhhhh, this is what i've been missing.

zoegirl: his arms were so strong, and he smelled so good, and he held me for what seemed like forever.

SnowAngel: sounds wonderful 🖤

zoegirl: i couldn't keep my hands off him. seriously, it

was like an addiction. i can totally see where that expression came from, that absence makes the heart grow fonder.

SnowAngel: huh, maybe i should i try that with logan. whaddaya think—should i send him off to SEA the world?

zoegirl: and on the way home, we *did* get to . . . you know. be more physical. his parents had a driver waiting for them in a limo, so for the car ride back it was just me and doug and maddie.

SnowAngel: doug didn't wanna take the limo?

zoegirl: no way! he wanted to be with me!

zoegirl: mainly we just snuggled, since maddie was in the front seat. but it was pure bliss.

SnowAngel: "pure bliss"? wowzers.

zoegirl: you know what i mean, cuz you have that with logan.

zoegirl: hey, let's go on a double date this weekend! you and me and doug and logan!

SnowAngel: uh . . . sure. i mean, lemme check with logan, but that would be fun.

zoegirl: not on friday, cuz on friday i want doug all to myself. but how about saturday? it could be a pre-valentine's thing, since valentine's day is the following tuesday.

SnowAngel: okey-doke—IF my nose is back to normal.

zoegirl: angela, logan won't care. he worships the ground you walk on . . . which is good, because otherwise i might worry that you'd steal doug away. (jk! i'm TOTALLY just kidding!)

SnowAngel: zoe! it makes me feel bad that you would even say that.

zoegirl: i'm sorry, i guess i'm just thinking about last year.

SnowAngel: well, don't. god.

zoegirl: but i know you would never do that. we're in a totally different situation now. we're both so lucky!

SnowAngel:	not to bring you down or anything . . . but are you doing all right with the whole jana weirdness? maddie finally gave me the complete story—sounds icky
zoegirl:	it was. i told doug about it, but he didn't understand why it creeped me out. so i explained jana's whole history with us, and turns out he didn't remember *any* of what happened in 10th grade. doesn't that blow your mind?
SnowAngel:	u think everyone should remember just cuz we do?
zoegirl:	well, yeah!
SnowAngel:	me 2 😊
zoegirl:	i mean, jana emailed that picture of mads to the whole entire school. you'd think doug would remember a topless photo!
SnowAngel:	maybe he never saw it
zoegirl:	everyone saw it. didn't they?
SnowAngel:	well, doug doesn't travel in the same circles as "everyone." that's part of his charm.
zoegirl:	yr right. and actually, that makes me happy. he does not need an image of a topless anybody in his mind.
zoegirl:	but anyway, i told him that from sophomore year on, jana's been nothing but trouble for all 3 of us. how on the one hand that made it hugely satisfying to see terri take her on, but on the other hand it gave me a chill. cuz now jana associates me with her moment of shame . . . and with jana you never know where that's gonna lead.
SnowAngel:	pissed and unstable—not a good combination. (plus you know her secret about Boo Boo Bear, hee hee)
zoegirl:	but in a way talking to doug about it was good, because he didn't see what the big deal was even

after i explained. it made me be like, "ok, time to chill. you have better things to do than worry about jana." i have doug back, and that makes everything ok.

zoegirl: g-nite, angela! I'M SO IN LOVE!!!!

Wed, Feb 8, 10:02 AM E.S.T.

mad maddie: YO! why aren't you at school, missy?! you didn't stay home cuz of your nose, did you?

SnowAngel: hey now, how shallow do you think i am?!

mad maddie: angela . . .

SnowAngel: well . . . yes. yes i did. you wld have 2 if you looked like me!

mad maddie: yr missing Senior Pet Day! how can you miss Senior Pet Day? yr the prez of the planning committee that came up with this swill!

SnowAngel: swill! the senior planning committee comes up with delightful activities to celebrate senior-ness. it does not come up with SWILL.

mad maddie: ted aronson brought a pig. he dressed him in tighty-whities.

SnowAngel: did you bring chumley the psycho kitty?

mad maddie: yeppers, on loan from my dear bro mark. he piddled on mr. bradley's carpet.

SnowAngel: mark?

mad maddie: good one. no, chumley.

SnowAngel: i'm so sorry i missed it

mad maddie: you should be. i can't believe your aunt sadie let you stay home cuz you think you LOOK bad. here i am in the fluorescently lit media center with chumley the psycho kitty digging gashes into my thighs, while yr languishing about eating bon bons and feeling sorry for yourself.

SnowAngel: the blister is at its peak of foulness, maddie. it is a pustule of terror.

mad maddie: ha. "The Pustule of Terror," coming soon to theaters everywhere.

mad maddie: which actress should we get to play you?

SnowAngel: ooo, excellent question. but if we're gonna make a movie, we have to make it of all 3 of us. and we're not calling it "The Pustule of Terror." we'll call it . . . hmm. "The Winsome Threesome: Senior Year." how 'bout that?

mad maddie: very nice. and now: the cast?

SnowAngel: i know who i want for me: leighton meester

mad maddie: dude, yr so not leighton meester. she is icy cool, and you are lovely and warm.

SnowAngel: *preens happily* i am?

mad maddie: how about taylor swift?

SnowAngel: hahahaha. i wld LOVE to be played by tay-tay, but her hair's the wrong color.

mad maddie: so she'll dye it a lovely light brown

mad maddie: or . . . i know! reese witherspoon!

SnowAngel: 2 old. i luv reese, but i don't wanna be played by an oldhead.

mad maddie: i've got it. hayden panettiere, only once again with a minor dye job

SnowAngel: ooo, i like hayden panettierre! she's approachable, not snotty, and she cares about clothes, but not in a show-off-y way. i say yes to hayden! 👍

mad maddie: what about me?

SnowAngel: oh, yr easy. mary-kate olsen, cuz yr so shy and retiring.

mad maddie: ha ha

SnowAngel: let's c . . . for real?

SnowAngel: we need someone who's beautiful, but not ladylike.

mad maddie: definitely not ladylike

SnowAngel:	someone who wears sweats instead of tiny tees. who's not afraid to chug a beer or tell a dirty joke. someone you'd want to party with.
SnowAngel:	i know! jennifer lawrence!
mad maddie:	**oh yeah, right!**
SnowAngel:	i'm serious! jennifer lawrence in one of her blondie phases. she's tough and beautiful, just like you.
mad maddie:	**i wish, but thx for the thought**
mad maddie:	**hold on—ow!**
mad maddie:	**sorry, chumley was doing some nipping.**
SnowAngel:	what about zo? i'd say katie holmes, except that her having a kid and being divorced kinda throws a wrench into that. katie's perfect in terms of the sweet-shy-smart category, tho.
mad maddie:	**plus the dark eyes and dark hair, especially now that zoe's grown it out. although personally i liked zoe's hair better when it was chin length.**
SnowAngel:	really? i like it long. now she can do french-twist-y things, very elegant.
mad maddie:	**but katie falls into the oldhead category too, so i'm axing katie.**
SnowAngel:	how about kristen stewart? KIDDING!
mad maddie:	**oh barf. the hair? sure. but *nothing* else, and certainly not that pouty-eyeliner thing she has going on.**
SnowAngel:	oh! ellen page! ellen page!
SnowAngel:	or wait, that girl from City of Bones, remember?
mad maddie:	**ellen's good, but she's a bit snarky for zoe. she'd have to lose the 'tude. the other actress you're thinking of is . . . wait a sec . . . lily collins.**
SnowAngel:	yeah! her!
mad maddie:	**how about this: we'll offer the job to ellen and lily both, and whoever accepts 1st gets the role.**
SnowAngel:	deal 👍

SnowAngel: who should we get for the role of snarky evil dragon lady?

mad maddie: otherwise known as jana?

mad maddie: it's our movie. she's not invited

SnowAngel: good point

mad maddie: altho i DO have a new chapter in the dragon tales. zoe and i were chatting by our cars this morning, and jana pulled up next to us in her station wagon. i took a sneaky-peek for Boo Boo Bear, but there was waaaaay too much crap. mcdonald's bags and coke cans and that ratty army blanket she keeps handy for who knows what.

SnowAngel: her skanky interludes?

mad maddie: probably—with Boo Boo Bear looking on!

SnowAngel: it's weird how a girl who cares so much about her appearance can be such a slob when it comes to her car.

mad maddie: i know

SnowAngel: if i had a car, i'd treat it right.

mad maddie: you could hide a horse in jana's backseat and she'd never know.

SnowAngel: did she say anything when she saw you guys?

mad maddie: she climbed out of her car and gave us an absolute death look, and zoe, being totally un-subtle, elbowed me in the ribs and said, "see? see? i told you!"

SnowAngel: what'd you do?

mad maddie: i burst out laffing—i couldn't help it.

mad maddie: jana was THIS close to marching over and scorching us with her fire-breath, i'm not kidding.

SnowAngel: you just draw ppl to you, don't you? yr so sweet and cuddly. 💣

mad maddie: why yes, i am

mad maddie: wanna know who i've drawn to me who i very

much wish was UN-drawn to me? and i'm not talking about jana. i'm talking about a certain someone who latched onto YOU when you lived in el cerrito last year, and who now, apparently, has latched onto ME.

SnowAngel: uh oh *chortles into hands*

SnowAngel: did you get another email from glendy?

mad maddie: glendy is YOUR nutcase, not MINE. why is she sending me her stupid freakin chain letters???

SnowAngel: why do you keep reading them?

mad maddie: you sure are glib for someone who's experienced glendy-love firsthand. she STALKED you, angela. and now she's stalking me!

SnowAngel: oh, muffin, you don't know what stalking is. has she bombarded you with care bears? noooo. has she invited you to dolphin-themed sleepovers? noooo. if she weren't the daughter of my dad's boss, i would have throttled her long ago. but luckily for glendy, she's zillions of miles away in california, so i deal with her by ignoring her—which is what you should do, you freak.

mad maddie: but why why why is she sending emails to someone she doesn't know?

SnowAngel: she must have gotten your addy from some group email i once sent, i dunno.

SnowAngel: she collects ppl like butterfly collectors collect butterflies.

mad maddie: i am not glendy's butterfly!

SnowAngel: if you go to her facebook page, you'll c she lists over 4,000 friends. now c'mon. does anyone other than famous ppl really have 4,000 friends?

mad maddie: the email i got from her today was titled "This Is Beautiful . . . And You Will Cry!" however, it was NOT beautiful, and i did NOT cry. it was about a made-up person who survived a hurricane or a tsunami or something, and there was a link to a fund where we cld send money. it makes me so mad that ppl try to exploit disasters real live ppl really do go thru.

SnowAngel: why don't you just block her messages?

mad maddie: cuz then i couldn't complain about them. duh.

mad maddie: at the end of the terrible disaster email, it said "let's see satan stop this one," followed by instructions to send it to 5 more ppl in 60 seconds, blah blah blah.

SnowAngel: of course glendy probably sent it to 60 more ppl in 5 seconds . . . make that 2,000 more ppl . . .

mad maddie: ack, g2g. chumley is hissing at pete mazer's iguana, and Peaches the Friendly Librarian is trotting over to break up the fray.

SnowAngel: good ol' peaches. give her a squeeze for me.

mad maddie: fo shizzle!

Thu, Feb 9, 4:15 PM E.S.T.

zoegirl: hurray for angela! you returned to school—AND YOU SURVIVED!

SnowAngel: barely. ppl stared, zo. it was one of those deals where everyone's eyes wld drift down to my nose then jerk back up, like, "oh, don't mind me. sure didn't notice that horrible blot on your face—nope, sure didn't!"

zoegirl: sweetie, your nose is so much less horrible than you think it is. i mentioned it to doug, and he said he wouldn't have even noticed if i hadn't pointed it out.

SnowAngel: gee, thx

SnowAngel: speaking of doug, what was up with his whole cheese rant?

zoegirl: what was up with you giving him such a hard time about it? everyone in the cafeteria was swiveling their heads to see what was going on. they were like, "ok, what's HER deal?"

SnowAngel: oh please. exaggerate much?

SnowAngel: he sounded so pretentious, that's all.

zoegirl: well i guess they have better cheese in other parts of the world, because the cheeses there aren't pasteurized or something.

SnowAngel: uh huh, whatevs. i LIKE american cheese.

zoegirl: so do i

SnowAngel: and not just cheese made in america, but actual orange squares of american cheese. it's the only kind for grilled cheese sandwiches.

zoegirl: all i'm saying is that *yr* the 1 who made a big deal out of it, not doug. and i guess it seemed a little . . . over the top. even kristin was like, "does it not bother you that angela spent the whole lunch period monopolizing your boyfriend? she talked to him more than you did!"

SnowAngel: omg, that is so not true! i can't believe kristin said that!

zoegirl: it wasn't in a malicious way. it was just an observation.

SnowAngel: friends aren't supposed to make "observations" like that.

zoegirl: ok, time out. forget i mentioned it, all right?

SnowAngel: no, it's not all right. what she said was completely rude!

zoegirl: we're changing subjects now

SnowAngel: says who?

zoegirl: i passed jana in the hall, and if i'm not mistaken, she actually *smiled* at me. isn't that bizarre? i keep expecting to find pig's blood on my locker or something, as payback for the whole Boo Boo Bear thing, and instead she smiles at me?

SnowAngel: no comment. i'm still annoyed with kristin.

zoegirl:	is it possible that what terri said to her—compliments of me—actually made her change her evil ways?
SnowAngel:	no. a spade is a spade is a spade—which AGAIN is why i'm surprised that kristin would act so uncool, cuz until now i didn't think she WAS a spade.
zoegirl:	okaaaay, time to change the subject
zoegirl:	will you go to planned parenthood with me? i've called and made an appointment for tomorrow afternoon.
SnowAngel:	whoa *jerks back in shock* didn't see that one coming!
zoegirl:	it's just that i'm pretty sure doug and i are gonna have sex, and i'm pretty sure it's gonna be sooner rather than later. i feel bad that i've made him wait this long!
SnowAngel:	he's been AT SEA, zoe. not a whole lot you could do from across the ocean.
zoegirl:	and when we do, i don't wanna be unprepared. i told the lady at planned parenthood that i wanna go on the pill, and she said i have to come in and talk to a counselor.
SnowAngel:	why the pill? why not condoms?
zoegirl:	well, because doug's a virgin just like i am, so disease-wise, we're both safe. i've thought about it, and the pill's the right choice for me.
SnowAngel:	you could do the patch, u know. that's what my aunt sadie uses.
zoegirl:	have you seen it?
SnowAngel:	it's just this brown plastic-y thing. it looks like a band-aid.
zoegirl:	i'm gonna go with the pill.
zoegirl:	will you come with me?
SnowAngel:	of course

SnowAngel:	does doug know?
zoegirl:	no, i'm going to surprise him
zoegirl:	hey! you should go on the pill too, for when you and logan decide to go for it!
SnowAngel:	i don't think so
zoegirl:	why not? don't you want to?
SnowAngel:	of course i do, just . . . there's no need to rush things. sometimes the wait makes it all the better.
zoegirl:	you're right, you're right, i don't mean to pressure you. i guess i'm just so happy that i'm in love, and i want you and logan to be that happy 2. i mean, you already are, of course. you know what i'm saying.
zoegirl:	if only maddie would find someone!
SnowAngel:	is she coming to planned parenthood with us?
zoegirl:	no, she promised to help her brother move out of their parents' house. can you believe mark and his girlfriend are finally getting a place of their own?
SnowAngel:	it's taken long enuff
SnowAngel:	how's pelt-woman doing, anyway? hairy as ever?
zoegirl:	hairy as ever, or so i assume. maddie still doesn't call her by her real name, if that tells you anything.
SnowAngel:	do we even know her real name?
zoegirl:	i don't remember. do you?
zoegirl:	omg, how horrible!
SnowAngel:	well, she probably doesn't know our names either. we're just "maddie's little friends."
zoegirl:	maddie's little friends who are off to planned parenthood . . .
SnowAngel:	ppl have no idea, do they? that we're growing up. 😨
zoegirl:	but *we* know . . . and one of these days they'll figure it out.
SnowAngel:	just hopefully not until after graduation. *wink, wink*

mad maddie: there is nothing—nothing, i tell you—worse than itchy toes.

SnowAngel: except for itchy palms. HATE itchy palms.

mad maddie: toes r worse. the itch is on the knuckle part, and it's driving me nuts.

mad maddie: but i actually didn't text to tell you that. i texted to tell you about vincent. i went to his house today and found him LOOKING AT PORN ON THE INTERNET!

SnowAngel: ewww!

mad maddie: i strolled into his room and there it was, up on the screen. i was like, DEAR JESUS, SAVE THIS BOY!

SnowAngel: what is it with guys and porn on the internet? do ALL guys like porn from the internet?

mad maddie: hmm. you want the true answer, or the angela-friendly answer?

SnowAngel: you don't think logan looks at porn, do you?

mad maddie: no, no, no. of course not.

SnowAngel: that's the angela-friendly answer, isn't it?

SnowAngel: oh, nvm

SnowAngel: my new friend andre doesn't look at porn on the internet, i know he doesn't.

mad maddie: what, cuz he's gay you think that? poor innocent angela.

mad maddie: and you don't have to say "my new friend." i go to school with andre too.

SnowAngel: yeah, yeah, yeah, but i'm SURE he doesn't look at porn. at least not the kind that vincent looks at.

mad maddie: well, with vincent, it's straight-up girl porn, and it's just who he is. i'm like, "ya gotta love him," u know?

SnowAngel: "ya gotta love him"??? maddie, PLEASE tell me yr not doing what i think yr doing!

mad maddie:	**which would be . . . ?**
SnowAngel:	crushing on vincent! falling for the bad boy!
mad maddie:	**whoa—me, falling for VINCENT?!**
SnowAngel:	i personally can't believe you're even friends with him, given that he's so tight with jana. how do you get your head around that?
mad maddie:	**i don't. don't know what the guy sees in her.**
SnowAngel:	have you asked him?
mad maddie:	**he says she's fun to party with. is that a guy response or what?**
mad maddie:	**anywayz, why the inquistion? you have andre, who's your "new friend." i have vincent, my spanish class friend. who entertains me.**
SnowAngel:	and makes you hot.
mad maddie:	**give me a break. that is not true, angela! and not that it's any of your beeswax, but he's got a thing for lila.**
SnowAngel:	uh, hate to say it, but it's not like you've let that stop you before. chive was totally dating whitney when you guys did your little fuck-buddy thing.
mad maddie:	**i am so not gonna respond to that. ancient history, a.**
mad maddie:	**and "fuck buddy" is hardly the term, since i never even got naked with the guy.**
SnowAngel:	next thing you know, it'll be YOU jaunting off to planned parenthood, and i'll be alone in the corner wearing black, a virgin forever.
mad maddie:	**save the drama for yo mama. vincent and i are just buds.**
SnowAngel:	u could look at porn together. and eat popcorn.
mad maddie:	**and as for being a virgin forever, you're way more likely to leave the V-club than I am—that is if things with logan are as good as you say.**
SnowAngel:	shuddup. when and if logan and i have sex is

mad maddie:	**yessss?**
SnowAngel:	hold on—mary kate just texted. LOTS of !!!!s.
mad maddie:	**dum di dum, dum di dum**
mad maddie:	**i'm practicing my typing . . . abcdefg**
mad maddie:	**STILL practicing my typing . . . hijklmnop**
SnowAngel:	ok, now THAT was weird
mad maddie:	**what?**
SnowAngel:	maddie, tell me the truth. is something up with zoe? has she been saying things about me to anyone?
mad maddie:	**what are you talking about?**
SnowAngel:	according to mary kate, paige said zoe thinks i was FLIRTING with doug at lunch.
SnowAngel:	*holds out hands in bewilderment* was i flirting with doug at lunch?
mad maddie:	**angela, you flirt with every 2-legged male on the planet.**
SnowAngel:	but it doesn't MEAN anything. zoe knows that.
SnowAngel:	do you think she seriously has a problem with me talking to doug?
mad maddie:	**yes, she probably thinks yer trying to STEAL HER MAN**
SnowAngel:	that's ridiculous!
SnowAngel:	omg, i'm gonna txt her and see what's going on.
mad maddie:	**angela, i was teasing!**
mad maddie:	**angela?**
mad maddie:	**BUT MY TOES R STILL ITCHING!**

Thu, Feb 9, 9:53 PM E.S.T.

SnowAngel:	zo, did u talk to paige jensen at any point today?
zoegirl:	i sat in front of her in AP English, but i wouldn't say we talked. why?
SnowAngel:	well, did u say anything to anybody that could have been passed on to paige? like to kristin, maybe?
zoegirl:	could you be a little more specific?

SnowAngel:	ok, this is stupid, but i'm just gonna say it. i know you think i was hogging doug's attention today, but do you honestly think i was FLIRTING with him?
SnowAngel:	cuz that was a LONG time ago when i somewhat (sorta) threw myself at him, and anyway i would never flirt with him cuz he's going out with YOU, which i would hope you would know!
zoegirl:	what? i *do* know that. when did i say you were flirting with him?!
SnowAngel:	and the more i think about it, the more it makes me mad. i don't wanna go around worrying about every last thing i say or do around him, so if you have a problem with the way i'm acting, would you plz just tell me instead of talking about me behind my back?
zoegirl:	angela. STOP.
zoegirl:	did paige say i was talking about you behind your back?
SnowAngel:	mary kate overheard paige talking to some junior, and paige said that you said i was embarrassing myself with doug, and that i needed to keep my hormones to myself!
zoegirl:	???
zoegirl:	i never said ANY of that!
SnowAngel:	r u sure?
zoegirl:	angela, i just 6 hours ago asked you as my dear friend to go to planned parenthood with me so that one day doug and i can have sex. would i do that if i thought you were flirting with him?
SnowAngel:	well, what about kristin? after all, she already told you what a harlot i am!
zoegirl:	kristin made *one comment* about how much you talked to him. i shouldn't have even told you.

SnowAngel:	what else aren't you telling me?
zoegirl:	nothing!
zoegirl:	*do* you still have a thing for him?
SnowAngel:	NO!
SnowAngel:	but if you didn't say any of the things paige says you did . . .
SnowAngel:	i'm confused. why would paige say you did?
zoegirl:	i have no idea. call her and ask.
SnowAngel:	yeah right. i've never even had a class with her. i'm gonna call her up and be like, "oh, btw, why were u talking trash about me?"
zoegirl:	then call mary kate and ask *her*. or call kristin. somebody is obviously mixed up.
zoegirl:	seriously, angela, i'm a little hurt you would think that of me!
SnowAngel:	well I'M a little hurt YOU would think that of ME!
zoegirl:	but i didn't! i *don't*!!!
zoegirl:	listen, i think we better end this convo, ok?!
SnowAngel:	zoe, wait!
zoegirl:	why, so you can yell at me some more?
SnowAngel:	agh. i'm SORRY. i'm sorry, i'm sorry, i'm sorry!
SnowAngel:	zo?
zoegirl:	i'm here. i just don't know where this even came from.
SnowAngel:	mary kate thought i should know, that's all.
zoegirl:	except there's nothing TO know. you're getting worked up over nothing.
zoegirl:	remember last semester when you made brownies to cheer me up, after my mom got mad at me for missing the early decision deadline for princeton? only i didn't *know* that's why you'd made them, and i didn't eat any, and you got really pissed?

SnowAngel:	i used aunt sadie's french chocolate. they were the most delicious brownies ever.
zoegirl:	you told me to tell you the next time you overreacted about something. well, here i am telling you.
SnowAngel:	ok, ok, ok
zoegirl:	you need to have faith in me. i love you, and i would never talk about you behind your back. all right?
SnowAngel:	except u did—with kristin
zoegirl:	ANGELA!
SnowAngel:	*baby deep breath. mama deep breath. big daddy deep breath*
zoegirl:	um . . . is this some new kind of therapy?
SnowAngel:	yes, i learned it from aunt sadie, who got it from 1 of her friends who teaches pre-school.
zoegirl:	and did it work? do you maybe want to tell me that you love me too?
SnowAngel:	of COURSE i do. and i'm sorry for freaking. i am.
SnowAngel:	*blinks humbly at friend* are we still on for tomorrow?
zoegirl:	we better be!

Thu, Feb 9, 10:20 PM E.S.T.

SnowAngel:	hey mads. zoe denied it all, but i called mary kate and she's SURE that's what she heard.
SnowAngel:	u don't think zoe's lying, do u?
mad maddie:	**i've never known zoe to be a liar**
SnowAngel:	yeah-huh. she lied to her mom when she said she'd apply to princeton early decision, when she never planned to actually do it.
mad maddie:	**that was zoe being passive-aggressive, not outright lying. and she DID get her application in eventually.**
SnowAngel:	well, maybe it's the same thing here. maybe she said something about me in a passive-aggressive sort of way, and it got twisted around.
SnowAngel:	but in that case why wouldn't she admit it?

mad maddie:	beats me
SnowAngel:	and if she DIDN'T say it, who did? i called kristin, and she swears it wasn't her. but who would have made something like that up?
mad maddie:	chill, angela
mad maddie:	if zoe says she didn't say it, she didn't say it.
SnowAngel:	but it bugs me! wouldn't it bug you if someone was saying un-true things about YOU?
mad maddie:	it's probably some dumb misunderstanding, but i'll keep my ears open tomorrow. if i hear anything i'll tell you!

mad maddie:	hey, zo. u guys doin' the deed at PP?
zoegirl:	we're here right now. eek!
zoegirl:	sad posters on walls. sad people in chairs. waiting my turn.
mad maddie:	text when u get back
zoegirl:	will do. thx for checking in!

SnowAngel:	hey, zo! pretend i'm whispering, k?
zoegirl:	whisper-texting?
SnowAngel:	yeah, to be polite.
SnowAngel:	but check out the girl wearing the "NO" shirt. is that a baby bump or is she just chubby?
zoegirl:	tough call. baby bump?
SnowAngel:	that's my guess. think that's why she wears the "NO" shirt now?
zoegirl:	she looks 14. sheesh.
SnowAngel:	no no no to unprotected sex! and to cat-eye eyeliner. just sayin'.
zoegirl:	that's why we're here. and have you ever seen me do cat-eye eyeliner?

Fri, Feb 10, 6:10 PM E.S.T.

zoegirl: well . . . i did it!

mad maddie: you are with pill?

zoegirl: i am with pill. is that weird or what?

mad maddie: what was it like? i want deets!

zoegirl: it was *crazy*. the woman i talked to was nice, i guess, but she was very . . . straightforward.

mad maddie: like how?

zoegirl: she had a plastic model of a vulva, for one thing. it sat on her desk like a flower arrangement.

mad maddie: ye gads

zoegirl: but it was more just the way she talked about everything. like she asked me what kind of "sex play" i'd engaged in, and she went through this checklist, bam bam bam, as if we were making a grocery list. AND she made angela stay outside in the waiting room, so i was all by myself!

mad maddie: what kind of sex play HAVE you engaged in?

zoegirl: 😑 really?!

zoegirl: and she asked me if i smoked—as if!

zoegirl: she told me that doug and i should use condoms even if i did go on the pill, and that we should *talk* about everything before we actually *do* anything. here's her rule: "the topic should come up and the condom should come out before your zipper goes down."

mad maddie: that's classic

mad maddie: you should have a plaque with that needlepointed onto it. you could hang it above your bed.

zoegirl: honestly, she made me want to swear off sex forever. it all sounds so complicated!

mad maddie: she's right, tho. if yr gonna have sex with someone, you should be able to talk to them about it.

zoegirl: and another hot tip: she said to consider the use of "lubricants," but never vaseline.

zoegirl: am i really going to be using . . . lubricants?

mad maddie: i dunno. r u?

zoegirl: AND she asked me if i'd had any abortions, and if so, how many.

zoegirl: i'm 17! are there really 17-year-olds out there who've had multiple abortions?

mad maddie: i'm sure there are. depressing, isn't it?

zoegirl: angela and i saw this one couple out in the waiting room. they were about our age, and the guy was holding the girl's hand and she was crying. it made me wonder if . . . you know. if that was what she was there for.

mad maddie: at least the guy came with her

zoegirl: true

mad maddie: but yr not gonna get preggo, cuz yr going on the pill.

zoegirl: right. RIGHT. i start the first sunday after my next period, which should be in a week or so. and once i've started, we're supposed to wait a month to be safe.

mad maddie: you've waited this long, what's another month?

zoegirl: well, that's kind of how i feel, to tell you the truth.

zoegirl: my counselor-lady said there might be side effects that come with taking the pill, like weight gain, moodiness, and "spotty darkening of the skin." doesn't that sound lovely?

mad maddie: lucky u

zoegirl: i told angela that part, and she turned pale. she was all, "why is it always the girls who get stuck with this crap? why can't the GUYS get spotty darkening of the skin?!"

mad maddie: ah, angela, how i love her

mad maddie: alexis winthrop came up to me today and asked if it was true that she's after doug, btw.

zoegirl: oh great

mad maddie: i told her no, of course

zoegirl: i don't understand. it's like 1 little seed got planted, and now it's growing into this huge thing.

mad maddie: ppl like gossip, especially when it's something bad.

zoegirl: not me! angela and i made a pact that if anyone says anything, we're just gonna ignore it.

mad maddie: it doesn't bother you?

zoegirl: are you kidding?

zoegirl: i asked kristin point blank if she talked about angela and doug with anyone else, and she swore up and down that the only comment she made was that one to me.

mad maddie: what about paige? did you ask her about it?

zoegirl: no. i almost did, but sitting there in english during the actual moment, i felt too ridiculous.

zoegirl: it's all so stupid, i figured just let it go.

mad maddie: makes sense.

zoegirl: you DO know i didn't say any of that stuff, right? about angela flirting with doug?

mad maddie: zoe, of course i know that

zoegirl: i mean, i might have *thought* she was being flirty, just for a sec. but i never said so out loud.

mad maddie: i know

mad maddie: i've noticed she HAS toned down the flirtation, tho. like today, she basically ignored him.

zoegirl: yeah, i noticed that too. part of me feels bad, but part of me's glad.

zoegirl:	although what am i saying? she's going out with logan, for heaven's sake.
mad maddie:	**oh, right, he's a great deterrent**

SnowAngel:	ok, little miss nosy pants. i have a list for you of all the reasons logan is so wonderful.
mad maddie:	**hey, i never said logan wasn't wonderful. i'm just not convinced he's wonderful for YOU.**
SnowAngel:	*clears throat and shakes out piece of paper*
SnowAngel:	Number 1. he loves me and always wants to be with me, even more than with his friends.
mad maddie:	**can u say "smother"?**
SnowAngel:	Number 2. he downloads songs onto my iPod and makes romantic playlists.
mad maddie:	**very sweet, i admit. have you ever made HIM romantic playlists?**
SnowAngel:	Number 3. he's extremely cute. even you can't deny that!
mad maddie:	**i never have! altho no more Hard Rock Cafe shirts. cld u tell him that, plz? no more Hard Rock?**
SnowAngel:	and Number 4. he doesn't look at internet porn!
mad maddie:	**hardy har har**
mad maddie:	**is that all you've got?**
SnowAngel:	noooo, that's not all. that's just all i came up with this very second, off the top of my head.
mad maddie:	**dude, i love logan—as a PAL. and i know you do too. i'm just not convinced he gets you hot and bothered.**
SnowAngel:	we have fun together. he gives great foot rubs, and he loves "mad men." he'll watch episodes back to back with me for as long as i want.
SnowAngel:	he's a catch—even aunt sadie says so. we have a *great* relationship!

mad maddie:	then why are you working so hard to defend it?
SnowAngel:	and i would like to point out that having a boyfriend who's also a "pal" is a good thing. in the long run that's much more important than getting hot and bothered.
mad maddie:	is it? i personally think you should go for both.
SnowAngel:	he's gonna inherit his dad's business one day, did you know that?
mad maddie:	u did NOT just say that
SnowAngel:	and tonite we're doubling with zoe and doug, so there. it's a pre-valentine's day thing.
mad maddie:	ooo-wee, that's sure to be fun.
SnowAngel:	well . . . to tell the truth, i'd back out if i could. i don't want to be around doug and have zoe accuse me of throwing myself at him again.
mad maddie:	angela, zoe DIDN'T accuse you of throwing yourself at him.
SnowAngel:	or of trying to lure him away or having pent-up feelings for him or whatever. but if she's gonna pretend there isn't all this tension floating around, then so am i.
SnowAngel:	HOWEVER, it's gonna be hard when it's just me and logan and zoe and doug. won't you come with us? please please pleasy please?
mad maddie:	can't. i'm going over to mark and pelt-woman's new pad for dinner. pelt-woman is making vegetarian lasagna in a desperate attempt to cover up the smell of kimchee.
SnowAngel:	huh?
mad maddie:	their new place smells like korean food from the ppl who lived there before them.
SnowAngel:	😐
mad maddie:	you know what's weird? i can't get used to the fact that mark moved out. you'd think i'd be, "wh-hoo,

more doritos for me!" but the house feels wrong
w/o him.

SnowAngel: u miss him. that's normal.

mad maddie: **i didn't say i missed him. who said anything about**
missing him?

SnowAngel: *deadpans* oh, right, cuz yr tough, strong maddie
who takes it all in stride. you luuuuuuuuuuv change.
you luuuuuuv change so much you can't wait to
dump this town and move to california!

mad maddie: **have you been talking to zoe? r you making fun of**
me?

SnowAngel: awww, mads, wld i do that?

mad maddie: **oh, nvm**

mad maddie: **have fun on your date!**

Sun, Feb 12, 10:00 AM E.S.T.

zoegirl: morning, angela. that was so fun last night,
wasn't it?

SnowAngel: uh, sure, we should do it more often 😊

zoegirl: was it weird that during the movie we were all . . .
you know? i felt kind of strange about it afterward.

SnowAngel: don't worry, it was fine

zoegirl: "fine"? just "fine"??? i doubt logan would like
hearing you call it that!

zoegirl: jk

zoegirl: anyway, we're all consenting adults. 😊

SnowAngel: exactly. of course. no need to talk about it again.
😗

zoegirl: i'm just so glad the four of us were able to spend
time together without there being any ridiculous
undercurrents. if anybody ever *did* think
you were secretly lusting after doug, they sure
wouldn't after last night!

SnowAngel: cuz i'm NOT lusting after doug. god!

zoegirl:	i know! i know, angela.
zoegirl:	but i am
zoegirl:	*swoons*
zoegirl:	although it's not lust; it's love. sometimes i think, what would i do without him? and then i feel so . . . i don't know, so un-me for feeling that way. although that's silly, because it *is* me feeling this way . . .
SnowAngel:	🙁
zoegirl:	didn't you think it was funny when doug did his walking-on-hot-coals impression? can you believe he actually DID walk on hot coals?
SnowAngel:	frankly, no
zoegirl:	but he did, in indonesia
zoegirl:	getting to see so many places *did* change him, but all in good ways.
SnowAngel:	he does seem more confident now. the way he holds himself, even.
zoegirl:	sometimes, even though i know i'm being silly, i get this tiny feeling of wondering whether i'm good enough for him. isn't that ridiculous? it's just that i know he's going to do important things in the world. i just *know* it.
SnowAngel:	so r U, zoe
zoegirl:	well, yeah. who said i wasn't?
zoegirl:	okay, i'm outta here. i'm meeting doug to study.
SnowAngel:	at 10 o'clock on sunday morning?!
zoegirl:	just because it's spring semester of our senior year doesn't mean we can slack off!

Sun, Feb 12, 11:23 AM, E.S.T.

SnowAngel:	maddie, i'm sorry to report that our zoe has gone over the edge. i fear she's becoming ONE OF THOSE.
mad maddie:	**one of what?**

SnowAngel: you know, one of those girls whose lives revolve
around their boyfriends. she hung out with him all
last nite, and now she's off with him AGAIN—on
a sunday morning when she should be lounging
around with messy hair and eating lucky charms
from the box!

mad maddie: let's see, three guesses what UR doing right now?

SnowAngel: *sniffs and pops special edition multi-colored whale
into mouth*

**mad maddie: doug JUST got back in town. she's excited, that's
all.**

SnowAngel: i guess *looks miffed anyway*

SnowAngel: can i tell u something pervy?

mad maddie: absolutely

SnowAngel: last nite after dinner, the 4 of us went and played
pool at coop's. then we went back to zoe's house
and watched HBO, her and doug on one sofa and
me and logan on the other. and the lights were off
and the door was closed and zoe's parents weren't
home . . . and it turned into this weird double Let's
All Make Out session. is that sick? that's sick, isn't it?

mad maddie: u were going at it in the same room? all 4 of u?

SnowAngel: i know! there was this pretense that we were
watching the movie, but no one was, and it was
just . . . icky!

mad maddie: so why'd u do it?

SnowAngel: i dunno! cuz everybody just . . . did. AND cuz i didn't
have any choice after the whole "angela's after
doug" debacle. not that i'm still obsessing over that.

mad maddie: paranoia will destroy ya . . .

SnowAngel: it's like, i had to make even more of an effort than
normal to be all rah-rah about logan, while at the
same time NOT act in any possible way that could
be considered flirty toward doug.

SnowAngel: but i also had to be jokey and normal with doug, cuz otherwise it would be like admitting that those rumors had actually existed. oh, and that i cared.

SnowAngel: it was exhausting.

mad maddie: so to counteract those rumors, you said, "what the hell, let's have an orgy"?

SnowAngel: at one point i heard doug whisper something to zoe about "lower, lower," and zoe giggled in an aren't-we-naughty kind of way. it was some random private joke, obviously, but it gave logan ideas, and i had to take his hand and move it higher higher higher. i was like, "logan, NO. we r not doing that in zoe's house with zoe and doug five feet away!!!"

mad maddie: u realize yr oversharing

SnowAngel: and of course it made me think about your "hot and bothered" comment, which pissed me off.

SnowAngel: so then zoe messaged me on facebook this morning to do a post-op on the date, and she was all glowing and giddy and a LITTLE embarrassed, but not nearly embarrassed enuff. it just made me think, what is my life coming to?

mad maddie: zoe's in love. it's sweet.

mad maddie: altho they do need to get their own room.

SnowAngel: *shakes off whole experience*

SnowAngel: i'm going to have a purging ritual, that's what i'm gonna do. aunt sadie bought this high-tech body wash yesterday with glycolic acid in it, and she said i could try it out. 🛁 supposedly it makes you itch like crazy, but afterward yr all silky and soft.

mad maddie: uh, sure, dude. enjoy your acid bath. as for me, i'm gonna park my butt in front of the TV and have a Netflix marathon. i'm talking all day and deep into the night . . . cuz tomorrow senior privileges kick in!!! yeah!!!

SnowAngel: aunt sadie is so confused about that, btw. she was like, "you mean, until now you COULDN'T sleep in? even if you had a free period 1st thing in the morning?" she thinks high school is like college or something.

mad maddie: **or maybe she just doesn't get the idea of NOT sleeping in. maybe she doesn't realize that other ppl have bosses/teachers who care.**

SnowAngel: i am very jealous that you'll be in your warm cozy bed while i'm in 1st period french.

mad maddie: **oh, babe. i feel for ya!**

Mon, Feb 13, 4:15 PM E.S.T.

zoegirl: hey, angela. i'm at java joe's. . . and guess who's working the counter?

SnowAngel: who?

zoegirl: margo pedersen! i'm the only customer, so she came over and hung out for a while. and angela, she broke up with ian!!!

SnowAngel: ian??? maddie's ian?

zoegirl: well, ian who *used* to be maddie's ian.

SnowAngel: but he never got over her, so i can still call him that.

SnowAngel: when did margo break up with him? and why?

zoegirl: today—and the reason she gave is cuz she doesn't want "a long-term commitment" when she goes to college.

zoegirl: she said she figured that since they were gonna break up anyway, they might as well do it now. she was all, "i don't want to be tied down. i wanna enjoy my senior year."

. SnowAngel: she cldn't enjoy it with ian?

zoegirl: that's what i said. and she said, "look, zoe. you and doug, if that's what you want, that's great. but i'm 18 yrs old, i'm not ready to settle down."

zoegirl:	she was pretty condescending, actually. like she felt sorry for me because i *was* settled down.
SnowAngel:	i'm sure she didn't mean it that way
zoegirl:	no, she did. but that just means that what she and ian had wasn't as real as what doug and i have.
SnowAngel:	so ian's a free agent, huh? *taps chin*
zoegirl:	but to break up with him the day before valentine's day, isn't that harsh?
SnowAngel:	crap—valentine's day!
zoegirl:	why "crap"?
SnowAngel:	nothing, nvm
zoegirl:	???
SnowAngel:	i don't have anything for logan, that's all. i thought saturday nite was our valentine's day deal. i thought that was our whole celebration. but yesterday logan said something about a "valentine's surprise," which means he's planning something else, which means i have to too. crap!
zoegirl:	go out and get him something. it's not hard.
SnowAngel:	what are you giving doug?
zoegirl:	😊 a unicycle
SnowAngel:	a UNICYCLE?
zoegirl:	i found it on craigslist. isn't that the perfect doug gift?
SnowAngel:	great, a unicycle
SnowAngel:	yr gonna make me look bad here, zo
zoegirl:	make logan something homemade, like certificates for one free snuggle. i'm doing that too. i cut the certificates out of fancy stationery and decorated them with love stickers.
SnowAngel:	i can't do that. he'd think i copied you
zoegirl:	you don't have to get him something big, just give him something from the heart.
zoegirl:	want me to go shopping with you?

SnowAngel:	no, that's ok
zoegirl:	**you sure? i'd be happy to.**
SnowAngel:	i'm sure.

Mon, Feb 13, 4:46 PM E.S.T.

SnowAngel:	maddie, i'm a bad person!!!!
mad maddie:	**why, what'd you do?**
SnowAngel:	tomorrow's valentine's day, and logan has a "surprise" for me. but i have nothing for him!
mad maddie:	**u need a ride to the mall?**
SnowAngel:	zoe already offered, and i turned her down. wanna know why?
mad maddie:	**why?**
SnowAngel:	cuz i didn't WANT to go valentine's day shopping with zoe. i didn't want to hear her go on and on about how in love she is when . . . when . . .
mad maddie:	**when what?**
mad maddie:	**once and for all, just say it.**
SnowAngel:	*turns into a tiny person with a very tiny voice*
SnowAngel:	when maybe i'm not. in love. *crawls under a rock and puts hands over head*
mad maddie:	**bravo, angela. clap, clap, clap.**
SnowAngel:	you've known it all along, i know. and maybe i have too—or maybe it took seeing how truly head-over-heels zoe is to realize how un-head-over-heels i am.
SnowAngel:	know what the worst part is? all this tension over not feeling in love with logan is making it hard to even have fun with him. when normally i DO have fun with him, lots of fun. just . . . more as a friend.
mad maddie:	**i'm soooo proud of you, a. if i were there, i'd give you a shiny gold star.** ⭐
SnowAngel:	the whole stupid rumor thing didn't help either, cuz it was like everybody could c what i couldn't. not

	that i was lusting after doug, just that i WASN'T lusting after logan.
SnowAngel:	altho i think it finally died out, don't you? the rumors?
mad maddie:	**uh . . .**
SnowAngel:	ok, if you have to say "uh," don't answer.
SnowAngel:	but about logan—what am i gonna do? 😕 just this afternoon he left a cherry mash for me in my locker, cuz he knows they're my fave. he's such a good guy. i don't wanna hurt him!!!
mad maddie:	**you gotta cut him loose, angela. you have no choice.**
SnowAngel:	but not the day before valentine's day! then i'd be just like
SnowAngel:	OMG, I FORGOT TO TELL YOU! MARGO PEDERSEN BROKE UP WITH IAN!!!
mad maddie:	**whoa, tone it down**
SnowAngel:	isn't that great? *happy dance, happy dance*
SnowAngel:	now you two can get back together!
mad maddie:	**angela, yr un-frickin-believable! one second yr moaning and groaning over logan, and the next yr jumping up and down about ian?**
SnowAngel:	i feel better now that i've gotten the logan thing off my chest.
SnowAngel:	*pats self in the chesty region* i do! i feel so much better!
mad maddie:	**well lucky u, but what about logan?**
SnowAngel:	i guess yr right—i have to break up with him. just not today, that would be heartless.
SnowAngel:	altho it prolly won't be as awful as i think. cuz when one person isn't into it anymore, usually the other person isn't either, right?
mad maddie:	**no**
SnowAngel:	what do you mean, no? the correct answer is yes, you blockhead!

mad maddie: uh huh. that's why there's so many songs about broken hearts. that's why ppl shoot their exes out of jealousy. cuz everyone's like, "oh, you want to break up? great! no problem! that's what i want too!"

SnowAngel: oh shut up *scowls at friend*

SnowAngel: i can't believe you suggested that logan might SHOOT me!

mad maddie: i did not just suggest

mad maddie: grrrr

SnowAngel: logan is not going to shoot me. logan might be sad, but logan'll be ok, and ultimately he'll be better off with someone who appreciates him.

SnowAngel: and now enuff about logan. aren't you excited to hear about ian?

mad maddie: angela . . . don't, k?

SnowAngel: but why????

mad maddie: i know it's this huge fantasy of yours that ian and i get back together, but whatever we once had . . . it was a long time ago.

SnowAngel: but

mad maddie: shush

SnowAngel: if only you'd

mad maddie: LET. IT. GO.

SnowAngel: is it cuz of vincent?

mad maddie: omg, yr unbelievable

mad maddie: no, angela, it's not cuz of vincent. it's just that we don't ALL need a boyfriend to make our lives feel complete.

SnowAngel: you're no fun at all

mad maddie: sure i am. i'm tons of fun.

SnowAngel: guess i better go buy logan a v-day present since yr being such a poop. tootles!

mad maddie: happy valentine's day, zo! wasn't that sweet what the senior guys did?

zoegirl: soooo sweet. totally sweet!

mad maddie: i wonder who came up with it? can you imagine a bunch of guys sitting around and one of them saying, "hey, here's a thought: let's deliver a bag of candy hearts to every girl in the senior class!"

zoegirl: what *i* can't believe is that doug managed to keep it a secret from me. he told me later that he made sure my bag had extra candy, though. because he is a big sweetie.

mad maddie: how'd the big sweetie like his unicycle?

zoegirl: he's out in my backyard right now, trying to get the hang of it. i can see him clinging to a tree branch, attempting to get his balance.

mad maddie: ha

mad maddie: what'd he get u?

zoegirl: a pair of hand-crafted earrings from somalia. he bought them when they docked there and saved them all this time. they're gorgeous.

mad maddie: uh huh. well, isn't that nice.

mad maddie: wanna know what i got for v-day? go ahead. ask.

zoegirl: uh oh . . .

mad maddie: A FRICKIN EMAIL CHAIN LETTER! FROM GLENDY!!!

zoegirl: oh no! what did this 1 say?

mad maddie: the subject line was "have a heart" (cuz it's v-day, get it?) and the message said, "hi, i am a 29-yr-old father whose baby has some terrible gut-wrenching disease. please forward this to your 2 million closest friends, cuz if you do then we'll get 32 cents a message and we can pay for our poor baby's operation." it ends with, "if you delete this . . . you seriously don't have a heart."

zoegirl:	ouch
zoegirl:	you deleted it, didn't you?
mad maddie:	on the bottom was a picture of a naked baby, butt in the air. there was a ribbon wrapped around the baby with a tag that said "from god."
zoegirl:	oh no!
mad maddie:	yr laffing, aren't u?
zoegirl:	i just think it's hysterical that you get chain letter thingies from glendy and you actually read them. you get what you deserve.
mad maddie:	gee, thx for your sympathy
zoegirl:	i get glendy's emails too, but they go straight to "junk" and i delete them. i don't understand why you don't.
mad maddie:	i dunno, cuz i'm perversely curious to c what horror she's dredged up next?
zoegirl:	then you can't complain about them.
mad maddie:	yes i can. that's the whole point.
zoegirl:	maybe she'll apply to santa cruz, since she's in-state. maybe you guys can room together.
mad maddie:	should i kill myself now?
mad maddie:	one of these days i'm gonna write her back. i'm just waiting for the right moment.
zoegirl:	be sure to tell me when you do. *that* i want to see.
zoegirl:	hey, have you heard from angela? i called her, but she didn't pick up—probably she's with logan. he found me today after french and told me he's got some great surprise for her. he was verrrrrrrry excited.
mad maddie:	oh man
mad maddie:	you know she wants to break up with him, right?
zoegirl:	WHAT?
zoegirl:	why???

mad maddie: cuz she finally admitted that he's more like a brother than a lover. ooo, that would make a good country song, wldn't it?

zoegirl: but that's not true! if you'd seen them on saturday . . . she sure wasn't *kissing* him like a brother!

mad maddie: cuz she was faking, and deep down you know it. you just want her to be in love with logan so that angela and logan can be twinsies with you and doug.

zoegirl: that's ridiculous

mad maddie: plus it made it easier for you to blow off those rumors, cuz if she was firmly with logan then of course she wasn't flirting with your bf.

zoegirl: oh god, maddie

zoegirl: you should have seen logan when he was telling me about her v-day surprise. he was like, "she likes blue, doesn't she? i know pink's her favorite color, but pink wasn't an option. but blue's good too, don't you think?"

zoegirl: he was so excited!

mad maddie: see, there's the imbalance. he was so excited, and she was like, "oh, crap. valentine's day."

zoegirl: you're depressing me. this whole conversation is depressing me.

zoegirl: first margo and ian, and now angela and logan?

mad maddie: it's senior year. these things happen.

zoegirl: i hate that attitude! just because it's senior yr doesn't mean everything has to fall apart—and people should just keep their mouths shut if all they're gonna be is negative.

mad maddie: by "ppl," do you mean me?

zoegirl: no, not you

zoegirl: but ok, take this for example. do you know what jana said to me today, totally out of nowhere? she stopped me in the hall and goes, "how are things with your boyfriend? keeping him on a short leash?"

mad maddie: heh?

zoegirl: she said it with a smirk, as if he *needs* to be kept on a leash. i guess she's been hearing those stupid rumors too. or . . . omigosh.

mad maddie: what?

zoegirl: was she the one who STARTED those rumors???

mad maddie: holy frickin crap!

zoegirl: all this time i've been thinking, whew, i got off easy with the whole Boo Boo Bear encounter. a couple thousand death stares, but nothing more.

zoegirl: was this her way of getting me back, by planting rumors about angela and doug?

mad maddie: jesus, how could we have been so STUPID?!

mad maddie: AND she has homeroom with paige. we're such idiots!

zoegirl: we don't know for SURE that it was her . . .

mad maddie: if it was, she's going to pay!!!

Tues, Feb 14, 8:42 PM E.S.T.

SnowAngel: LADIES! i haz news! you both out there?

mad maddie: angela, where have you been? i've been calling forever!

SnowAngel: i know, but i was unable to answer the phone. wanna know why?

zoegirl: why?

SnowAngel: cuz i was 2 busy DRIVING MY JEEP!!!!!! *squeals and laffs spazerifically*

zoegirl: your jeep? what jeep?

mad maddie: wait a minute, please don't tell me . . .

zoegirl: no

SnowAngel: yes

mad maddie: NO

SnowAngel:	YES! 😊 😊 😊
zoegirl:	**LOGAN GAVE YOU A *JEEP*???**
SnowAngel:	i know, isn't it incredible?! 🚙
SnowAngel:	he took me to collier park and led me to the playground area, and parked on the street was this sweet baby-blue Suzuki Samurai. he goes, "nice car," and i said, "yeah." he goes, "you should take it for a ride," and i was like, "uh huh, sure, whatever." and he goes, "no, seriously. look—the keys r in the ignition." and i was like, "what dummy left the keys in the ignition?"
SnowAngel:	finally he took me by the shoulders, looked me in the eyes, and said, "angela, it's yours. happy valentine's day."
mad maddie:	**whoa, that's a helluva v-day present**
SnowAngel:	his uncle IS the decatur car king, you know. i've given him so much hell over those cheesy radio commercials, but now i'm like, "car king, i love you!!!"
SnowAngel:	OMG!!! I HAVE A JEEP!!!!!!!!!!!!!!!!!!!!!!!!!!!!
zoegirl:	**but angela . . . you can't *keep* it!**
SnowAngel:	why not?
zoegirl:	**you know why! cuz yr planning on breaking up with him!**
SnowAngel:	maddie! *growls at friend*
mad maddie:	**oops—guess i let the cat out of the bag**
SnowAngel:	*regains composure like a glorious summer day*
SnowAngel:	well OBVIOUSLY i'm not gonna break up with him now! duh!
zoegirl:	**cuz he gave you a *car*?**
SnowAngel:	yep
SnowAngel:	i mean, what an amazingly generous thing! he's like . . . oprah!
mad maddie:	**i can't believe he gave you a jeep—altho that does**

show good taste on his part. if your parents were
here, no way would they let you keep it.

SnowAngel: but they're not, and aunt sadie thinks it's extremely
romantic. she's gonna put me on her insurance,
and we're just gonna . . . not exactly mention it,
that's all. 😶

zoegirl: angela, i can't get my head around this. how much
do you think he spent?

SnowAngel: $2000, he told me. his uncle cut him a deal.

zoegirl: two thousand dollars???

SnowAngel: it's used. der. but logan sez it's been really well
maintained (whatever that means). 😃

zoegirl: angela, i think that's . . .vz

zoegirl: i mean, it's incredibly nice . . .

mad maddie: MORE than nice

zoegirl: but it just doesn't seem right. you can't just give
someone a CAR!

SnowAngel: well, he did

zoegirl: what did you give him?

SnowAngel: erm . . . a very lovely gift certificate to barnes & noble

mad maddie: for how much?

SnowAngel: that hardly matters, now does it?

mad maddie: you need to give it back.

SnowAngel: i'm not giving it back.

mad maddie: but you don't even love him!

SnowAngel: love can grow! love can bloom! 🌷

zoegirl: ANGELA!!!

mad maddie: ohhhh, i just figured out what's going on here.
zoe's rethinking those hand-crafted earrings . . .
aren't you, zo?

zoegirl: what?! i *adore* my earrings!

zoegirl: r you suggesting i'd rather have a car?

mad maddie: heavens, no. who in their right mind would rather
have a car than earrings?

SnowAngel: you guys, please don't spoil this for me. you KNOW how much i've wanted a car, for like my whole life. and logan wanted to do this—for me.

SnowAngel: i think everyone should just be happy, k?

mad maddie: come pick us up—i wanna see these wheels of yours!

mad maddie: plus, we've got news to share about our evil nemesis, the dragon lady.

zoegirl: we've MAYBE got news. MAYBE.

SnowAngel: i'll be right over 👍

SnowAngel: zoe, you in?

zoegirl: ohhh . . . ok. i've just gotta call doug and tell him i'll be late for our study date.

SnowAngel: there in a flash, chickies. i'll be the one in the jeep!!!!

Wed, Feb 15, 6:33 PM E.S.T.

mad maddie: hey, a. i saw yr "zoom zoom zoom" status, so i am making the wildly brilliant deduction that you're out driving yr jeep.

mad maddie: txt me when you get in, k? i hunted down jana. i want to give you the full report!

Wed, Feb 15, 10:39 PM E.S.T.

SnowAngel: hey, mads. sorry i missed you.

mad maddie: that's ok. how's the jeep?

SnowAngel: *sighs in rapture*

SnowAngel: jeep is WONDERFUL. i feel like such a princess! 👸

mad maddie: you R a princess

SnowAngel: i'm gonna treat logan right, i really am. i think i wasn't being fair to him . . . before.

mad maddie: ehh, what will be, will be. i'm washing my hands of it.

mad maddie: ready to hear what happened with jana?

SnowAngel: *sits criss-cross-apple-sauce at maddie's feet*
spill!

mad maddie: i was totally straight-up. i cornered her by her locker and said, "did you tell paige jensen that zoe said angela needed to keep her hormones to herself?"

SnowAngel: *blushes* i really don't like hearing it put that way, even if zoe DIDN'T say it.

mad maddie: being the callous and soul-less person she is, jana laughed and said, "no, but i wish i did. that's priceless!" so i said, "bullshit. you tried to get zoe in trouble with angela, but it didn't work. zoe would have never said that about angela, and angela would have never believed zoe said it anyway."

SnowAngel: except we both did. just for a teeny tiny second . . . but still.

mad maddie: jana doesn't need to know that. what matters is that your friendship was strong enough to get thru it.

SnowAngel: OUR friendship, all 3 of ours. you talked us thru it, ya know.

mad maddie: nonetheless, jana tried to screw with us, and she must face the consequences.

SnowAngel: IF she really was the one who said it . . .

mad maddie: oh, she was. her smugness was undeniable.

SnowAngel: did you tell zo? is she mad?

mad maddie: she is, but not mad ENOUGH

mad maddie: i told her i was gonna get jana back, and she was all, "no, no, just leave it." but it's about sticking up for what you believe in—and i believe in us.

SnowAngel: so wha'cha gonna do?

mad maddie: i don't know, but i'll think of something!

SnowAngel: zo? are you tweeting lyrics from weird esoteric indie bands? are you becoming THAT GIRL???

SnowAngel: it's cuz of doug, isn't it?

SnowAngel: uh huh. i'm looking up the "so look to the stars" line . . .

SnowAngel: omg, i soooo called it! it's from that band he was talking about yesterday! This Season's Color or This Season's Spice or . . . something. omg, zoe, plz keep liking your OWN music? plz???

SnowAngel: or maybe the star song is great. i dunno. GRRRR.

SnowAngel: either way, i was just txting to giggle about maddie and how bad-ass she's being. i think she sees it as defending our honor, which is sooo sweet. what do you think she's gonna do???

SnowAngel: i also wanted to tell you that i've re-thought the whole logan thing for real, and i don't think i've been giving him a fair chance. we were in a rut, that's all. but he's a great guy. he's a wonderful guy, and i would be insane to throw that away.

SnowAngel: and no, it's not just the jeep.

SnowAngel: i thought you'd be happy to hear that, that's all!

SnowAngel: PS—i'm not TOTALLY superficial. i mean, i like looking at stars too.

mad maddie: hungry! hunnnngry!

SnowAngel: go to snack machine. buy delicious food item. insert delicious food item into mouth.

mad maddie: can't. i'm supposedly recording grades for ms. hathoway. i'm also working on a brilliant way to get back at jana, but don't ask what it is.

SnowAngel: what is it?

mad maddie: i just told you, i'm not telling! let's just say it's

a friendly reminder that all actions come with
repercussions.

SnowAngel: when will this friendly reminder take place?

mad maddie: **hopefully tomorrow, so stay alert.**

SnowAngel: yes, ma'am. so i'm googling jeep accessories, and
i'm considering a "cherry" theme—do you think
that would be stupid? like, they have steering wheel
covers and all that, all decorated with cherries. 🍒

mad maddie: **my brother mark has a sheepskin steering wheel
cover.** 🐑

SnowAngel: i don't want a sheepskin steering wheel cover. i
want a cherry steering wheel cover. shld I poll my
english class?

mad maddie: **i'm sure mrs. mahan wld love that. excellent use
of class time.**

mad maddie: **hey, i talked to vincent during culture studies, and
he's having a party tomorrow night. happy time!**

SnowAngel: uh oh. you say happy time, i say DANGER. is this
when you guys r finally gonna end up in a closet
with your hands all over each other?

mad maddie: **god, angela, could we get off that already?
seriously.**

SnowAngel: i'm just *teasing*

mad maddie: **well stop. it's like you're refusing to let me be an
actual mature adult.**

SnowAngel: an actual mature adult who's salivating over the
prospect of a parent-free house party with an
endless supply of beer?

mad maddie: **exactly**

SnowAngel: wh-hoo! then i'll be the designated driver—IN MY JEEP!

mad maddie: **i'm all over that. l8rs!**

Fri, Feb 17, 9:06 AM E.S.T.

mad maddie: **yes! score! do i rock or what?**

zoegirl:	omg, jana must be livid! yr CRAZY, mads!
mad maddie:	that'll show her to mess with my buds
mad maddie:	did angela hear?
zoegirl:	dunno—didn't c her at her locker
zoegirl:	g2g, history quiz. but big high 5!!!!

Fri, Feb 17, 9:45 AM E.S.T.

SnowAngel:	wahhhhh! no fair! mary kate told me i missed it!!!!
mad maddie:	aw, man! it was classic. WHY WERE YOU NOT IN HOMEROOM TO HEAR IT?
SnowAngel:	cuz i forgot my shoes. *bonks head on desk* i got all the way to school, and then i was like, "oh, crap. i'm barefoot!"
mad maddie:	god, angela. only you.
SnowAngel:	well if you had TOLD me you were gonna plant a phony announcement, maybe i would have been there on time!
SnowAngel:	mary kate said you got the office lady to call jana out as a liar in front of the whole school???
mad maddie:	please, it was far more sophisticated than that.
mad maddie:	it said, and i quote, "congratulations to jana whitaker, winner of our first annual liars club award. jana, your free copy of 'Lies and the Lying Liars Who Tell Them' can be picked up at the office."
SnowAngel:	noooooo! 😦
mad maddie:	loretta, she's the office lady, wanted to know what the liars club was, and i told her it was a student organization dedicated to rooting out social injustice. she was like, "it's so nice to see young ppl getting involved in a worthwhile cause."
SnowAngel:	is there an actual book called "Lies and the Lying Liars Who Tell Them"?

mad maddie: yeppers. i saw it one day on mark and pelt-woman's coffee table, and i remembered the title. i went to B&N last night and bought a copy.

SnowAngel: that's awesome

SnowAngel: how did ppl react when they heard the announcement? how did JANA react?

mad maddie: megan said jana tried to play it off as "ha ha, very funny," but that it clearly got under her skin. even if ppl didn't know the full story, they know jana, and they could put 2 and 2 together.

mad maddie: she said jana and terri spent all homeroom talking about what a bitch i was, but do i care? no, i do not.

SnowAngel: jana and terri r tight again?

mad maddie: i guess. but megan said that as soon as jana was out of the room, terri turned to margaret and was like, "i'm sorry, but that was too perfect!" and then they both cracked up.

SnowAngel: i can't believe i missed it. *pouts*

SnowAngel: what's gonna happen when jana never shows up at the office to pick up her book?

mad maddie: i hope loretta will announce it again. and when jana still doesn't show up, i'm hoping she'll have someone deliver it to her in person.

SnowAngel: you r bad, maddie—and i luv it!

Fri, Feb 17, 5:18 PM E.S.T.

SnowAngel: hey there, sweetie. what'd ya think of maddie's homeroom announcement?

zoegirl: i thought it was funny, even tho it was totally unnecessary. but funny.

SnowAngel: you reap what you sow, that's what i say. in fact maybe i'll make that my senior quote.

SnowAngel: have you decided what your senior quote will be?

zoegirl:	no, but i'm not terribly worried about it since we have over two months to decide. i've got too many other things to worry about—ack!
SnowAngel:	well, to thank maddie for sticking up for us, i had a great idea: we shld invite ian to vincent's tonite. whaddaya think?
zoegirl:	uh, i think maddie would kill you
SnowAngel:	so i should go for it?
SnowAngel:	she really needs to start going out with ian again. he would be soooooo much better for her than vincent.
zoegirl:	you keep giving maddie a hard time about vincent, but i honestly don't think she's interested in him.
SnowAngel:	that's what SHE says. i want ian on her radar anyway.
zoegirl:	why do you not like vincent? just because he's buds with jana?
SnowAngel:	there is that, which is a huge strike against him. but it's more that i just don't wanna see her get in trouble again. like with chive.
zoegirl:	vincent's not chive, though
zoegirl:	i think you give her a hard time about vincent cuz she gives you a hard time about logan. that's what i think.
SnowAngel:	WHAT? plz.
zoegirl:	well . . . whatever
zoegirl:	will jana be at this party?
SnowAngel:	probably. yikes, i didn't think of that.
SnowAngel:	she confronted maddie in the hall today, did you hear? she said, "i know you did it, bitch," and maddie said, "no, but i wish i did. that's priceless."
zoegirl:	she quoted jana back to jana? oh great—so now jana's doubly mad. i *told* maddie not to do anything!

SnowAngel: well she did

SnowAngel: ok, i'm off. gonna go call ian!

Fri, Feb 17, 8:18 PM E.S.T.

SnowAngel: oh, ma-a-a-die! i is here. where u b?

mad maddie: den. near tv. come!

SnowAngel: kk. i haz small pressie for u. well, small-medium. well,
             medium-medium. medium-large? can I bring?

mad maddie: if it's a drink, hell yeah!

Sat, Feb 18, 9:45 AM E.S.T.

zoegirl: angela, i need to talk.

SnowAngel: *stretches luxuriously and remembers evening
             of decadence* last nite was a blast, wasn't it?
             even with jana lurking in the corners and giving us
             murderous glances. i almost peed my pants when
             maddie made that comment about her being a
             witch, cuz it was so true. like she was muttering
             incantations and putting curses on us with her evil
             mind.

zoegirl: can we not talk about jana?

SnowAngel: apparently she's got some "plan" up her sleeve
             to get back at maddie. mary kate overheard her
             talking about it, but she shut up as soon as she
             realized mk was listening.

zoegirl: seriously, i don't wanna talk about jana, k?

SnowAngel: righty-o *flicks jana into little witchy-poo trash can*

SnowAngel: omg, i've got "just give me a reason" totally stuck
             in my head. *sings soulfully with hand to heart: "just
             give me a reason, just a little bit's enough!"*

zoegirl: you and andre were so cute dancing together.

SnowAngel: i LOVE andre. i should kidnap him and make him live
             in my closet, and just take him out to hold every nite
             like a teddy bear.

SnowAngel:	he said i could be his fag-hag, did i tell you that?
zoegirl:	yes, about 1,000 times
zoegirl:	what does logan think of that?
SnowAngel:	of what? of ANDRE?
zoegirl:	it kinda seemed like you weren't hanging out with him much. logan, i mean.
SnowAngel:	we hung out plenty—what r you talking about? and if maybe we're still working on things, so? it's like the song says: "we're not broken, just bent." we'll fig it out.
SnowAngel:	anyway, how would YOU know, miss disappearing act? maddie and i looked all over for you when "thrift shop" came on so we cld belt it out together. you were nowhere to be found!
zoegirl:	well, that's why i wanted to talk. i'm feeling kinda weird about life, but i don't *want* to be.
SnowAngel:	yesssss? tell auntie angela all about it.
zoegirl:	well, doug and i somehow ended up alone in vincent's brother's room. at 1st we were just fooling around, but then things got . . . pretty involved.
SnowAngel:	"pretty involved"? that's such a zoe-way of putting it.
SnowAngel:	kinda skanky that you used vincent's bro's room, tho.
zoegirl:	i know!
zoegirl:	and then right in the middle, doug stopped and said, "do you want me to put on a condom? i've got one."
SnowAngel:	*shrieks*
SnowAngel:	little dougie had a condom? he actually went out at some point in time and bought A CONDOM??? zoe, that is SO cute!
zoegirl:	it wasn't *cute*, it was awful! it means that he's been thinking about it 2. you know—about having sex!

SnowAngel:	well DUH
SnowAngel:	what did you say?
zoegirl:	i handled it completely wrong. i said, "now?!" and he said, "why not? it's as good a time as any."
zoegirl:	after that i pretty much stopped interacting, and eventually he got the point.
SnowAngel:	have you told him about the pill?
zoegirl:	no, i couldn't make the words come
SnowAngel:	zoe . . .
zoegirl:	why do i act this way?! WHY? i *love* doug. i should be able to talk to him about anything!
zoegirl:	i just didn't wanna have sex with him right that second, in vincent's brother's room, with me afraid the whole time that someone was gonna come in.
SnowAngel:	sweetie. listen. you did the absolute right thing.
SnowAngel:	you and doug will figure it out . . . and until then, there's plenty of other things you 2 can do to keep yourselves occupied. 😊
zoegirl:	i start tomorrow, btw. the pill.
SnowAngel:	i hope you don't get "spotty dark spots" or whatever.
zoegirl:	gee, thanks
SnowAngel:	just lookin' out for ya
SnowAngel:	so r you good? you feel less weird about things?
zoegirl:	yeah. thanks for listening!

Sat, Feb 18, 1:18 PM E.S.T.

mad maddie:	**a word plz, angela**
SnowAngel:	*she awakens! she rises! celestial chorus fills the air*
mad maddie:	**now that i've had time to sober up, would you mind telling me when you invited ian to vincent's party???**
SnowAngel:	omg, that was so fantastic, wasn't it? i was like, "ian, wow! what a kawinkidink!"

mad maddie:	a kawinkidink. uh huh. u told me u had a pressie for me, medium or medium-large, and then u brought IAN to me???
SnowAngel:	now, maddie, no need to get hung up on details. he was there, you were there, you guys had fun . . .
SnowAngel:	you DID have fun, didn't you?
mad maddie:	it was good to see him, i suppose
SnowAngel:	did you talk about margo?
mad maddie:	no, we didn't talk about margo. why wld we talk about margo?
mad maddie:	mainly we talked about college. he thinks santa cruz sounds cool—i liked the way he looked at me when i told him that's where i want to go. like he thought i was brave for marching off so far.
SnowAngel:	i wish you WEREN'T so brave. i wish you would just go to UGA with me—athens is only an hour away!
mad maddie:	ian's gonna be in athens, you know. he applied to UGA's honors program.
SnowAngel:	i applied to the dumbshit program. i need to leave time for my busy social life. 😊
mad maddie:	i wish we would hear already. i mean, you and ian have nothing to worry about—you'll both get into georgia. but what if i get a really skinny letter from UCSC and it's a rejection?
SnowAngel:	then like i said: just come with me! and ian!!!
mad maddie:	go dawgs! woof woof!
SnowAngel:	u think i'm joking, but i'm not
SnowAngel:	u did apply, didn't u?
mad maddie:	as a back-up, sure. but i'm not going to georgia
SnowAngel:	but why not???? just think how much fun we would have together. and if we could only get zoe to come, things would be absolutely perfect!
mad maddie:	zoe? at georgia? zoe's not going to georgia. zoe didn't even apply to georgia.

SnowAngel: which is stupid, cuz doesn't her mom know the
                president of the university? she'd be a shoo-in.

mad maddie: she'd be a shoo-in anywayz.

**mad maddie: nah, zoe's gonna end up at princeton, cuz that's
                where her mom went.**

SnowAngel: i thought her top choice was kenyon.

**mad maddie: it is, but she's gonna end up at princeton, that's
                my prediction. the pressure from her parents will
                be 2 strong.**

SnowAngel: oh hush. lemme live in my fantasy-land until the very
                last minute.

SnowAngel: anyway, how'd we get started on college? i
                thought we were talking about vincent's party.

**mad maddie: vincent is wacked. last nite he pulled me aside
                and offered me a vicodin tablet "to smooth things
                out." then he changed his mind, saying, "nah, i
                better not corrupt you."**

SnowAngel: doesn't he know yr already corrupted?

mad maddie: not in that way, i'm not

SnowAngel: where'd he get the vicodin?

**mad maddie: from his bro, who i'm pretty sure does some
                farming on the side.**

SnowAngel: farming?

**mad maddie: as in pharmaceuticals. and i think you should be
                proud of me for not being tempted.**

SnowAngel: i AM proud of you. i'm also proud of you for not
                letting vincent be your fuck-buddy.

SnowAngel: i wanted to apologize for that, actually. for assuming
                you were after him.

mad maddie: i'm NOT after him. i never have been after him. god.

SnowAngel: well, yeah, i realized that after watching y'all last
                nite. *gulps and sucks it up* i realized that maybe
                i wasn't being very fair toward him. or you.

madmaddie: thank u! i've been wondering what your deal was!

SnowAngel:	he's cool, i admit it! *lashes self with rope of thorns*
SnowAngel:	when he and i were in the kitchen, he was totally cracking me up. AND he had only good things to say about you. he thinks yr a good influence, poor guy.
mad maddie:	**a good influence, right. that's why he offered me vicodin.**
SnowAngel:	well, we'll just gloss over that bit.
SnowAngel:	you and vincent r pals, just like me and andre.
mad maddie:	**amazing, isn't it? turns out i AM capable of being pals with a guy and not jumping his bones . . .**
SnowAngel:	a HOT guy at that, who doesn't happen to be gay.
SnowAngel:	can i ask a question, tho? why is his brother white, when vincent is tan-colored?
mad maddie:	**ha! vincent says they get that all the time.**
mad maddie:	**frank is irish–puerto rican, and vincent is puerto rican–irish**
SnowAngel:	???
mad maddie:	**their mom is light-skinned, their dad is dark-skinned. i guess each kid came out looking different.**
SnowAngel:	oh. ok.
mad maddie:	**so did you talk to zoe, find out where she disappeared to?**
SnowAngel:	just as we suspected—off with doug.
mad maddie:	**doin' da freak between da sheets?**
SnowAngel:	omg, where do u come up with these expressions???
SnowAngel:	ALMOST doin' da freak b/w da sheets. doug pulled out a condom, and zoe froze up and put an end to things.
mad maddie:	**zoe, zoe, zoe**
SnowAngel:	it's only gonna make it harder, you know. once they have sex, it's only gonna make it harder for them to split up in the fall.
mad maddie:	**who says they're gonna split up?**

SnowAngel:	well PHYSICALLY they will, cuz neither of them applied to the same schools. that's what i mean.
mad maddie:	**which in all likelihood means they WILL split up, cuz of the whole long-distance thing. they'll break up . . . and then they'll get together during christmas break . . . and then they'll break up again . . .**
SnowAngel:	stop, yr depressing me!
mad maddie:	**or who knows? maybe they'll be the couple who proves everyone wrong.**
mad maddie:	**holy moly, i've gotta piss like a racehorse.**
SnowAngel:	oh, now that's lovely
mad maddie:	**it's a hangover pee. it was worse this morning, and i sooo didn't wanna crawl out of bed to go to the bathroom.**
mad maddie:	**i found myself thinking, if only i was wearing a Depends . . .**
SnowAngel:	delete! delete! *erases image of maddie in diaper*
mad maddie:	**that would turn ian on, huh?**
mad maddie:	**peeing now, fyi. la la la.**
SnowAngel:	maddie! TMI!
mad maddie:	**oh, whatev. everyone pees. i, however, am now pee-free!**
mad maddie:	**i realized we hadn't discussed the j-word, and i have a new example of her ridiculosity to share.**
SnowAngel:	uh oh, did she put into action her EVIL PLAN? *cues special effects guy for thunder and lightning and a shower of hoppy toads*
mad maddie:	**i suppose—altho it was so stupid it just made me laugh.**
mad maddie:	**me, megan, vincent, and vincent's bro were standing around talking, right? and vincent and frank were giving megan hell cuz she kept doing that phlegm-clearing thing cuz of her cold.**

SnowAngel:	she was doing that all night! it was driving me crazy!
mad maddie:	**frank was like, "i know—yr a hooker. THAT'S why yr sick!"**
SnowAngel:	huh?
mad maddie:	**it was mildly funny at the time. megan said no, she wasn't a hooker, and frank goes, "ohhhh, then yr a slut!"**
SnowAngel:	ok, vincent may be cooler than i thought, but i am SO not impressed with frank. *makes disapproving granny face*
mad maddie:	**anywayz, jana had been lurking about during this whole exchange, and when frank said that, she inserted herself into the convo and goes, "WHO'S the slut? WHO'S the slut?"**
SnowAngel:	and who WAS the slut?
mad maddie:	**me, apparently. isn't it shocking? didn't she totally put me in my place?**
SnowAngel:	i don't get it. what have you done that's slutty recently?
mad maddie:	**RECENTLY?!!!**
SnowAngel:	lol 🙊
mad maddie:	**omg, i can't believe u!**
SnowAngel:	sorry sorry sorry, i'm TERRIBLY sorry. *kisses maddie's unslutty butt repeatedly*
SnowAngel:	so what did u say?
mad maddie:	**i said, "jana, jana, jana . . . must we have such a potty mouth? Boo Boo Bear would NOT approve!"**
SnowAngel:	*claps hands in delight* for real?!
mad maddie:	**no. i just looked at her like *yr such a dumbshit.* it wasn't worth the trouble of a reply.**
SnowAngel:	damn! i mean, DARN. (sorry, Boo Boo Bear!)
mad maddie:	**it's too bad, really, that after my extremely impressive "lying liars" display, that's all she could come up with.**

SnowAngel:	um . . .
mad maddie:	**yesss? you have a comment you would like to make?**
SnowAngel:	just that it couldn't have been all she could come up with
mad maddie:	**what r u saying?**
SnowAngel:	that one little remark, it couldn't have been the "plan" mary kate overheard her talking about. cuz if it was, then she's . . . i dunno. feeble.
mad maddie:	**vincent said she's going thru some tough shit—not that i care. maybe it's affected her brain.**
SnowAngel:	don't tell me that—then i have to feel sorry for her!
SnowAngel:	what kind of tough shit?
mad maddie:	**i dunno, just that it has to do with her stepmonster. blah blah blah.**
mad maddie:	**and DON'T feel sorry for her. god. if you need to feel sorry for someone, feel sorry for ME. i'm the one she called a slut!**
SnowAngel:	poor old madikins!
mad maddie:	**and poor old angela-kins. she basically called you a slut 2, or have you forgotten? she just tricked everyone into blaming it on zoe.**
SnowAngel:	point taken
SnowAngel:	just watch your back, k? betcha a million dollars she's up to something more.
mad maddie:	**pah, she's feeble.**

	Sun, Feb 19, 10:09 PM E.S.T.
zoegirl:	well, i did it. i took my very 1st pill.
mad maddie:	**nice work. have you told doug?**
zoegirl:	i decided i want to take them for at least a week and THEN tell him. that way i can be, "oh, and btw, i'm on the pill now." you know, very blasé.
zoegirl:	it's strange, i feel sometimes like i *need* to be

blasé with him—but only when i'm not with him. when i'm actually with him, i *can't* be blasé. does that make sense?

mad maddie: no

zoegirl: i know, it doesn't to me either!

zoegirl: it's like i'm being sucked into him. at times i feel this need to resist, but then i get near him and i think, "omg, i would die without him." as in literally die.

zoegirl: i know it sounds crazy.

mad maddie: you shouldn't let him control you that much, zo.

zoegirl: he doesn't *control* me. i just love him.

mad maddie: uh huh, same difference. jk.

mad maddie: hey, i found the most awesome webseries—you've gotta check it out. it's by this chick named amy winfrey who makes animated cartoons. there's muffin films, making fiends, and big bunny.

zoegirl: uh . . . ok. do you not wanna talk about doug anymore?

mad maddie: big bunny's my fave. it's about 3 kids who go into the forest even tho they're not supposed to, and they meet this humongous bunny who says things like, "do not run, tasty children!"

mad maddie: they ask the bunny if he's seen their dog, and he says, "noooo, i have seen no fluffy crunchy doggies around here. maybe the yummy puppy has gone home!"

zoegirl: huh

mad maddie: there's a theme song and everything. go to <ins>big-bunny.com</ins>.

zoegirl: um, ok, when i get a chance.

Mon, Feb 20, 5:55 PM E.S.T.

mad maddie: angela, yr on my bad list!

SnowAngel:	i am? why?
mad maddie:	**and i quote: "Tonight your true love will realize how much they love you between 1 and 4 in the morning. Tomorrow the shock of your life will occur if you break the chain, and you will have bad luck for 10 years if you don't pass this on to 15 people."**
SnowAngel:	uh oh *takes big tiptoe steps backward*
mad maddie:	**you know who it's from, don't you?**
SnowAngel:	er . . . glendy?
mad maddie:	**YES, glendy! aaargh!**
SnowAngel:	can i help it if she likes you? yr very likable, maddie.
SnowAngel:	did you break the chain?
mad maddie:	**what do u think?**
SnowAngel:	uh oh, hope yr ready for the shock of your life . . .
mad maddie:	**that stuff is such garbage. who believes that crap?**
SnowAngel:	i sent out a chain letter when i was 10. a snail-mail chain letter, one of those where yr supposed to put your name on the bottom of the list and send a dollar to the person on the top of the list. i was supposed to receive thousands of dollars within the next month, but i never did.
mad maddie:	**go fig**
SnowAngel:	i was very hardcore about it, 2. i sent it to my camp buddies and used all sorts of emotional blackmail, like, "c'mon, trish, i know YOU won't let me down." i feel bad about it now.
mad maddie:	**you should. you should write them all an apology.**
SnowAngel:	um . . . i'll keep it in mind
mad maddie:	**hey, wanna do something? go somewhere?**
SnowAngel:	YEAH! i was supposed to go with logan to pick out an interview suit for summer internships, but i'll call and tell him i can't.
mad maddie:	**shld i invite zoe?**

| SnowAngel: | sure, but i bet she's with doug |
| SnowAngel: | cya in a jiff! |

Mon, Feb 20, 6:04 PM E.S.T.

SnowAngel:	oh ha ha, maddie. very funny.
SnowAngel:	i just checked my email, and what should i see waiting for me in my inbox?
SnowAngel:	yr supposed to send it to 15 DIFFERENT ppl, you freak!
SnowAngel:	yr still gonna get the curse unless you send it to 14 other ppl!!!!!!!!

Tues, Feb 21, 4:33 PM E.S.T.

mad maddie:	angela, yr not trying to play some kind of trick on me, r you? to make me think i'm cursed?
SnowAngel:	huh?
SnowAngel:	OHHHHH, cuz of that chain letter from glendy. what happened? did you drop a dr pepper on your foot? ha ha!
mad maddie:	angela, i'm not joking. i came home to 17 voicemails on our HOME phone. our land line! and they're all from guys saying they wanna . . . do stuff with me. or TO me.
SnowAngel:	what?!
mad maddie:	they know my name. and some of them are really really sick.
SnowAngel:	OMG
SnowAngel:	who r they from?
mad maddie:	i don't know, i don't recognize any of them.
SnowAngel:	could it be vincent? could he be pranking you?
mad maddie:	these r, like, old guys. all DIFFERENT guys, some with accents and some really gruff and . . . no, it's not vincent.
mad maddie:	i don't actually think it was you, either. obviously.

SnowAngel: it's jana. it's jana, isn't it?!! THAT'S what the slut remark
               was all about!

mad maddie: **she must have written my name and number in a
               gas station bathroom . . . or maybe put an ad on
               a dating website?**

SnowAngel: call 1 of the guys back and ask where he got your
               number

mad maddie: **NO!**

mad maddie: **they think i'm a call girl or something. i'm totally
               creeped out, angela.**

SnowAngel: ok, listen. if anyone calls, DON'T pick up.

mad maddie: **i already unplugged the phone, but the voicemail's
               digital and i can't figure out how to deactivate it.
               what if ppl leave more messages? what's gonna
               happen when my parents get home?**

SnowAngel: yr there by yourself?!!

SnowAngel: i'm coming over. you shouldn't have to deal with
               this alone.

mad maddie: **that would be really really great, actually.
               thanx, a.**

SnowAngel: i'm on my way!!!

Tues, Feb 21, 10:00 PM E.S.T.

zoegirl: **how's mads?**

SnowAngel: by the time i got over there, there were 33 voicemails
               for maddie. by the time i left, it'd gone up to 68,
               and the only reason there weren't more was cuz the
               voicemail thingie *finally* got to the "this mailbox is
               full" level!

zoegirl: **were they all the same sort of thing?**

SnowAngel: uh huh. i plugged the phone back in so i cld listen
               to them—altho i NEVER answered the phone when
               it rang—and they said things like, "hey, baby, i'll
               satisfy your every fantasy," and "if u want someone

well-equipped, then i'm your man. gimme a ring
and let's get dirty."

zoegirl:	ewww!
SnowAngel:	some were even worse. some i couldn't even listen to—i just hit "delete" and then wanted to go take a boiling hot shower.
zoegirl:	did anyone say where they got her number?
SnowAngel:	no—they just said, "i heard u were looking for some action" or "slut for grabs? hell yeah. call me."
zoegirl:	poor maddie!
zoegirl:	how could there be so *many*?
SnowAngel:	i dunno. whatever jana did, she did it in a big way— more than just scribbling something on some wall.
zoegirl:	so we're sure it's jana?
SnowAngel:	i am. aren't u?
zoegirl:	i just have a hard time believing that even she would do something so . . . VICIOUS. and dangerous! hasn't she heard about all the girls who've been molested by chatroom lurkers and stuff like that?
SnowAngel:	i can't believe i was almost feeling sorry for her, cuz of her personal problems or whatever.
SnowAngel:	this goes so much further than what maddie did. this is just WRONG.
zoegirl:	did mr. and mrs. kinnick show up?
SnowAngel:	they got in around 9:00. maddie didn't tell them about the messages cuz she doesn't want her dad thinking about her like that . . . even tho none of it's true.
SnowAngel:	she's really shaken up, zo. and she NEVER gets shaken up!
zoegirl:	i'm gonna do some hunting around on the internet. maybe i can figure this out.

good idea. and tomorrow let's stick close to maddie so she feels safe!

Wed, Feb 22, 4:14 PM E.S.T.

mad maddie: so much for keeping the parents in the dark. guess how many calls the moms got while i was at school?

zoegirl: oh no. i thought you unplugged the phone again!

mad maddie: yes, but apparently she plugged it back in when she needed to use it. anyway, twenty-frickin-six voicemails! i guess ppl aren't quite as busy being pervy in the daylight hours as during the night, but still.

zoegirl: holy crap

mad maddie: the 1st guy asked her to pass on a message about his big cock. isn't that charming? and then she answered the 2nd call, assuming the 1st was a wrong number, and that guy said, "is this maddie? you don't sound 18." the moms goes, "this is maddie's mother. who IS this?" and the guy laughed and asked if she was the one who taught me to be so nasty.

zoegirl: oh. my. god. she must have had a heart attack.

mad maddie: pretty much. she called my cell, and i had no choice but to tell her about last night. then she called the police, and they said to get a phone log so we can find out where the calls came from.

zoegirl: good idea

mad maddie: yeah, only lots of the numbers were blocked.

zoegirl: agh

mad maddie: so mom started asking the callers for their names. can u imagine? most ppl just hung up at that point, but eventually this one guy said he'd gotten our number from craigslist.

zoegirl:	from CRAIGSLIST??? maddie. omg.
mad maddie:	**tell me about it. i knew ppl used it to find roommates, apartments, cars . . . stuff like that . . . but i didn't know till now that there's also a "casual encounters" section, and that's where you can find ME, apparently.**
zoegirl:	oh. my. god. maddie, i am sooooo sorry.
mad maddie:	**i want u to go find it, ok?**
zoegirl:	the ad?
mad maddie:	**the moms tracked it down, but she won't tell me what it said, which makes me think it must be REALLY bad.**
zoegirl:	you don't want to c for yourself?
mad maddie:	**no**
zoegirl:	oh. ok.
mad maddie:	**so go look and then report back.**
mad maddie:	**craigslist. atlanta. casual encounters.**
zoegirl:	got it. be back soon!

Wed, Feb 22, 4:36 PM E.S.T.

zoegirl:	hey angela. i'm supposed to talk to maddie, but i wanted to talk to you first.
SnowAngel:	about the want-ad thingie? i've seen it. it's sick.
zoegirl:	it literally made me *feel* sick.
zoegirl:	i feel terrible, like it's all my fault!
SnowAngel:	how is it YOUR fault?
SnowAngel:	oh, cuz of Boo Boo Bear. right.
SnowAngel:	zo, this is sooooo much worse than Boo Boo Bear OR the lying liars club. it's in a whole different league.
zoegirl:	i'm gonna tell my mom and see if jana can be prosecuted for sexual harassment and identity theft. what she did is SO wrong. and dangerous! what if someone did a reverse phone number search and found out where maddie lives?

SnowAngel:	that is a GREAT idea, zo. but the listing is down now, right? gone from craiglist forever?
zoegirl:	doubt it's down yet, but i reported it as inappropriate. hopefully it'll be gone soon.
zoegirl:	but about maddie—do i tell her the truth about the post? *all* of it?
SnowAngel:	well, i don't know how you can't. she deserves to know.
zoegirl:	let's tell her together. okay?
SnowAngel:	oh. um.
zoegirl:	she needs us both for moral support.
zoegirl:	i'm going to do a group text. you better reply!

Wed, Feb 22, 4:45 PM E.S.T.

zoegirl:	hi, maddie. we have some answers for you.
mad maddie:	"we"?
SnowAngel:	*waves dispiritedly* hey, mads.
mad maddie:	uh oh, i'm not liking the whole tag-team thing going on here. is it that bad?
zoegirl:	yesssssss . . . kind of?
SnowAngel:	yes, definitely. don't sugar-coat it! AND it's totally illegal, so zoe's gonna get her mom to step in. jana's gonna be so incredibly busted!
mad maddie:	will u tell me already???
zoegirl:	aaargh
zoegirl:	the ad says you're looking for guys to fool around with, and that you like to . . . do it in front of others.
zoegirl:	and i wish i didn't have to tell you this, but jana included a picture.
SnowAngel:	that one from sophomore year, of you with no shirt on.
zoegirl:	angela!
SnowAngel:	what? i wanted to make sure she knew which one!
zoegirl:	which other one would i mean, her class photo?

SnowAngel:	well we said we were gonna tell her the truth, but yr downplaying it cuz you feel responsible. yr making it sound like some harmless innocent thing!
zoegirl:	saying she likes to do it in front of others is some harmless innocent thing???
mad maddie:	STOP!
mad maddie:	just paste the damn thing in!
zoegirl:	it's been taken down. i checked, and it's gone now.
mad maddie:	can't you hit your back button? find the page when you first opened it?
zoegirl:	i thought you didn't wanna see it.
mad maddie:	i don't, but you guys r making it sound 10,000 times worse than it is, i'm sure.
mad maddie:	zoe?
mad maddie:	angela?
mad maddie:	what, r you both cowering in the corner?
SnowAngel:	*glowers at zoe for being such a wimp* you heard her, zo. just show her and be done with it!
zoegirl:	oh GOD. but i'm not including the picture!
zoegirl:	here's the stupid ad, word for word:

I like to put on a show, so not only do you have to be very hung, talented (long lasting, multiple cummer), but you have to be ok fucking a sexy 18 yr old in front of other guys. There would never be too many—three, four, or even five, I'm on the chubby side as you can see, but that just means more of me to go around. If you meet the critiria and you're interested, call me, guys! (404) 555-0176

SnowAngel:	maddie? u there?
mad maddie:	she spelled "criteria" wrong
SnowAngel:	cuz she's a dumbass, that's why!

mad maddie: the ad doesn't mention my name. how did they know my name?

zoegirl: from the caption on the photo

mad maddie: which says . . . ?

SnowAngel: um . . . "misbehaving maddie"

SnowAngel: but remember: jana's gonna be in serious trouble for this. she is NOT gonna get away with it!

mad maddie: well, yeah, fantastic—except she is

mad maddie: the moms wants to press charges, too, so she emailed the craigslist ppl. there's no way to prove who wrote the ad. nobody's name is attached to it but mine.

zoegirl: but you can just tell them who it was!

mad maddie: and they'd believe me because . . . ?

zoegirl: what about an IP address? can't they find the IP address the ad was sent in from?

mad maddie: anonymous. apparently there are ways to route your IP addy through zillions of other addies so that there's no way to know where the root source was.

zoegirl: well, i'm sure my mom'll have some ideas. jana *stole* your identity, that's a criminal offense.

mad maddie: i'm gonna tattle on her like a kindergartener? no way.

zoegirl: but your mom does know, right? that it was jana?

mad maddie: no

SnowAngel: WHY???

mad maddie: i told her it wasn't me (duh), but that i didn't know who it was.

mad maddie: i'm not giving jana the satisfaction of seeing me all teary-eyed and hiding behind my mommy's skirt. and don't either of YOU tell, either. don't tell anyone!

zoegirl: maddie . . . don't be like this. you've gotta let us help.

mad maddie:	**you? or your mother?**
zoegirl:	both!
mad maddie:	**forget it**
mad maddie:	**we're gonna have to change our phone number, that's what the police said. it makes me so frickin mad.**
SnowAngel:	want me to come get you, sweetie?
SnowAngel:	i'm gonna come get you and we'll all 3 go out for ice cream.
mad maddie:	**no, don't. in fact i'm turning off phone. i don't feel like talking. bye.**
SnowAngel:	maddie?
SnowAngel:	did u really leave?
zoegirl:	i think she really left.
zoegirl:	crap crap crap. i hate jana so much!!!
SnowAngel:	especially cuz you know she's laughing her butt off.
zoegirl:	you realize why maddie doesn't wanna go to the principal, right? and why she doesn't want me going over her head to my mom?
SnowAngel:	cuz she doesn't want them getting involved?
zoegirl:	no, cuz she doesn't want anyone else to see the ad. anyone who already hasn't, that is.
SnowAngel:	ack—i didn't think of that.
zoegirl:	did maddie seem . . . i dunno. mad at me? cuz i know this all started with the Boo Boo Bear thing, but she kept it going with the liars club prank. i mean, she's part of this too.
SnowAngel:	she's mad at the world. wouldn't you be?
SnowAngel:	oh, i want to KILL jana!!!!
zoegirl:	only the sucky thing is, you can't. i don't want you getting on jana's bad side too.
SnowAngel:	there's gotta be SOMETHING we can do.
zoegirl:	"we" as in you and me? that'll just escalate things.
SnowAngel:	so?

zoegirl:	so jana's a nutcase. if we could bring the police in, or the school administrators, then sure. but if it's just you who does something? who knows what she'll do to get you back?
SnowAngel:	i'm not just gonna let it go. i refuse.
SnowAngel:	i'll figure something out—just wait and see!

Thu, Feb 23, 11:01 AM E.S.T.

SnowAngel:	did you hear annc. about getting sized for grad. robes? how r we supposed to think about grad robes at a time like this?!
zoegirl:	impossible. maddie is shattered. she's trying to hide it, but i can tell.
SnowAngel:	does vincent know anything? about jana and the ad?
zoegirl:	i asked. he said no.
SnowAngel:	i saw her in the hall and she was gloating—makes me so mad!
zoegirl:	okay, but don't do anything!!!
SnowAngel:	gonna anyway. bye!

Thu, Feb 23, 5:14 PM E.S.T.

SnowAngel:	all right, maddie. you can stop worrying about jana!
mad maddie:	**i can?**
SnowAngel:	*beams with satisfaction*
SnowAngel:	i fixed HER wagon, i'll tell ya!
mad maddie:	**you fixed her . . . ? huh?**
SnowAngel:	i drove over to her house after school. that's right, i went to the DRAGON LADY'S LAIR. *spooky horror noises*
SnowAngel:	i rang the doorbell multiple times to make sure no one was home, and then i went around to the back, turned the doorknob, and wala. breaking and entering, baby.
mad maddie:	**you broke into jana's house?! yr insane!**

SnowAngel: i had my cover story ready if anyone had answered the door, but i knew jana herself wasn't there, cuz i mad-dashed out of school right when 6th period ended and jana's trash heap car was still in the parking lot.

SnowAngel: anyway, the house was unlocked, so i didn't technically break in. i just entered.

mad maddie: yeah, the cops'll give you a medal. what were you thinking???

SnowAngel: i was thinking that no one plays such a dirty trick on my maddie and gets away with it. i was thinking that jana needs a taste of her own medicine.

SnowAngel: so i scoped out the house (smelled like cigarettes) and found the room which had to be jana's, cuz of all the DVDs strewn about and the horrible black wall-hanging. and then i left a little something on her pillow. i got the idea from the senior boys.

mad maddie: you gave jana a bag of candy hearts?

SnowAngel: nooooooo. and not a dead rat, either, altho i swear i would have if i happened to have a spare dead rat. that's what i WANTED to put on her pillow.

SnowAngel: what i left was a note, which i typed on one of the school's computers so it can't be traced. it said, "hello, jana. what a beautiful room you have. hope you don't mind that i popped by, and hope you don't mind that i . . . never mind. seriously, don't give it a 2nd thought. did i tell you what a beautiful room you have? so many exquisite things, just begging to be touched." and then at the bottom, "p.s. people who are nice don't get visits from strangers."

mad maddie: angela . . .

SnowAngel: what?

mad maddie: that's extremely stalker-ish, for one thing. is that what you were going for?

SnowAngel: exactly! *claps hands in glee* now she'll be forever
               wondering who came in and what they did!

mad maddie: no she won't. she'll know right away it was you.

mad maddie: what DID you do, other than leave the note?

SnowAngel: nothing, really. i swished her toothbrush in the toilet
               and shuffled around the makeup on her counter,
               basic stuff like that. but for all she knows, i could
               have done anything.

mad maddie: wow

mad maddie: but i still don't understand WHY.

SnowAngel: what do you mean? to teach her that she can't
               mess with the winsome threesome! so that SHE'LL
               feel violated like YOU felt violated!

mad maddie: who said i felt violated?

SnowAngel: maddie . . . why r you being this way?

SnowAngel: i thought you'd be cackling with delight!!!

mad maddie: well, i'm not

mad maddie: we have a new landline number now. the moms
               changed it first thing this morning.

SnowAngel: i'm sorry she had to do that, but at least that'll take
               care of the craigslist problem.

mad maddie: it makes me so angry. not that it's even that big a
               deal, a new phone number, but just the fact that
               jana could waltz in and screw with my life like
               that . . . and with my *parents'* lives like that . . .

mad maddie: so i decided not to care, only now you've started
               it all up again.

SnowAngel: no i haven't. i've ended it.

mad maddie: do you really think that? tell me yr not that naive.

SnowAngel: *looks silently and reproachfully at friend*

mad maddie: aaaargh

mad maddie: i've got a headache, i've got to go. please don't
               guilt-trip me, that's the LAST thing i need!

mad maddie: angela, you still there?

SnowAngel: yes, i'm nursing my wounds and feeling annoyed.

SnowAngel: i broke into jana's house for you and you can't even say thanks!

mad maddie: well that's why i'm back. so . . . thanx.

SnowAngel: gee, that was so very heartfelt

mad maddie: and to admit that maybe it was a TEENY bit funny . . . and satisfying . . . and brilliant . . .

SnowAngel: *perks up* yeah?

mad maddie: but why did you say you fixed her wagon?

SnowAngel: i dunno, it's an expression my grandmom uses. *adopts crabby old-lady persona*: "i fixed HER wagon, ehh ehh ehh!"

mad maddie: it makes no sense

SnowAngel: such is life

mad maddie: what did zoe think of your little crime spree?

SnowAngel: oh, zoe *shakes head*

SnowAngel: she's not happy. AND she thinks yr mad at her.

mad maddie: well frankly, i was. just her whole "i'll bring in my big bad mommy" attitude . . . it pissed me off.

SnowAngel: why? she was just trying to help.

mad maddie: i know, i know. it's just, i don't want her MOM fighting our battles for us. god.

mad maddie: but then i realized, what else can i expect? it's not like zoe's gonna go storming in herself. that's just who she is.

SnowAngel: i did, tho. cuz i am Big Bad Angela. *preens and feels tougher than zoe*

mad maddie: and guess what? now yr gonna be next on jana's hit list.

SnowAngel: i don't care. jana is NOT gonna ruin our senior yr.

SnowAngel: *gives maddie big wet smoochie* 😊 luv ya!

zoegirl: ok, angela, i know yr phone's off, cuz when i called it went straight to voicemail. but i just had a run-in with the j-word, and you need to know about it.

zoegirl: i was sitting at my locker trying to organize my binder. i wasn't even THINKING about jana, when suddenly she comes barreling over to me and says, "you can tell angela i know it was her. tell her i'm gonna kick her a**!"

zoegirl: i was like, who talks like that? are you for real?

zoegirl: i don't want to demonize her, because i know she's a real live human being with wants and needs and all that. blah blah blah.

zoegirl: but face it. she *is* stunted and immature and oozing with bad energy. she just IS.

zoegirl: and i hope she grows out of it, and maybe one day at our 20th reunion we'll, you know, all share a chuckle . . . although that seems extremely unlikely, if not downright impossible.

zoegirl: AAARGH, i'm getting all worked up, when the only reason i'm texting is to warn you of her wrath. so watch out, that's all i'm saying!

SnowAngel: ASS, zoe. yr allowed to say it! ass ass ass! ass-poopy!

zoegirl: did you just say . . . ass-poopy?!

SnowAngel: and GOD, why do you have to be so nice all the time? we will NOT be sharing a chuckle with jana at our 20th reunion. we will not be sharing a chuckle with jana at our 100th reunion! i suppose it's to your credit that yr trying to be all fair-minded or whatever (gag), but honestly? it's just annoying.

zoegirl: angela, jana was showing serious psychotic break material by threatening you like that.

zoegirl:	has she said anything to you in person?
SnowAngel:	of course not, cuz i put her in her place and she knows it. *squishes jana with thumb and grinds into icky mess*
SnowAngel:	SHE is the ass-poopy. i learned that term on "Bones," btw. have you ever watched that show?
SnowAngel:	or, hrmm. maybe it was ass-booby . . . ?
zoegirl:	she's not gonna let this go, you know.
SnowAngel:	oh, whatever. blah blah blah.
SnowAngel:	let's go out tonite and put it all behind us. wanna?
zoegirl:	i can't, i've got plans with doug
SnowAngel:	BOR-RRRRING
SnowAngel:	i'm gonna call maddie and see if SHE wants to go out, since yr now being a you-know-what. (here's a hint: it rhymes with gas-woobie)

Sun, Feb 26, 7:01 PM E.S.T.

SnowAngel:	hey, sweet tater. have you figured out what yr going as for alter-ego day tomorrow?
mad maddie:	"alter-ego day," good god.
SnowAngel:	don't take that tone with me. you love the special senior days as much as anyone!
mad maddie:	do i? i mean, seriously. who comes up with this shit?
SnowAngel:	*pouts in a steely-eyed sort of way*
mad maddie:	oh, wait! it's YOU! YOU come up with this shit!
SnowAngel:	ha ha, yr soooo hilarious
SnowAngel:	so what r you gonna go as?
mad maddie:	let's c. i'm normally the coolest chick on the planet, so for my alter-ego i guess i'll go as . . . the president of the senior planning committee!
mad maddie:	jk again. whew, i crack myself up.
SnowAngel:	i think i'll go as a big ol' slob, since normally i'm so stylish and hip. which means I'LL go as YOU!

mad maddie: could ya try being the tiniest bit original? could ya?

SnowAngel: i told zoe to go as a stoner, since in real life she's Miss Straight-A Super Student. but she's afraid the administration would disapprove, so she's going as a biker babe.

mad maddie: A BIKER BABE???? ZOE????

mad maddie: what is she gonna wear?

SnowAngel: i dunno, we didn't get that far.

SnowAngel: what do you think jana'll go as?

mad maddie: hmm, what is the opposite of evil incarnate . . . ?

SnowAngel: ZOE!!!! *rolls about in glee*

mad maddie: lol. good one, a.

SnowAngel: ah, me. *pats self on back with extendable hand*

SnowAngel: i'm gonna go figure out my outfit for tomorrow. see ya in the morning?

mad maddie: yeah, only tomorrow's my day to sleep in, so don't look for me before 2nd period. byeas!

Mon, Feb 27, 9:02 AM E.S.T.

SnowAngel: ello, biker babe! yr looking verrry hot!

zoegirl: ello, rain cloud angela! you're looking very . . . gloomy!

SnowAngel: seen mads?

zoegirl: not yet. saw jana in her geek-wear, though. so tacky.

SnowAngel: can you say, ego?

zoegirl: ego!

Mon, Feb 27, 5:13 PM E.S.T.

mad maddie: hey there, sunshine. r you back in your traditional pink?

SnowAngel: u kidding? i've decided black is a good look for me. i will soon start using one of those ultra-long cigarette holders and slink about discussing art.

85

mad maddie:	**only u don't know anything about art**
SnowAngel:	fashion, then. i'll suck in my cheeks and be heroin-chic. except heroin-chic is so yesteryear.
SnowAngel:	didn't you think it was thoroughly egotistical of jana to show up dressed like a nerd?
mad maddie:	**it would be the same as if zoe had come as, like, a drooling idiot, cuz basically she'd be saying, "look how smart i think i am, if this is what i consider to be my opposite." but zoe would never do that.**
SnowAngel:	i liked your preppy attire. the pink-and-green belt was an excellent touch.
mad maddie:	**ms. hathoway said, "well, madigan, you certainly clean up nice." i said, "enjoy it while you can, cuz i am never tucking my shirt into my pants again."**
SnowAngel:	hee hee
SnowAngel:	and andre in his football uniform thingie, i loved that
mad maddie:	**and the captain of the football team in a tutu**
SnowAngel:	he shouldn't have worn tights, tho
mad maddie:	**especially w/o underwear**
SnowAngel:	i'm bored, and aunt sadie's going out with friends. logan said he'd bring me pizza, but i turned him down. if he and i could just hang out and have fun, i'd be all over it. but he always wants to fool around.
mad maddie:	**the nerve**
SnowAngel:	so can i come over?
mad maddie:	**yeah baby!**

Tues, Feb 28, 4:34 PM E.S.T.

mad maddie:	**oh man, you should see my room. i can't stop laughing.**
zoegirl:	pourquoi?

mad maddie: angela came over yesterday, and we took a pad of sticky notes and jumped on my bed and stuck them to the ceiling.

zoegirl: ha

mad maddie: then i found 5 more pads, blue green purple pink and orange. we jumped off my chair and desk and stuck them ALL OVER. i totally forgot how trashed it was until i got home from school.

zoegirl: aw! i wish i could have been there!

mad maddie: me 2. i need more of that, just good times with my buds.

zoegirl: we have had some pretty good times over the years, haven't we?

mad maddie: some FABULOUS times.

mad maddie: hey, did you ever check out big bunny?

zoegirl: as a matter of fact, i did. maddie . . . big bunny has teeth.

mad maddie: yeppers

zoegirl: and maddie, big bunny ate that poor little puppy.

mad maddie: nuh uh. didn't you listen to big bunny's story about the giant orange wolf?

zoegirl: the giant orange wolf who found a puppy whose nose was like an olive and whose legs were like four well-stuffed sausages?

mad maddie: and you will recall that big bunny—i mean the big orange wolf—did NOT eat the puppy, cuz he wasn't hungry at the moment. he put the puppy in a bag for later.

zoegirl: ick, maddie

mad maddie: blame that amy winfrey chick. she made it up!

mad maddie: anywayz, there's 6 more episodes. you have to watch them all to find out what happens.

zoegirl: uh huh

zoegirl: g2g—there's someone at the door.

mad maddie: come back and visit me l8r. and be sure to drink plenty of milkshakes and eat lots of sausage!

Tues, Feb 28, 5:15 PM E.S.T.

mad maddie: hey, not trying to bug you, but i'm downloading songs from itunes. want me to send you my playlist when i'm done?

zoegirl: yes please!

mad maddie: who was at the door?

zoegirl: two jehovah's witnesses. my instinct was to give them the polite brushoff, but then i thought, why? shouldn't i see what they have to say?

mad maddie: uh . . . no

zoegirl: they're people just like we are. it can't hurt.

mad maddie: yeah, but it can waste your time—time which would be far better spent downloading songs from itunes, for example.

zoegirl: plus, it doesn't say much about me if i'm not willing to consider other perspectives.

zoegirl: so i invited them in, and they were nice. they were both women, and one of them wasn't much older than us, like maybe 19 or 20. she just got married last month.

mad maddie: too young, too young

zoegirl: she goes to Bible study every week, and she and her husband are committed to lifting up their lives to God. well, whom they call "Jehovah."

zoegirl: can you imagine believing in something so much that you go door to door trying to spread the word?

mad maddie: no, and i think it's obnoxious that they do. organized religion gives me the heebie-jeebies.

zoegirl: they left me a book called "knowledge that leads to everlasting life," which we're gonna discuss the next time they come.

mad maddie:	**you invited them BACK?**
zoegirl:	in an up-in-the-air sort of way. they said, "can we come again?" and i kind of agreed.
mad maddie:	**good lord**
zoegirl:	what was i supposed to say?
zoegirl:	the girl, tina, was so pretty. she had really long hair, and she wore a skirt and a blouse. she seemed so . . . innocent.
mad maddie:	**don't let them convert you, that's all i'm gonna say**
zoegirl:	oh please
mad maddie:	**don't "oh please" me. i'm serious!**
mad maddie:	**time for din-din. tootles!**

Wed, Mar 1, 5:01 PM E.S.T.

SnowAngel:	my steering wheel cover arrived! my steering wheel cover arrived! *gambols about strewing cherries thru air*
zoegirl:	did you end up ordering the seat cover, too?
SnowAngel:	yes, it's spifftacular. plus an ADORABLE dangly cherry to hang from my rearview mirror. 🍒
SnowAngel:	next i'm gonna get a Barbie to prop in front of the gear shift. mary kate has a Barbie propped in front of her gear shift, and it cracks me up.
zoegirl:	but do you really want to copy mary kate?
SnowAngel:	then i'll get a Care Bear! yeah! *gets really excited* cuz isn't there 1 with cherries on its tummy???
zoegirl:	last year glendy gave you a care bear and you got all freaked out. you threw it away, remember?
SnowAngel:	that's cuz it was from glendy. *makes strangled sound as if being smothered in saran wrap*
SnowAngel:	if there's a Care Bear with cherries on it, then i'm definitely getting it. i'm not letting 1 bad experience taint my whole Care Bear career. 🙂

zoegirl:	what does logan think of your cherry theme?
SnowAngel:	he makes fun of it to carl and brannen, but mainly just to tease me. he's like, "i get her a jeep—a tough rugged jeep!—and she's already dolling it up. women!"
zoegirl:	i've noticed that he brings that up a lot, the fact that he gave it to you.
SnowAngel:	but he DID give it to me. i guess he's got the right to brag.
zoegirl:	it doesn't bug you?
SnowAngel:	no. does it bug YOU?
zoegirl:	why would it bug me?
SnowAngel:	good question, why WOULD it? i thought you wanted me and logan to be hunky-dory, so why r you looking for problems?
zoegirl:	i want things to be hunky-dory if they ARE hunky-dory, but i don't think you should fake it just for the sake of the jeep.
SnowAngel:	what a horrible thing to say! omg, zoe!
zoegirl:	angela, wait, i don't mean it in a *bad* way.
SnowAngel:	what other way IS there?
zoegirl:	well, then i'm sorry
zoegirl:	just delete that whole remark, ok?
SnowAngel:	*crosses arms over chest*
zoegirl:	maybe i'm just having troubles of my own. maybe i'm feeling bad and taking it out on you.
SnowAngel:	why? did something happen with doug?
zoegirl:	he's annoyed with me because i don't want to go to tilman barnwell's party with him on friday. but it's going to be that whole popular crowd. i feel awkward around them.
SnowAngel:	did you explain that to doug?
zoegirl:	no. i mean, all of a sudden doug IS friends with them, and i don't want to hold him back. but at

	the same time, i'm like, "wouldn't you rather spend friday night with me? *alone*?"
SnowAngel:	so what r you gonna do?
zoegirl:	go with him, i guess. since he wants me to.
SnowAngel:	ah-ha! so your rltnshp with doug ISN'T perfect—even you have to make compromises!
zoegirl:	i never said it was perfect!
zoegirl:	and of course i have to make compromises. i never said i didn't!
SnowAngel:	well, then let's not fight about it. *thwacks all stupidness away* there, it's gone.
SnowAngel:	here's something to change the subject: guess where aunt sadie's going tonite?
zoegirl:	where?
SnowAngel:	to a POLE-DANCING party! *snickers into cupped hands*
SnowAngel:	it's the new rage among the 30s set, apparently. she and a bunch of her girlfriends r getting together, and a real live exotic dancer is going to teach them how to do pole-dances.
zoegirl:	i don't understand. WHY?
SnowAngel:	to learn how to turn on their men?
SnowAngel:	also it's supposed to be good exercise . . .
zoegirl:	will they . . . wear costumes?
SnowAngel:	good grief, i hope not. some of aunt sadie's friends r, shall we say, rather generously endowed. i'm not really wanting to envision them in g-strings.
zoegirl:	wowzers
zoegirl:	i don't really know what to say.
SnowAngel:	next month she's supposed to go to a lingerie party—and the friend who's hosting that one wants *aunt sadie* to host a sex toy party!
zoegirl:	what happened to tupperware??? do these 30-year-olds not need tupperware anymore?

SnowAngel:	no, cuz they're 2 busy gyrating around poles. who can store leftovers at a time like that? 😊
SnowAngel:	want me to ask aunt sadie if you can tag along?
zoegirl:	**no thanks**
SnowAngel:	if you change your mind, just holler!

Wed, Mar 1, 11:30 PM E.S.T.

SnowAngel:	omg, zoe, i have to give you the report on aunt sadie!
SnowAngel:	zoe!!! WAKE UP!
SnowAngel:	oh fine, whatever
SnowAngel:	so aunt sadie stumbled in half an hour ago, all tipsy and giggling and loud, and she woke me up so she could do her dance for me. 😲 😲 😲
SnowAngel:	she had to use the bedroom door since she didn't have a pole, but she's gonna buy 1 from the exotic dancer, who's name was marge. isn't that a terrible name for an exotic dancer? MARGE?
SnowAngel:	anyway, her dance was all full of leg kicks and shimmies and shakings of the boobs, and IT WAS AWFUL!!!
SnowAngel:	it's so weird when you realize that grown-ups are ppl too, and that they do really stupid and embarrassing things just like we do.
SnowAngel:	she told me her inner thighs are super-sore. she also told me (prepare thyself) that the whole thing made her really horny.
SnowAngel:	my innocence? gone!!!

Thu, Mar 2, 9:55 AM E.S.T.

mad maddie:	**dude! megan got accepted to clemson!**
SnowAngel:	yahootie!!!
mad maddie:	**she got her letter yesterday. it was big and fat, so she said she had a good feeling about it.**

SnowAngel:	aw, that's awesome
mad maddie:	**i know! but at the same time, it's like, YIKES. she's our first friend to get an acceptance, you know? not counting bryce's early decision to UVA.**
SnowAngel:	first but not last, hopefully!
mad maddie:	**can you sneak out of class? i'm gonna go meet megan and mary kate in the quad and you shld come, too!**
SnowAngel:	can't. mrs. e haz eagle eyes.
mad maddie:	**let's take megan out for lunch, then. we need to celebrate!**

Fri, Mar 3, 6:17 PM E.S.T.

mad maddie:	**hey, zo. is tonite tilman's party?**
zoegirl:	yes, won't you *please* come? i'd feel so much more comfortable if you were there!
mad maddie:	**no way, that crowd's too power suit for me.**
mad maddie:	**remember how mean they were to doug back in 9th grade?**
zoegirl:	they weren't ALL mean to him. anyway, doug says they were ok one-on-one. it was just when they got together that they ganged up on him.
mad maddie:	**and that makes it soooo much better**
zoegirl:	paige and holly and those girls are going to be there, and i'm going to feel like the biggest dork. i wish i didn't have to go!
mad maddie:	**you don't! you R allowed to say no, you know!**
zoegirl:	but i already said i would. doug would be *really* pissed if i backed out now.
mad maddie:	**has doug changed that much, that he would be "pissed" if you didn't obey his every command?**
zoegirl:	it's not like that
mad maddie:	**then what is it like?**
zoegirl:	just forget about it

zoegirl:	i've got to go
mad maddie:	**well . . . all right. try your best to have fun!**

Sat, Mar 4, 10:09 PM E.S.T.

mad maddie:	**hey, girl! i'm over at vincent's. whatcha doin?**
SnowAngel:	logan fell asleep during "Pitch Perfect." he's very cute when he's asleep, but he's not such great company.
mad maddie:	**maybe you should let HIM pick the movie every once in a while. ever thought of that?**
SnowAngel:	*pushes "reject" button* bleep!
SnowAngel:	i watched the end of it myself, and now i'm on facebook looking at pics from tilman's party. zoe shows up in none of them, interestingly enough. tilman's parents seem to have been there, tho, which must have been loads of fun.
SnowAngel:	but i'd much rather chat with you. HI! 🐵
mad maddie:	**vincent and his bro r playing foozball, and later on some other ppl r coming over. you guys should join us.**
SnowAngel:	that's ok. i'm kinda liking having a low-key nite, to tell the truth.
mad maddie:	**i hear ya**
mad maddie:	**vincent gets a kick out of you, tho. your name came up earlier, and he said he thought you'd be good in bed.**
SnowAngel:	WHAT?!
mad maddie:	**he's not hitting on you. he just thinks yr cool.**
SnowAngel:	i am cool
SnowAngel:	why did my name come up?
mad maddie:	**i was telling him about the whole j-word soap opera and why he shouldn't believe anything she says. apparently she bad-mouths me all the time, and vincent gets stuck listening to it all, poor baby. but**

	too bad, it's his own fault for being friends with her.
SnowAngel:	is he STILL friends with her? even after the craigslist thing?
mad maddie:	he thought that was funny—and yes, i smacked him for it. he thought it was even funnier that you broke into her house and left a stalker note.
SnowAngel:	you TOLD him?!
mad maddie:	he says jana's stepmonster is having an affair, that's what jana thinks, and that's why she's full of rage. whatevs.
SnowAngel:	maddie, i can't believe you told vincent that i was the one who broke into her house! what if he tells jana?!
mad maddie:	ooo, you'd be so busted! ooo! cuz right now she thinks it was the tooth fairy, you know.
SnowAngel:	fine, maybe she has her suspicions. there is no reason for him to CONFIRM it.
SnowAngel:	i would like to point out, however, that it's been over a week and she hasn't done anything to get back at me. i don't think she's gonna.
mad maddie:	you just keep having those happy thoughts, sweetie.
SnowAngel:	why did vincent say that about me being good in bed???
mad maddie:	no reason, it was just where the convo ended up going. he had a soul station playing on Pandora, and he was like, "B-L-double-M, man."
SnowAngel:	what's B-L-double-M?
mad maddie:	black love-making music. B-L-double-M.
mad maddie:	and you have to say it that way. you can't say B-L-M-M.
SnowAngel:	uh . . . ok
SnowAngel:	is that a term he made up? sounds racist.
mad maddie:	it's not racist. it's amusing.

SnowAngel:	just cuz something's amusing doesn't mean it's not racist.
mad maddie:	**dude, chill. vincent likes soul, and vincent likes sex. AND he's a "person of color," so he can't be racist.**
mad maddie:	**anywayz, it's better than U-H-D-H-M**
SnowAngel:	what's that?
mad maddie:	**uptight honky dry-humping music**
SnowAngel:	ha
mad maddie:	**what would UHDHM be, you think? faith hill? celine dion?**
SnowAngel:	justin bieber
mad maddie:	**EWWWW!**
SnowAngel:	so, not to go on and on about this . . . but did vincent say WHY he thought i'd be good in bed?
mad maddie:	**probably cuz you make him laugh. plus he thinks you've got CAJONES.**
SnowAngel:	hmmph
SnowAngel:	did he say if he thought zoe would be good in bed?
mad maddie:	**nope, just you**
mad maddie:	**i don't think zoe is the 1st person who comes up when guys talk about sex . . .**
SnowAngel:	yet if they only knew . . .
mad maddie:	**how'd tilman's party go? i thought about calling to ask, but didn't. i think i annoyed her last night.**
SnowAngel:	we talked this morning. turns out it was a party for grown-ups, but the grown-ups could bring their kids, and doug wanted zoe there for moral support. cuz DOUG was nervous—isn't that funny?
mad maddie:	**why was he nervous?**
SnowAngel:	cuz even tho doug hangs out with tilman and that crowd at school, he doesn't really know them all that well.
SnowAngel:	plus doug had already told his mom that zoe was

coming, so when zoe tried to back out, it made doug get uptight. not that he explained that to zoe at the time . . .

mad maddie: **unnecessary drama, baby**

SnowAngel: but zoe said the party itself was fine. she said it actually ended up bringing them closer, cuz they had to talk that stuff out. she said, and i quote, "he's amazing. i feel soooo lucky."

mad maddie: **that's her problem, that she feels "lucky"! HE'S the one who should feel lucky!**

SnowAngel: absolutely

mad maddie: **but with zoe these days it's totally one-sided.**

mad maddie: **i miss the old zo, the one who thought for herself.**

SnowAngel: i know she's worried about next year, but who isn't?

mad maddie: **i say live in the present and enjoy each moment as it comes.**

mad maddie: **speaking of—guess who i had coffee with this afternoon?**

SnowAngel: who?

mad maddie: **ian—but don't get all excitedl it was just coffee.**

SnowAngel: *squeals in a super-high-pitched voice*

mad maddie: **i told you not to get excited**

SnowAngel: *squeals again*

SnowAngel: did you call him, or did he call you?

mad maddie: **he called me. it was sweet.**

SnowAngel: AND?

mad maddie: **and we had coffee. actually, i had chai.**

SnowAngel: *puts hands on hips* madigan kinnick, give me details right now!

mad maddie: **we had a good time talking. it was nice cuz it made me think maybe things can be normal b/w us again.**

SnowAngel: just "normal"?

mad maddie: listen, i already broke up with the guy once. no way i'm gonna put him thru that again.

SnowAngel: AH HA! but yr thinking about it!

mad maddie: i'm NOT thinking about it, that's the point.

SnowAngel: but yr acknowledging the possibility exists.

SnowAngel: anyway, if you did start seeing each other again, who says you'd break up?

SnowAngel: and ANYWAY, shouldn't ian be the one who gets to decide whether he's willing to risk it?

mad maddie: whoa there, bessy

mad maddie: he asked me out for coffee. he didn't ask me to marry him. altho he did pay for my chai . . .

SnowAngel: *perks up* he did?

mad maddie: and my cheesecake

SnowAngel: he DID?

mad maddie: and i have to admit, he looked pretty hot. he hadn't shaved cuz he's been sick, and his stubble was so damn sexy.

SnowAngel: STOP! UR GONNA MAKE ME PIDDLE MYSELF!

mad maddie: okey-doke, i'm outta here. i'll call you tomorrow— we can go out for donuts.

SnowAngel: yes ma'am!

Sun, Mar 5, 3:30 PM E.S.T.

mad maddie: krispy kreme? half an hr?

SnowAngel: cya there!

Sun, Mar 5, 9:33 PM E.S.T.

SnowAngel: hey, zo. i wish you could have come out with us today. we missed you!

zoegirl: next weekend we'll do something together, i promise.

SnowAngel: we better, cuz time is going by way too fast and we have to spend as much of it together as possible.

zoegirl:	i know, i know
SnowAngel:	i'm SERIOUS, zo!
zoegirl:	you don't think i realize that? i do. but the same's true for doug. i wish you could understand that.
zoegirl:	he wanted to go for a walk by the chatahoochee. what was i gonna do, say no?
SnowAngel:	a little time apart's not gonna kill you. in fact, it'd probably be good for you. isn't that what those relationship articles say, that yr supposed to maintain your own friends and interests?
zoegirl:	???
zoegirl:	i AM maintaining my own friends and interests. just because we didn't hang out this weekend doesn't make me a bad friend!
SnowAngel:	i never said you were a bad friend. i just love you, and it makes me sad that i never get to c you.
zoegirl:	well please don't guilt-trip me about it. i feel like i'm under so much pressure these days! and if i don't do everything just right, everyone hates me!
SnowAngel:	???
SnowAngel:	where is THIS coming from?
zoegirl:	never mind. we're *all* under pressure, i know that. that's why doug wanted to go for a walk, cuz he hasn't heard from oberlin yet and it's driving him crazy.
SnowAngel:	take a deep breath. everything's gonna be ok.
zoegirl:	it's just that so much is riding on this year. i feel like if i make one false step, everything's going to come tumbling down. and with the whole college thing looming over us . . .
zoegirl:	i'm going to miss everyone so much. i'm already dreading saying good-bye.
SnowAngel:	then don't! come to UGA with me! ☺

SnowAngel:	with your record, you could apply tomorrow and get in.
zoegirl:	that's a sweet thought . . . but i don't think so
SnowAngel:	why not? make doug apply 2, and you could BOTH go to UGA.
zoegirl:	i know you're trying to make me feel better, but you're actually not.
zoegirl:	my top choice is still kenyon, assuming i get accepted.
SnowAngel:	*pouts*
SnowAngel:	why kenyon? what makes kenyon so much better than georgia?
zoegirl:	because it's small, because it's got a great liberal arts program, because it's got a strong writing faculty. it's just a really good fit.
SnowAngel:	you sound like yr quoting from a brochure
SnowAngel:	anyway, UGA has all of those things
zoegirl:	plus kenyon's 2 hours away from oberlin
SnowAngel:	zoe, you can NOT make your college decision based on doug!
zoegirl:	i'm not!
zoegirl:	i just . . . i don't want to go to a state school, all right?
SnowAngel:	*draws back*
SnowAngel:	ok, now i'm a little offended. a state school's not good enough for you?
zoegirl:	*please* don't, angela!
zoegirl:	i just told you how stressed out i feel—you're supposed to be nice to me!!!
SnowAngel:	maddie says yr gonna end up at princeton cuz that's where your mom went.
zoegirl:	maddie's not the ruler of the universe. and i'm not going to end up at princeton, because i'm not gonna get in.

SnowAngel:	you don't know that
zoegirl:	yes i do . . . because i sabotaged my application.
SnowAngel:	*faints*
SnowAngel:	for real??
zoegirl:	i wrote my essay about swinging on the playground at memorial park and how liberating it is. which is true, but not exactly princeton material. and how i think there should be a National Pigtails Day, where everyone says "screw it" to being grown-up and wears their hair in pigtails.
SnowAngel:	
zoegirl:	uh huh
SnowAngel:	oh
SnowAngel:	do you really think that, that there should be a Nat'l Pigtails Day?
zoegirl:	don't you? just to escape from the go-go-go of it all?
SnowAngel:	i suppose. i'm just kinda surprised that YOU do.
SnowAngel:	first you "missed" the early decision deadline, and then you sabotaged your application. why didn't you tell us?
zoegirl:	i don't know, i just didn't. but i am now.
SnowAngel:	what's your mom gonna do?
zoegirl:	what *can* she do?
zoegirl:	if i don't get in, i don't get in. case closed.
SnowAngel:	i'm floored, that's all i can say.
zoegirl:	i've got to go, it's time to take my pill. i have to take them at the same time every night or they won't work.
SnowAngel:	for real?
zoegirl:	i picked 10 o'clock, because that's when i usually brush my teeth and get ready for bed. but then when i was a week and a half into it, i realized that

wasn't such a good idea, because when i go out, i
have to bring one with me. like at tilman's party. i
brought my pill in my pocket, wrapped in a sliver
of aluminum foil, and at 10 o'clock i snuck off to
the bathroom and swallowed it.

SnowAngel: sounds complicated

zoegirl: welcome to my life. *everything* is complicated!

Mon, Mar 6, 6:14 PM E.S.T.

zoegirl: hey, mads. i needed a distraction from
homework, so i watched big bunny episode 2.

mad maddie: **YUMMY episode 2, you mean. that's what it says
when you click on it. yummmmmmmy.**

zoegirl: i'm thinking that susie and lulu and the round-
headed boy should stop visiting big bunny.
the "sofa" he put out for them? it was a giant
baguette!

mad maddie: **yes, but while they were sitting there, he told that
delightful story about the turnip. wasn't that a
delightful story?**

zoegirl: that story made no sense!

mad maddie: **"it is from eating veg-uh-tuh-buls that i got to be
sooooo big and strong. yessss, veg-uh-tuh-buls."**

zoegirl: uh huh. then why, when lulu said she'd bring him
some carrots, did he request a kitty instead?

mad maddie: **he wants a delicious tender kitty to pet and love!
weren't you paying attn?**

zoegirl: i think lulu and the round-headed boy need to
listen to susie. that's what i think.

mad maddie: **i love susie. susie's my hero**

zoegirl: of course she is, she's a mini-maddie.

mad maddie: **why, cuz she's surly?**

zoegirl: and churlish. yes.

mad maddie: **susie's the only 1 with brains. she TOLD lulu and**

	round-headed boy not to go back into the forest, but they did anyway.
zoegirl:	she went too, don't forget
mad maddie:	cuz she's a good friend! she had to take care of them.
mad maddie:	you noticed, however, that she was the only 1 of the 3 who did NOT take a seat on the french-bread sofa?
zoegirl:	i don't want lulu to bring big bunny a kitten. lulu better not bring big bunny a kitty, maddie.
mad maddie:	watch and c (heh heh heh . . .)
zoegirl:	you're so weird
zoegirl:	hey, did you hear the latest? supposedly terri spotted jana's stepmom in some guy's car who *wasn't* jana's dad, and terri, being the good friend that she is, let it slip to everyone.
mad maddie:	what a pal
zoegirl:	i know, can you imagine?
mad maddie:	it would totally suck. it would be beyond humiliating. but given that jana has no problem humiliating ME, i can't muster up much sympathy.
zoegirl:	at least it's distracted her from getting back at angela.
mad maddie:	true dat!

Tues, Mar 7, 5:15 PM E.S.T.

SnowAngel:	🙁
zoegirl:	what?
SnowAngel:	jana left a DEAD BIRD in the passenger seat of my jeep!!! (and i'm so not kidding, much as i wish i was.)
zoegirl:	noooooo!
SnowAngel:	yessssss!
zoegirl:	but we thought she wasn't going to do the evil revenge thing! we thought she'd forgotten!

SnowAngel:	well, she didn't. and you know what's weird? i almost put a dead rat on her pillow, except i didn't have a spare dead rat. where in the world do you think she found a dead bird?
zoegirl:	angela, whoa. you've got to give me a minute to process this.
zoegirl:	a DEAD BIRD? i don't understand!
SnowAngel:	have you not yet grasped the fact that when it comes to jana, there IS no understanding? maybe it was a voodoo thing. or maybe she's jealous of my beautiful cherry-themed jeep, since her station wagon is such a heap. maybe the bird actually died in her backseat, i wouldn't be surprised!
zoegirl:	how did she put the bird in there? did you leave the jeep unlocked?
SnowAngel:	what is this, blame-the-victim time? it's got zip-up windows. it's not that hard to break into.
zoegirl:	then you should get the window fingerprinted!
SnowAngel:	*hedges just a teeny bit* except that i SUPPOSE it's possible i left the window open myself. *eensy-weensy niggle*
zoegirl:	did you or didn't you?
SnowAngel:	i was in a hurry to get to homeroom! i can't always be leaning over and zipping up windows when i'm late to homeroom, can i?
SnowAngel:	anyway, i doubt there's any law against leaving dead birds in someone's car.
zoegirl:	you're *sure* it was jana who did it?
SnowAngel:	yr NOT? who else would it be? who else would have such a psychotic brain as to scoop up a dead bird and deposit it in someone's open window?
zoegirl:	point taken
zoegirl:	so what did you do?
SnowAngel:	i made logan remove the bird with his jacket, and

	i gave it a proper burial. it wasn't its fault it was the pawn of the evil jana.
zoegirl:	but you don't think she actually "killed" it. that's creepy, the idea of jana killing a living creature.
SnowAngel:	no, it wasn't mauled or anything. it was just dead.
zoegirl:	freshly dead?
SnowAngel:	ewww! how am i supposed to know?
zoegirl:	what are you going to do? are you going to say anything to jana?
SnowAngel:	hmm, lemme think. "nice bird, thanks for the memories"?
zoegirl:	i think that once and for all you should just let it go. let her have her moment of triumph, pathetic as it is, and move on.
SnowAngel:	yr saying do NOTHING? just sit here and take it like a . . . dead-bird-taking person?
zoegirl:	yes, because you're bigger than this. you're a bigger person than jana.
SnowAngel:	*rolls eyes and fails to feel noble*
SnowAngel:	i'm gonna go lysol the heck out of the place where the bird was. i could get bird flu, you know. and perish.
zoegirl:	you're being very brave. i'm proud of you for not retaliating.
SnowAngel:	hmmph!!!

Tues, Mar 7, 11:50 PM E.S.T.

mad maddie:	angela! newsflash! newsflash!
mad maddie:	it came to me in a sparkling moment of clarity: jana was GIVING YOU THE BIRD. as in stick up middle finger, fold down others? jana gave you the frickin bird.
mad maddie:	you've gotta give her points for cleverness, actually. or not.

mad maddie: i'm feeling smug for figuring it out, that's all!

Wed, Mar 8, 11:04 AM E.S.T.

mad maddie: um, mary kate said she spotted you in study hall.

mad maddie: shall i repeat myself? in. study. hall. all by yourself. care to explain?

SnowAngel: study hall is sexy, don't you know? plus I needed a nice lonely computer to use, with no busybodies peeking over my shoulder.

mad maddie: how come?

SnowAngel: *grins evilly* i'm ordering a crate of baby chicks to be delivered to jana's house. bwahaha!

mad maddie: wtf???

SnowAngel: just click on the "submit" button and . . . wala! order #2453 completed and paid for. YES.

mad maddie: dude, explain

SnowAngel: well, it's obvious that zoe wasn't gonna do anything, even tho in a perfect universe she would have. but no. she thought we should "let it go," as if that was an option.

mad maddie: see? now you know how i felt!

SnowAngel: i never said i didn't!

SnowAngel: you stepped in to defend her when jana started those rumors, and then I stepped in to defend YOU after the craigslist nightmare. it is soooo her turn!

mad maddie: if zoe were an eye-for-an-eye girl. but she's not. she's a pacifist.

SnowAngel: there is time for peace and there is time for war. and a dead bird in my jeep means war.

mad maddie: and war means . . . a crate of baby chickens?

SnowAngel: it was aunt sadie's idea. she and her sorority sisters sent a crate of chicks to some girl in college. you can buy them from farmresource.com.

mad maddie: um, sweetie? jana left a dead bird—i repeat, a DEAD bird—in your jeep. and now, as a way of thanking her, yr sending her a crate of fresh victims?

SnowAngel: omg

mad maddie: uh huh

SnowAngel: omg, OMG, OMG!

SnowAngel: what have i done? *bashes in head with keyboard*

mad maddie: just go back and cancel the order, you doof!

SnowAngel: right. gotta run!!!!

Thu, Mar 9, 4:45 PM E.S.T.

zoegirl: did angela hear back from the farm supply place? were they able to stop her order?

mad maddie: nope, by the time she got a human being on the phone, the order was already processed. however, the nice man did offer her a discount on fertilizer.

zoegirl: angela is insane. what was she thinking?

mad maddie: she was thinking that jana needed to be put in her place, and since it was obvious YOU weren't gonna do anything . . .

zoegirl: *me*? why would i do anything?

zoegirl: did angela *want* me to do something?

mad maddie: ???

mad maddie: of course she did. she wanted you to rush in like her knight in shining armor, just like i rushed in for you and she rushed in for me.

zoegirl: well . . . but . . .

zoegirl: it was a dead bird, maddie. not a mortal wound to her soul.

mad maddie: dead bird, mortal wound to soul . . .

mad maddie: i'm just sayin

zoegirl: great. so you and angela think i'm a sucky friend,

and i've basically murdered a crate of baby chicks. that's just great.

mad maddie: the chicks r scheduled to arrive tomorrow—they haven't been murdered YET.

Fri, Mar 10, 8:17 PM E.S.T.

zoegirl: hey, angela! sorry i didn't call you back—i went to R.E.I. with doug.

zoegirl: but just to be clear, it's not that i didn't *want* to call you back, i was just busy. and i just happened to be with doug. but that doesn't mean i was picking him over you. you know that, right?

zoegirl: where r you? r you intercepting the chick delivery???

zoegirl: call me!!!!

Fri, Mar 10, 9:09 PM E.S.T.

mad maddie: dude, i heard back from angela, and it's not good. the UPS guy was a tool and refused to give her the package, even after she explained the situation.

zoegirl: so where are the chicks now? and where is she?

mad maddie: well. i had my boy vincent do some detective work, and jana DID receive the crate. angela can be happy about one thing: jana's stepmonster was LIVID. i guess the chicks messed up her newly refinished floor.

mad maddie: she told jana to get rid of the chicks or else, so jana took them to tony marcus's house, who's gonna use them to teach his doberman how to attack.

zoegirl: WHAT?!!!

mad maddie: so that's where angela is, racing over to tony's to rescue the chicks from the jaws of death. i would have gone with her, but i'm at starbucks waiting for ian. vincent calls it "starfucks," btw.

zoegirl:	that's so sick that tony marcus would torture baby chicks. why would anybody do that?
zoegirl:	wait a sec, did you say *ian*?!
mad maddie:	**but i like starbucks. i like their frappuccinos.**
zoegirl:	i like starbucks too, and i'm proud of you for not calling it starf***s. i'm even more proud of you for having a date with ian. but now i'm going to try calling angela again!!!

Fri, Mar 10, 10:33 PM E.S.T.

SnowAngel:	i got the chicks!!! i got the chicks!!!
mad maddie:	**yay! they're all safe and sound?**
SnowAngel:	all but 1, which was dead when i got there. ☹ tony swears it had a heart attack just from hearing his dog bark, but i dunno. do baby chicks have heart attacks?
mad maddie:	**did it have any bite marks on it?**
SnowAngel:	oh god, i'm not sure. i didn't really look . . .
mad maddie:	**poor chickie**
SnowAngel:	i know, i feel sooooo bad. like, i should have zoe say a prayer for it or something!
SnowAngel:	but at least i saved the others. they're in aunt sadie's bathtub, slipping and squawking around. and pooping. they poop A LOT. i'm a bit worried about what aunt sadie's gonna say . . .
mad maddie:	**did zoe reach you? she's been hyperventilating all nite.**
SnowAngel:	yeah. we talked. and—omg! she told me you were at starbucks waiting for ian???
mad maddie:	**yep, he's here now, sitting right next to me. we r having a fool-around-on-the-computer date, cuz turns out we're geeks. who knew?**
SnowAngel:	did you just call it a DATE?! and what do you mean, fool around? as in FOOL AROUND fool around?

mad maddie: i mean we've both got our laptops and we're doing random computer stuff, you freak. and showing each other. in fact ian's reading over my shoulder and trying to grab my phone this very second.

SnowAngel: *shrieks and claps hand to mouth*

SnowAngel: he's not really, is he?

mad maddie: no. but i did tell him about the chicks, and he thinks you did a good thing by saving them.

SnowAngel: i had to. i'm the 1 who . . . you know. put them in peril.

mad maddie: nonetheless, baby. big thumbs-up.

mad maddie: so there's a party at ethan's tomorrow—gonna go?

SnowAngel: yep, i'm going with andre. well, technically i'm going with logan, but i told logan i'd meet him there. which didn't make him happy, but . . .

SnowAngel: bleh. sometimes i just don't want to deal with it.

SnowAngel: does that answer your question?

mad maddie: uh, sure, altho a simple "yes" would have been sufficient.

SnowAngel: don't know what i'll do about the chicks, tho . . .

mad maddie: dude, i'm outta here. want me to tell ian "hi" for you?

SnowAngel: i want you to give him a big smoocheroo for me. on the lips, with lots of tongue action.

SnowAngel: bye! 😊

Sat, Mar 11, 9:44 AM E.S.T.

zoegirl: hi, angela. how are the chicks doing this morning?

SnowAngel: they're pooping machines—it's unbelievable! aunt sadie made me take them out of the tub and scrub it with bleach, so now they're living in my room in a box. only they keep hopping out and peck-peck-pecking all over my room.

SnowAngel:	hey, would YOU like a cute baby chick? or 2 or 3? i'm giving them away fo fwee!
zoegirl:	no thanks
SnowAngel:	rats. can you think of anyone who would?
zoegirl:	er . . . maybe a petting zoo? or a farmer?
SnowAngel:	ooo, yeah! do you know any petting zoo owners or farmers?
zoegirl:	sorry
SnowAngel:	*grrrr-ness*
SnowAngel:	zoe, listen. i have a question for you and yr gonna think i'm being facetious, but i'm not. do you pray?
zoegirl:	um, yeah. why?
SnowAngel:	like, every night? do you get down on your knees?
zoegirl:	i don't get down on my knees, but yes, i pray every night. why?
SnowAngel:	what do you pray about?
zoegirl:	just stuff that's going on in my life. i ask for help dealing with it. and i say thanks for all the good things in my life, like you and maddie and doug.
SnowAngel:	honestly? you thank God for me??? *gets teary-eyed*
zoegirl:	i think it's important to be grateful, that's all.
zoegirl:	are you secretly thinking that sounds incredibly stupid?
SnowAngel:	not at all! i think it's awesome.
SnowAngel:	will you say a prayer for that one chick? the one who died?
zoegirl:	why don't *you* say a prayer for it?
SnowAngel:	cuz you've had more practice.
SnowAngel:	1 little prayer, plz? it would make me feel so much better.
zoegirl:	sure, of course
SnowAngel:	and while yr at it, would you pray that i develop

	phenomenally lustrous hair and a flawless complexion? and that i win a shopping spree at macy's?
zoegirl:	angela!
SnowAngel:	jk—but not about the chick 😊
SnowAngel:	you going to ethan's tonite?
zoegirl:	no, doug and i are going to watch a movie and cuddle.
SnowAngel:	a pox on your head
SnowAngel:	well, if you change your mind, you should come!

Sat, Mar 11, 9:57 AM E.S.T.

SnowAngel:	one more thing. i bet you floss, too, don't you?
zoegirl:	of course. don't you?
SnowAngel:	no comment
zoegirl:	angela! you really should floss EVERY DAY!!!

Sat, Mar 11, 11:00 PM E.S.T.

mad maddie:	we miss you, zo! come to ethan's and drag doug with you!!!
zoegirl:	er . . .
mad maddie:	andre keeps singing songs from "The Book of Mormon." so random, and yet so very, very entertaining.
mad maddie:	and *someone* has a lampshade on his/her head. the classic party move, and it's REALLY AND TRULY HAPPENING, RIGHT IN FRONT OF MY EYES. 👀
mad maddie:	wanna know who?
zoegirl:	sure
mad maddie:	then get off yer butt and get over here!
zoegirl:	it sounds fun! it really does. but i'm good.
zoegirl:	but thanks for asking!

mad maddie: omg, ethan's party turned so soap-opera-ish last night. u REALLY shld have been there.

mad maddie: zo? anyone? helloooooo?

mad maddie: well, here's the short version: angela made logan cry.

mad maddie: if you wanna know more, call me!!!

mad maddie: hey, sweetie. you doing ok?

SnowAngel: hey, mads. i'm FINE, i just feel like a huge jerk.

mad maddie: how's logan?

SnowAngel: *blows out big puff of air*

SnowAngel: he's sad. i dunno.

SnowAngel: but we talked some more after we left ethan's, and i guess we got things resolved. for now, anyway.

mad maddie: it kinda surprised me, the way you were acting last nite. you just . . . didn't seem like you.

SnowAngel: i know! i didn't FEEL like me! i get that way whenever i'm around logan these days. it's so bad, maddie. i become this mean callous person who treats him like shit, even tho he's such a great guy. and the worst thing is, he LETS me!

mad maddie: ooo, that's not good

SnowAngel: he likes me too much! i never thought that could be a problem, but it is! *pulls hair from scalp*

mad maddie: angela . . .

SnowAngel: what?

SnowAngel: no, don't. i know what yr gonna say. but i CAN'T break up with him. he gave me a JEEP, maddie.

mad maddie: is the jeep really that important?

SnowAngel: aaargh

SnowAngel: no not as in "i'm so materialistic that i'll keep going out with you so i can have a car." it's more the fact that . . .

SnowAngel: GOD, maddie. HE GAVE ME A JEEP. that's the nicest thing any guy's ever done for me. what kind of heartless bitch would break up with him after that?

mad maddie: er . . . the kind of heartless bitch who at least wouldn't be treating him like shit anymore?

SnowAngel: i wish HE would break up with ME. that's what i keep hoping will happen. is that horrible?

mad maddie: pretty much

mad maddie: but i love you anywayz. you know that.

SnowAngel: so does logan, apparently *buries face in hands*

mad maddie: i tried to reach zoe so i cld catch her up on everything, but she was—sooprise—unavailable. prolly with doug, prolly doing something ridiculously wholesome like having brunch with him and his parents.

mad maddie: i almost told her that she and doug are starting to look alike, like those owners who look like their dogs. but i showed restraint.

SnowAngel: what a good girl you are

mad maddie: change of subject: what did jana say when you were playing quarters? i saw your face get all hard.

SnowAngel: oh GROAN. it was just jana being jana, as usual. she goes to serena patterson, "it's so sad to see a hottie like logan go to waste, isn't it? cuz he sure isn't getting any from angela. HE's the one who would appreciate a good chick, if you know what i mean."

mad maddie: did you say anything back, like "better a good chick than a dead bird"?

SnowAngel: ha, i wish

SnowAngel: but no, i took the high road and didn't even mention the dead bird incident. so there.

mad maddie: that'll show her!

zoegirl:	angela, what happened at ethan's party?
zoegirl:	maddie hinted that there was drama, but then added to the drama by not telling me. will you please explain?
SnowAngel:	it's really not that interesting but fine.
SnowAngel:	andre and i showed up around 9, and i could tell logan was all excited to see me. but i wasn't excited to see him. and i guess i kinda . . . didn't make much of an effort. i somehow talked to other ppl for most of the night, and i guess it made logan feel bad.
zoegirl:	because you were ignoring him?
SnowAngel:	not IGNORING him, just . . .
SnowAngel:	i didn't set OUT to ignore him, i just didn't wanna be with him.
zoegirl:	why?
SnowAngel:	cuz my head is messed up! cuz i'm a mean, stupid, horrible person!
zoegirl:	how did he end up crying???
SnowAngel:	well, at one point i ended up out on the patio with vincent, who was listening to me go on about how frustrated i am with the whole situation. and that in itself was strange. i mean, me? having a heart-to-heart with vincent?!
SnowAngel:	part of it was the beer, i'm sure. you know how drinking can either make things better or worse depending on what mood you were in to start with?
zoegirl:	not really
SnowAngel:	last night it just made me feel down on everything. it wasn't much fun.
zoegirl:	doesn't sound like much fun
SnowAngel:	anyway, maddie realized that logan was upset, and she came and told me that i should talk to him. but

	i said no. so she went to talk to him herself, and a few minutes later he appeared by my side and said, "angela, come on, let's go for a walk."
SnowAngel:	we went and sat on a wall outside ethan's house, and he told me he thought he loved me. isn't that just peachy? and that he didn't understand what was going on. that's when he started crying, which made ME cry. it was awful!
zoegirl:	poor logan!
SnowAngel:	and poor me! don't forget poor me!
zoegirl:	so how did you work things out? or rather, *did* you work things out?
SnowAngel:	i told him i didn't know WHY i was acting that way, and that i was sorry for being such a terrible girlfriend. and last nite i really did feel sorry. but now i just feel blah about it again.
zoegirl:	oh, angela
SnowAngel:	usually i'm the 1 chasing after whatever guy i'm crushing on, you know? and now the situation's reversed, and i can't get my head around it.
SnowAngel:	the problem is, i honestly do like him . . . just not in a pulse-racing way. but why can't i just CHOOSE to like him that way? why can't i let my head decide instead of my heart???
zoegirl:	i can't believe he said he loves you.
zoegirl:	what did you say back?
SnowAngel:	i buried my head against his chest and didn't meet his eyes. but i DIDN'T say "i love you, 2." at least i was honest that way.
zoegirl:	wow
SnowAngel:	on the plus side, it's almost spring break, which means we'll be apart for a week. which sounds horrible, i know, but maybe being in california will clear my head.

zoegirl:	i wish i were going to california. but no, i get to visit my grandparents in tennessee.
SnowAngel:	please remember: i'm going to EL CERRITO, where i will prolly see the dreadful glendy. altho i guess it's better than poor maddie, who has to stay at home and clean out her room.
zoegirl:	geez louise, we're pathetic
SnowAngel:	you got that right
SnowAngel:	i have to go feed the chicks. cya tomorrow!

Mon, Mar 13, 5:25 PM E.D.T.

mad maddie:	oh, zo-eeee!
zoegirl:	hey, mads. what's up?
mad maddie:	whoa! yr actually there!
mad maddie:	how long do i have before doug comes over?
zoegirl:	haha, very funny
mad maddie:	???
zoegirl:	grrrr . . . 3o minutes. we have a physics exam to study for, because of course mr. franklin is making us take an exam the week before spring break.
zoegirl:	but we can chat till then
mad maddie:	wow, i'm honored
mad maddie:	did mr. franklin read you guys the announcement about "senior games week"?
zoegirl:	if he did, i missed it. what's senior games week?
mad maddie:	i swiped mr. gerard's copy, lemme read it to you.
mad maddie:	"Dear Teachers, We are asking that you please mention these following senior lunch games to your classes. If you can, act excited. On Tuesday we will have Ice Sledding in the cafeteria, which will include prizes. On Wednesday we will be having a game called Cheese Heads, in which students will wear fro wigs and try to catch cheese

balls in their hair. On Thursday, the big one, we will be holding a root beer chugging contest!!!"

zoegirl: omg. angela's behind this, isn't she?

mad maddie: no doubt. isn't it classic?

zoegirl: they should just give us bonus free periods. if they want to do something for us, that's all they need to do.

mad maddie: "cheese heads." it kills me. and i love the part about, "if you can, act excited"! when mr. gerard came to that part, he glanced up with his typical deadpan expression and said, "yippee."

zoegirl: it's insulting, the idea that throwing cheese balls at each other will make us forget how stressed we are.

mad maddie: and don't forget the "big one," a root beer chugging contest!

mad maddie: but I'M not stressed. who says we're stressed? the only one who's stressed is you, zo.

zoegirl: you're not stressed? really?

mad maddie: spring semester grades don't even matter. you've gotta lighten up, cupcake.

zoegirl: ack—maybe you're right

zoegirl: tina and arlene suggested that too, although not in those words.

mad maddie: who the hell r tina and arlene?

zoegirl: the jehovah's witnesses who visited me. they came back today.

mad maddie: yr now on a first-name basis?

zoegirl: i invited them in and we had a nice chat. i served them pepperidge farm cookies.

mad maddie: jesus, zoe. what would your mom say if she knew you were inviting strangers into the house and giving them cookies?

zoegirl: but my mom wasn't here, and anyway, all she

	talks about these days is when i'm going to hear from princeton.
zoegirl:	*she's* the reason i'm stressed. well, part of the reason.
mad maddie:	**so what did you and tina and arlene talk about?**
zoegirl:	if i tell you, you're going to be rude, but i don't care.
zoegirl:	we talked about everlasting life.
mad maddie:	**uh huh**
mad maddie:	**and what did you learn about everlasting life?**
zoegirl:	i didn't "learn" anything. tina and arlene talked about the peaceful paradise that's waiting for us after we die, and i was like, "yeah, that would be nice."
mad maddie:	**it WOULD be nice. doesn't mean it's true.**
zoegirl:	doesn't mean it's not, either
zoegirl:	tina, she's the one who just got married, she looked so . . . i don't know. open and honest when she talked about it. her whole face lit up.
mad maddie:	**cuz she's trying to suck you in. it's all an act.**
zoegirl:	no it's not. why are you so cynical?
zoegirl:	i haven't figured out what makes jehovah's witnesses so different from normal old Christians. so far it seems like it's just that they call God "Jehovah."
mad maddie:	**and that they go door to door invading ppl's privacy, trying to cram jehovah down their throats.**
zoegirl:	i was thinking how hard that must be, the whole door-to-door thing. i bet people are mean to them all the time. (case in point: YOU!)
mad maddie:	**i wouldn't be mean. i just wouldn't invite them in for cookies.**
zoegirl:	i think they're brave. it may not be what you or i

would do with our lives, but that doesn't make it wrong.

mad maddie: whatevs

mad maddie: did they give you any more reading material?

zoegirl: yeah, a book called "The Greatest Man Who Ever Lived." i gave them a $5 donation for it.

mad maddie: $5 for a book you neither asked for nor wanted?

zoegirl: in the illustrations, jesus looks like that cute guy from "white collar." only not a criminal.

mad maddie: maybe that's to keep all the j.w. girls hot for christ.

zoegirl: uh huh, i'm sure that's what they were thinking

mad maddie: whoa—i'm fading here, zoe. i'm gonna go take a nap.

zoegirl: it's almost six o'clock! you can't take a nap, you'll be up all night!

mad maddie: vicious cycle, isn't it?

mad maddie: buenas noches!

Tues, Mar 14, 8:17 PM E.D.T.

SnowAngel: hey, zo. i just got the saddest email from my sister!

zoegirl: poor chrissy. what's going on?

SnowAngel: it's sooooo freshman yr. it's almost laughable, except i know how much this stuff can hurt.

SnowAngel: her email was all about this girl named mackenzie, who lies.

zoegirl: mackenzie lies? about what?

SnowAngel: er, everything? apparently she's 1 of those girls who can win ppl over when she wants to, but then she stirs things up by spreading rumors and everybody gets mad at her.

SnowAngel: shit—i just realized! she's a 9th-grade jana!

SnowAngel: anyway, chrissy made the mistake of telling mackenzie some personal private things about this

	other girl named jo ellen, and now she's worried mackenzie's gonna blab.
zoegirl:	why would chrissy tell mackenzie anything if she knew mackenzie's reputation?
SnowAngel:	according to chrissy, she was mad at jo ellen at the time.
zoegirl:	so what happened?
SnowAngel:	i'll paste in her email so you can read it yourself.

oh and i'm so smart. i told mackenzie some stuff about my friend jo ellen and i'm scared she's gonna tell to get back at me for not sitting with her at lunch. if she does, i'm in deep doo doo cuz it'll start this whole big war all over again. should i tell jo ellen wut i said about her or lyke leave it alone???

zoegirl:	sheesh, tough call
SnowAngel:	it's all so silly, and yet i feel bad for her.
SnowAngel:	aren't you glad we're past that? i mean, yeah, we have our problems, but we have learned SOME things, ya know?
zoegirl:	er . . .
SnowAngel:	what? why r you ER-ing?
zoegirl:	not to be rude, but are you *sure* we're past all that?
SnowAngel:	are you referring to jana? the REAL jana? such a different situation, omg!
zoegirl:	how is it so different?
SnowAngel:	for the record, jana started everything, or do you not remember?
SnowAngel:	SHE started it and SHE continued it and SHE is the person to blame. and btw, i've decided not to let her comment about logan go unpunished!
zoegirl:	ok, let's try again. *how* is it so different?

SnowAngel:	you don't get to have an opinion, cuz you have wimpily refused to get involved. *sticks out tongue*
zoegirl:	well . . . i think it's sweet that chrissy writes you for advice, even if she has no idea how unqualified you are to offer any. she misses her big sis.
SnowAngel:	she'll see me in 5 days. i fly out to el cerrito on sunday.
zoegirl:	what r you gonna do about the chicks?
SnowAngel:	holy crap! (literally!)
SnowAngel:	what AM i gonna do about the chicks?
zoegirl:	i can't take care of them, because i leave for tennessee that same day. i'm *dreading* the car ride with my parents. all they're going to talk about is college, i just know it.
SnowAngel:	blech
zoegirl:	how are they, anyway? the chicks. when do i get to meet them?
SnowAngel:	whenever you get your butt over here. how bout right now?
zoegirl:	i would, but i just can't. too much homework.
zoegirl:	have you named them?
SnowAngel:	yes, but i kept getting them mixed up. so now i call all of them "squishy." they're the collective squishy.
zoegirl:	*are* they squishy?
SnowAngel:	when you squeeze them, yes. but not in a yucky way.
SnowAngel:	they're growing on me, the little squishies. altho 1 of them pooped on my pillow.
zoegirl:	you let them on your bed?
SnowAngel:	they like it when i bounce them.
zoegirl:	okaaaay
zoegirl:	moving on . . . how are things with logan?
SnowAngel:	

zoegirl:	what does that mean?
SnowAngel:	it means that things r fine and not fine.
SnowAngel:	we're on cruise control. we're both just kinda . . . going along.
zoegirl:	well, could be worse, i guess
SnowAngel:	yeah. thanks for not saying anything obnoxious. *makes face to show idiocy of it all*
zoegirl:	you're a good person, angela. you'll do the right thing!

mad maddie:	dude! i'm at ian's and i've got news. zo? angela? PLZ tell me yr both out there. are you????
SnowAngel:	i iz! hi!
zoegirl:	i'm here too. what's going on?
zoegirl:	except, wait, don't tell us yet. let me tell doug one thing . . .
zoegirl:	ok, i'm all yours. spill!
mad maddie:	I GOT ACCEPTED TO SANTA CRUZ!!!!
SnowAngel:	omg!!!!
zoegirl:	maddie!!!!! yay!!!!!!
mad maddie:	i know! it's incredible!
SnowAngel:	*squeals and hugs sweet maddie*
SnowAngel:	tell us every single detail!!!
mad maddie:	well, i got home from school and saw this big thick envelope on the kitchen counter, with "Santa Cruz Admissions Office" as the return address. i got really fidgety and just started screaming, right there in the house. no one was there but me, so i could be as loud as i wanted.
zoegirl:	omg!!!
mad maddie:	i took a deep breath and tried to calm down, but my hands were shaking. i opened the envelope and pulled out a folder that said, "Welcome to

	Santa Cruz." inside was a letter that said, "Dear Madigan. You're In!"
mad maddie:	isn't that cool? i LOVE that, that instead of being all prissy and formal, they're like, "you're in! yahootie!"
SnowAngel:	oh, maddie, i am soooooo happy for you!
mad maddie:	i ran out to my car all jumping and hopping around and drove to ian's, cuz i knew neither of you would be home yet. i showed him my letter and he hugged me really hard and lifted me into the air. it was AWESOME.
zoegirl:	i'm so proud of you, maddie!
SnowAngel:	me 2!!!
zoegirl:	but it's scary, too. out of the 3 of us, this is our first college acceptance. which means that others (hopefully) are coming, and which means it's really going to happen . . . we're really going to graduate and leave and never be together again!!!
SnowAngel:	what are you talking about? we're gonna be together FOREVER. you think college is gonna change that?
zoegirl:	well . . . it's not going to be the same, no matter how much we want it to.
SnowAngel:	don't SAY that!
SnowAngel:	we're gonna be friends when we're 90. we'll grab our walkers and meet at maddie's house for a pole-dancing party. we'll gossip about who died and who got divorced and who's got the biggest wattle. OKAY???
mad maddie:	who's got the biggest what-ull?
SnowAngel:	WATTLE. it's, like, a fold of skin that hangs down low and wobbles under your throat. turkeys have them, as do old ladies. aunt sadie does neck-tightening exercises to prevent 1 from coming on.

zoegirl: my grandmom has a wattle.

zoegirl: you think they're genetic?

SnowAngel: probably. you should get aunt sadie to show you her exercises, altho she looks extremely silly when she does them. *widens eyes and stretches mouth into "O" shape, then rotates lips all around*

mad maddie: girlies, i've gotta run. the rents will probably wanna take me out to dinner to celebrate.

SnowAngel: hug hug, kiss kiss! yr amazing, miss college stud girl!

zoegirl: you really are. way to go!!!

Wed, Mar 15, 9:03 PM E.D.T.

mad maddie: omg, i hate my parents

SnowAngel: oh no. why?

mad maddie: this should have been such a happy day, but now it's turned bad and it's all their fault. i HATE them!

SnowAngel: talk to me. did something happen at dinner?

mad maddie: at dinner? no, cuz they went to dinner WITHOUT me. i got home and there was a note on the kitchen counter saying they'd gone out for chinese.

mad maddie: isn't that cold? the moms must have known what the UCSC letter meant, and even so they went out w/o me.

SnowAngel: maybe they thought you were celebrating on your own

mad maddie: they could have called me. they could have checked.

mad maddie: and then when they DID get home and i told them my good news, the dads didn't say a word. the moms said, "well, congratulations, but you know santa cruz isn't our top choice."

SnowAngel: ouch

mad maddie: i started to tell her about going over to ian's and what a rush it was, and midway thru my story the moms held up her hands and said, "wait, wait, wait. do you realize you've said the word 'like' in front of almost every word you've said?" and then she MIMICKED me, saying "and then ian, like, hugged me, and, like, it was awesome!"

SnowAngel: ewww. why was she being so mean?

mad maddie: she goes, "madigan, you say you don't want to be a typical teenager, that there r bigger things in store for you. but talking like that makes you sound better suited to a community college than some fancy school in california. so try not to use the word 'like' at all, just eliminate it from your speech entirely. now start over and tell your story again!"

SnowAngel: oh, maddie, ICK. i am not liking your mother AT ALL right now.

mad maddie: i waited until she finished her lecture, and then i looked at her and said, "i can't believe you just said that, when i was so happy and trying to share that with you." i told her that i had absolutely no desire to tell my story again, and then i left the kitchen and came up here.

SnowAngel: *reaches thru time and space and gives friend tremendous bear hug* i'm SO sorry!

SnowAngel: DON'T let her ruin your excitement!

mad maddie: she already did

SnowAngel:

mad maddie: i'm gonna make a list of things NOT to do when i have kids, including "burst their bubble for no good reason." seriously, what does she stand to gain from making me feel like crap?

SnowAngel: just remember: you DID get accepted. she can't take that away from you.

mad maddie: thanx, a

mad maddie: g'night.

Wed, Mar 15, 9:20 PM E.D.T.

SnowAngel: hey, zo. did you hear how jerky maddie's parents r being?

SnowAngel: are you there? or are you at doug's?

SnowAngel: if you're at doug's, you can STILL text me back, you know.

SnowAngel: *shakes it off* tomorrow's another day, full of fresh beginnings and root-beer-y goodness. bye!

Thu, Mar 16, 1:03 PM E.D.T.

mad maddie: WHO won the chugging contest?

SnowAngel: YOU did!

mad maddie: and WHO won the victory lap belching contest?

SnowAngel: YOU did!

mad maddie: das rite, cuz i da king

SnowAngel: i take it yr feeling better?

mad maddie: well blow me down. reckon maybe i am.

SnowAngel: hurray! and da crowd goes wild!!!!!

Thu, Mar 16, 4:19 PM E.D.T.

SnowAngel: i've come up with a plan to pay jana back for her slut-meister remark, hee hee hee.

mad maddie: r you sure you want to keep going with this, a? you saw what she did to me when i didn't let it go.

SnowAngel: which is exactly why i REFUSE to let it go. i am NOT letting her feel all high and mighty, like we're just going to roll over and play dead like that poor bird.

mad maddie: ah, christ. what do you have up your sleeve?

SnowAngel:	not telling *hunches shoulders and rubs hands together like mad scientist*
mad maddie:	**have you decided that you enjoy being devious, angela? are you gonna enter into a life of crime?**
SnowAngel:	i dunno. think they have a "life of crime" major at UGA?
mad maddie:	**yeah, it's called poli-sci**
SnowAngel:	was that some kind of political joke? cuz you know i don't get political jokes.
mad maddie:	**oh lordie**
SnowAngel:	but since we're talking about college . . . what about you and santa cruz? is your mom being more normal?
mad maddie:	**i talked to zo during our free, and her theory is that the moms is scared to let me go. that the whole me-going-away-to-college thing is a big deal for her, and that's why she's being such a snot.**
SnowAngel:	but you're 18 years old, you have to live your life.
mad maddie:	**i know, that's what i said.**
SnowAngel:	so yr gonna go to santa cruz? for sure?
mad maddie:	**well, i haven't sent in my "statement of intent to register," but i will.**
SnowAngel:	i'd have thought you would have mailed that baby back the second you got it.
mad maddie:	**i have until may 1st**
mad maddie:	**when are you supposed to hear from georgia?**
SnowAngel:	WE are supposed to hear from georgia by april 1st (you applied too, remember!)
SnowAngel:	zoe's supposed to hear from kenyon and princeton around then too.
mad maddie:	**i kinda wish it would just slow down, don't you?**
SnowAngel:	*faints dead away*

SnowAngel:	what happened to "hasta la vista, baby" and "i can't wait to get out of this dump"?
mad maddie:	**that's all still true. that doesn't mean it has to happen tomorrow.**
SnowAngel:	omg, yr growing sentimental in your old age!
mad maddie:	**what?! no i'm not.**
SnowAngel:	wait till i tell zoe! you ARE gonna miss us, aren't you?
mad maddie:	**jesus, angela . . . more than you can possibly know.**
SnowAngel:	*hold out arms* c'mere, ya goof!
mad maddie:	**no thx**
SnowAngel:	c'mere! *clasps maddie to chest and rocks back and forth*
mad maddie:	**erm, i'm leaving now. i'm freeing myself from your clasp and leaving, k?**
SnowAngel:	bye, you old darling! mwah!!!

Fri, Mar 17, 10:10 AM E.D.T.

zoegirl:	angela, i just saw maddie in the hall. she told me you're starting the jana war again. i am *not* happy about this!
SnowAngel:	i'm downloading fake health service letterhead as we speak. but don't worry, it's "for entertainment purposes only." *throws back head and laughs*
zoegirl:	angela, stop! this has gone on long enough!!!
SnowAngel:	oh piddle
SnowAngel:	don't you wanna hear what i'm gonna do with this fake health service letterhead?
zoegirl:	NO. i'm serious, angela. what if peaches sees what you're printing? you could get expelled!
SnowAngel:	peaches LUVS me. i can do anything i want, cuz i tell her how fabulous her book displays are.
SnowAngel:	and now, your attn plz. *clears throat and shakes out paper* "Dear Ms. Whitaker, It has come to our

attention that an outbreak of gonorrhea has been traced to your recent sexual activity. Please call our clinic at your earliest convenience to discuss treatment options. You will also need to set up an apppointment with our on-site counselor, who can help you come up with an action plan to cut back on your slutty behavior. This is a matter of the utmost concern."

zoegirl:	oh angela
SnowAngel:	i know!!! c'est magnifique!
zoegirl:	the health service would never use the word "slutty." if anything, they'd say "promiscuous."
SnowAngel:	ooo, thanks for the tip
zoegirl:	angela!
SnowAngel:	what? jana made a comment suggesting that i don't "put out" enough. fine. i'm just suggesting that being a slut isn't necessarily the way to go, either.
zoegirl:	please don't send it to her. please?
SnowAngel:	who said anything about sending it to her? i'm gonna print up multiple copies and accidentally-on-purpose drop them in various school bathrooms.
SnowAngel:	it's a hard job, but someone's gotta do it!

Fri, Mar 17, 5:16 PM E.D.T.

mad maddie:	IT'S SPRING BREAK!!! WOOT!!!!!
zoegirl:	i feel like a huge load has been lifted off my shoulders! except for the fact that i still have to go to tennessee with my parents, who are going to drive me insane. and except for the fact that yes, i saw angela's health service handiwork, which means that everyone in the school saw, which means that jana once again is going to be on the warpath.
zoegirl:	but except for that, i feel so much better!
mad maddie:	let it go, baby. just let it all go.

zoegirl:	right, you're so right. and as a reward for getting thru another tough week, i treated myself to big bunny episode #3.
mad maddie:	"as a reward for getting thru another tough week"? is that really how you operate?
zoegirl:	you say that as if it's weird. do you think it's weird?
mad maddie:	i just think you should give yourself rewards any time you feel like it.
zoegirl:	but then they wouldn't be rewards. they would just be . . . random good things.
mad maddie:	and the problem is . . . ?
zoegirl:	you have your pop-tarts and dr pepper; i have my rewards. okay?
mad maddie:	whatevs
mad maddie:	so you saw that lulu DID bring big bunny a kitty, hmmm?
zoegirl:	yes. and when susie told lulu to take the kitty back, big bunny told that horrible story about "another" susie who sold herself to the devil and had a pet hell-hound.
mad maddie:	ah, yes. and then the faux susie repented at the last second and went to heaven. a classic morality tale.
zoegirl:	i do like ol' susie
mad maddie:	cuz you have good taste. she is a prophet of the modern times.
zoegirl:	let's do something tonight, want to? just you and me and angela, since we won't see each other for a week. i might not even have a cell signal, because my grandparents live in the boonies!
mad maddie:	i think that's a great idea. you sure doug won't mind?
zoegirl:	don't be silly. let's meet at angela's so we can play with the chicks. i'll call and tell her we're heading over!

SnowAngel: hello, hello, sleepy maddie! i know you're awake! admit it!

mad maddie: i'm poking around on pinterest before going to bed. pinterest is the devil, you know. do i *need* to know how to turn an ordinary can of V-8 juice into a charming and folksy lantern? no. do i suddenly feel an intense craving to turn an ordinary can of V-8 into a folksy lantern? yes.

SnowAngel: do you have any cans of V-8 lying around?

mad maddie: what are you, nuts? why wld i have cans of V-8 lying around?

SnowAngel: as I suspected.

SnowAngel: so, moving on, that was fun tonight, huh? i love you guys with every single bit of my heart, and sometimes i feel like we haven't been making enough time for each other. i'm so glad zoe suggested it!

mad maddie: did you like how it turned out that doug was out with HIS buds, and that's why she was available all of a sudden?

SnowAngel: i'm not gonna quibble. but yeah, i did notice when she let that slip.

SnowAngel: oh well, we got to have her all to ourselves. that's all that matters.

mad maddie: you, me, zo, and the collective squishy.

SnowAngel: speaking of . . . are you sure they can't come live with you over break? pretty please with chicken feed on top?

mad maddie: no can do, the moms has all these spring-cleaning plans that don't involve 11 baby chicks.

SnowAngel: well, have you called your brother yet to see if he and pelt-woman can take them?

mad maddie: chill, i'll call them in the morning. yr not leaving till sunday!

SnowAngel: be sure to tell them how extremely cute and lovable they are! and how hugging a chicken is good for your soul!

mad maddie: will do. catch ya on the flip side, homie!

Sat, Mar 18, 3:33 PM E.D.T.

SnowAngel: uh oh

mad maddie: uh oh, what-oh?

SnowAngel: well . . .

SnowAngel: i crashed the jeep

mad maddie: WHAT?

SnowAngel: but not bad! just a little! *holds thumb and forefinger verrrry close together*

mad maddie: angela! u ok?

SnowAngel: i'm fine, but before i go any further, you need to know that honestly, it wasn't my fault. it was aunt sadie's. she's the one who ordered "The Firm." "The Firm" is this set of exercise DVDs she's been wanting, and it arrived today.

mad maddie: what happened to pole-dancing? didn't she just buy that ridiculous pole thing?

SnowAngel: a girl needs variety in her exercise routine—that's what she said. plus the pole was giving her bruises.

mad maddie: ack, didn't really wanna hear that

mad maddie: so what does this have to do with crashing your jeep?

SnowAngel: well, the mailman left aunt sadie's package at the end of the driveway by the mailbox, which he shouldn't have done. he's supposed to bring it to the door.

SnowAngel: omg, it's the POSTMAN'S fault!

mad maddie: dude. WHAT HAPPENED?!

SnowAngel: so i was driving back from jamba juice, and there was aunt sadie's package, just sitting by the side of

133

	the road. being the good niece that i am, i thought i'd bring it to the house.
SnowAngel:	so i opened the door of the jeep and leaned down to get it.
SnowAngel:	and . . .
SnowAngel:	well . . .
mad maddie:	**yes?**
SnowAngel:	i kinda fell out
mad maddie:	**you "kinda" fell out?**
SnowAngel:	ok, i DID fall out, the jeep is very high off the ground! you know that!
SnowAngel:	and it was still in gear, and of course aunt sadie's driveway *wld* go downhill, so there i was sprawled on my butt while the jeep rolled along on its merry way!
mad maddie:	**oh, angela**
SnowAngel:	i was like, wait! come back!
mad maddie:	**and . . . ?**
SnowAngel:	it ran into the garage door 😖
SnowAngel:	it's not TOO banged up, mainly just the fender. and there's a big dent in the garage door. but logan is so pissed!
mad maddie:	**why? it's not HIS car.**
SnowAngel:	he's just . . . i dunno. he thinks i wasn't being careful enough. i thought he would laugh when i told him— i honestly did—but he got all silent on the other end of the phone and then said, "see? this proves that you don't care as much about me as i care about you."
mad maddie:	**cuz you wrecked the jeep?**
SnowAngel:	i know!
mad maddie:	**i mean, it's true what he said, but that's kinda a random connection to make.**

SnowAngel:	i was like, "logan, this has nothing to DO with you!" it's so exhausting, soothing his ego all the time.
SnowAngel:	anyway, he's gonna take the jeep to this guy his uncle knows who does body work, which i do appreciate.
mad maddie:	**unbelievable**
SnowAngel:	i know, he's taking offense over NOTHING
mad maddie:	**no, unbelievable that he's coming over, BAM, to fix the jeep for you.**
mad maddie:	**doesn't that make you feel bad, angela? doesn't it make you feel icky inside?**
SnowAngel:	well . . .
SnowAngel:	hmmm. *gazes off with look of unresolved anguish*
mad maddie:	**???**
mad maddie:	**what do YOU have to be anguished about?**
SnowAngel:	logan's part of this relationship too, you know. if he thinks i don't care enough, then he should break up with me!
mad maddie:	**have you told him that?**
SnowAngel:	i scraped my knee on the driveway, i'll have you know, i could have lost a limb!
mad maddie:	**good lord**
SnowAngel:	yes, and yr being a big poopy pants for not being more sympathetic.
SnowAngel:	but lookie here, logan just pulled up—so i guess i'll go to HIM for solace and comfort. at least he'll give me the attention i deserve!
mad maddie:	**and what will you give him?**
SnowAngel:	i'll give him . . . a great big hug!
SnowAngel:	*thumbs nose at friend and flounces off*
SnowAngel:	make that *LIMPS*!

Sat, Mar 18, 3:50 PM E.D.T.

| SnowAngel: | *hobbles back to bedroom* *drops onto bed* |

SnowAngel: i forgot to ask due to all the trauma. did mark and
pelt-woman say they'd take the squishies?

mad maddie: maybe

SnowAngel: did they???

**mad maddie: yes, IF you can get them to them. but how are you
gonna deliver them, huh?**

SnowAngel: i will very nicely ask logan to drop them off after he
takes care of the jeep. so there!

Sat, Mar 18, 11:32 PM E.D.T.

zoegirl: angela! i wanted to make sure i said good-bye
before you left!

SnowAngel: i was just emailing pelt-woman instructions on taking
care of the squishies. i sent written notes with logan,
but i wanted to add a few small details, like that the
smallest squishy really likes music, anything by taylor
swift.

SnowAngel: what's up with you?

zoegirl: i'm kinda wired. i just gave doug his very first
blow job.

SnowAngel: *falls backward out of computer chair*

SnowAngel: WHAT?!!

zoegirl: it was a going-away present, since i won't see him
for a week. i feel so proud of myself!

SnowAngel: well, for sure. you can list it right up there with your
other accomplishments: straight As, honor council,
giving head . . .

zoegirl: it wasn't all that fun for *me*, but i think he really
liked it, and that made me happy.

zoegirl: but my jaw got really tired.

zoegirl: have you ever given logan a blow job?

SnowAngel: no, and i don't plan 2. i have . . . odor issues.

zoegirl: hmm. yes, i can see that.

zoegirl: but i was just like, "this is doug, and i love him."

	and i hope you don't think it's bad that i'm talking about all this, i just needed someone to process it with! i mean, it's a really big deal!
SnowAngel:	sweetie, of course
SnowAngel:	anyway, he prolly talks to his friends about what you guys do and don't do, don't you think?
zoegirl:	oh god, he better not!
SnowAngel:	so: spit or swallow?
zoegirl:	i swallowed, but i don't think i'm going to next time. i'll just tell him very politely so he's not offended.
SnowAngel:	erm, i bet he'll be ok with it. what's he gonna say, "nuh uh, no way! in that case, no blow jobs for YOU, missy!"
zoegirl:	i don't *want* a blow job
SnowAngel:	you know what i mean
zoegirl:	doug tried to go down on me (geez, that sounds dorky), but i was like, "no no no no no. that's ok."
SnowAngel:	why?
zoegirl:	like you said, the whole odor thing. but in reverse. ack, i'm blushing just talking about it!
SnowAngel:	what about plain old sex? if yr embarrassed to have him go down on you, won't you be embarrassed to have sex?
zoegirl:	that's different
zoegirl:	but . . . maybe
zoegirl:	i'll cross that bridge when i come to it, which i guess will be soon, because pill-wise i'm one day away from being safe. can you believe it? but i leave for tennessee tomorrow, so there goes that good timing.
SnowAngel:	which means you'll have more time to get ready. 👍
zoegirl:	exactly

zoegirl:	i'm gonna go brush my teeth (again!), and then i'm going to bed. and then i won't see you for a week! sad!
SnowAngel:	no worries. we'll be reunited soon!!!

Sun, Mar 19, 8:19 PM P.D.T.

SnowAngel:	hey, madikins. i'm txting from the lurvely el cerrito to tell you to have a good spring break!!!
SnowAngel:	u there?
SnowAngel:	no?
SnowAngel:	well, i saw yr tweet about how yr mom is already making plans to turn yr room into a study, and ooo, that's cold.
SnowAngel:	dr. phil sez parents aren't supposed to convert their kids' rooms until they've been gone for at least a year. otherwise it sends the wrong message.
SnowAngel:	okay, back to me. omg, mads, it's WEIRD to be here! chrissy looks so much older. her clothes r hipper than mine, which is extremely scary and wrong.
SnowAngel:	well, they're not REALLY hipper. c'mon. but too hip for comfort.
SnowAngel:	but i'm glad i'm here, despite the fact that my right ear is all pluggy from the airplane. and you know what occurred to me as i was in the cab? next year when i visit my family in el cerrito, i can pop over and visit YOU in santa cruz! IF you send in your thingie, that is. have you yet? cuz yr kinda taunting me by not, you know! it makes me get my hopes up for georgia!
SnowAngel:	okey-dokey, smokey. fam's taking me out for thai.
SnowAngel:	kissies!!!

Tues, Mar 21, 3:33 PM E.D.T.

mad maddie: i just made myself a whomping good peanut-

butter-and-banana sandwich. anyone who slices
their banana instead of mushing it up with the
peanut butter is tragically misguided. agreed?

mad maddie: ahhhh. so now YOU'RE away-from-phone,
angela. naughty girl. wha'cha doing, shopping
for souvenirs in bee-yoo-tee-ful san francisco?
today is the day you're going to san fran, right?

mad maddie: you better bring me some of that cantaloupe-
flavored gum you got last time. and i want a
t-shirt with "i heart san francisco" on it, or your
ass is grass.

mad maddie: speaking of asses, i saw logan at the drugstore
this morning. he was wearing those khakis that
make his butt look fat, and all i cld think was, why
oh why haven't you plucked those from his closet
and burned them?

mad maddie: i went over to say hey, and he was totally no-eye-
contact-boy, like he didn't wanna talk. wassup
with that?

mad maddie: ok, enough talking to myself. l8rs!

Thu, Mar 23, 6:12 PM P.D.T.

SnowAngel: saw yr instagram pic of that waffle. that was weird,
mads.

mad maddie: weird? or delightful?

SnowAngel: BUT i figured that meant you had yr phone out and
on, and sure enough you do! so yay! hello!

mad maddie: hello, cali girl, hello!

SnowAngel: i can't talk for long, cuz we're going over to mr.
boss's for dinner, where i will have to c the dreaded
glendy. *sticks arms out and walks like a zombie*

SnowAngel: want me to pass on any messages for you? 🙂

mad maddie: yeah, to quit sending me her stupid chain letters.
i got one yesterday about those damn bonsai

kittens FOR THE 2nd TIME. she already sent me one about the damn bonsai kittens, and now here she is doing it again!

SnowAngel: what bonsai kittens?

mad maddie: you don't know about bonsai kittens??? there's someone in the universe who hasn't heard of bonsai kittens?

mad maddie: here, let me enlighten you. first i'll paste in what she said at the top of the email:

i'm crying as i'm typing. this can't be happening!!!!!!!!!!!!!!!! we HAVE to stop this!!!!!!!!!!!!!!!!!!!! !!!!!!!!!!!!!!!!

mad maddie: and here's the body of the message:

A site that we were able to shut down last year has returned. We have to try to shut it down again! (bonsaikitten.com) A Japanese man in New York breeds and sells kittens that are called BONSAI KITTENS. That would sound cute, if it weren't kittens that were put into little bottles after being given a muscle relaxant and then locked up for the rest of their lives!! The cats are fed through straws and have small tubes for their feces. The skeleton of the cat will take on the form of the bottle as the kitten grows. The cats never get the opportunity to move. They are used as original and exclusive souvenirs. These are the latest trends in New York, China, Indonesia, and New Zealand. This petition needs 500 names, so please put your name on it!!! Copy the text into a new email and put your name on the bottom, then send it to everyone you know! THIS NEEDS TO BE STOPPED NOW!!

SnowAngel: omg, that is the most awful thing i've ever heard in my life!

mad maddie: yeah, only IT'S NOT TRUE. there is no such thing as bonsai kittens, nor is there rat urine on or in your coke can, nor is there a mass murderer out there who lures women from their homes with a crying baby. NONE OF IT IS TRUE!!!!

SnowAngel: a mass murderer lures women out of their houses with a crying baby?! ooo, that's freaky. what does he do, leave the baby on the porch or something? what does he do with the baby afterward???

mad maddie: yr yanking my chain, right?

mad maddie: THERE IS NO CRYING BABY! THERE ARE NO BONSAI KITTENS!!!!!

mad maddie: just go to urbanlegends.com. you can look up anything and see if it's real or bogus.

SnowAngel: oh, wow, you just used the word "bogus." *touches maddie reverently*

mad maddie: shuddup

mad maddie: so i talked to zo yesterday. she's all fluffy with pride cuz she's officially safe birth-control-wise.

SnowAngel: has she told doug?

mad maddie: yeb'm. she couldn't muster the courage in atlanta, but she was able to from tennessee when they didn't have to be face to face. apparently she had to hike up a quasi-mountain in order to get a strong enough signal to call him. isn't that so zoe?

SnowAngel: awww. was he excited?

mad maddie: they didn't have phone sex, if that's the kind of excited you mean.

SnowAngel: no, that's not what i meant 😊

SnowAngel: she prolly told him long-distance cuz she wanted to give him something to look forward to. something to keep her on his mind.

mad maddie: why? doug wouldn't stray, not in 1000 yrs.

SnowAngel: i know, but it's part of zoe's deal with him to be paranoid anyway. i'm sure she's missing him like crazy.

mad maddie: are you missing logan like crazy?

SnowAngel: hmm, how to respond . . .

SnowAngel: well, i saw a really cute boy at the embarcadero, and i totally lusted after him. like, bad hormone crazy-lust. does that answer your question?

mad maddie: it should tell YOU something, that's for sure

SnowAngel: i know, which is why—*deep breath*—i'm gonna break up with logan as soon as i get back in town. i am, and no wimping out. and no worrying about the jeep, which of course i'll offer to give back.

SnowAngel: r u proud?

mad maddie: yes, i am

SnowAngel: this trip has been good for me, just to give me clarity on it all. it's NOT fair to logan to keep going out with him. he's such a good guy. he deserves better.

mad maddie: right on

SnowAngel: and i'm gonna drop the whole jana thing, i truly am. even if she does something to get back at me for the health center letter (which you've got to admit was frickin brilliant).

SnowAngel: but we're seniors. we should be above this crap.

mad maddie: wow, i almost believe you. but let's hold off on that 1 till yr back in the same state with her, k? i don't want you holding yourself to unreasonable standards.

SnowAngel: i just wanna rid my life of pointless shit, that's all. i want my life to matter!

Fri, Mar 24, 10:00 AM P.D.T.

SnowAngel: hey, sweet zoe! i know yr busy seeing relatives and eating lots of hush puppies. i'm just leaving you a message so you'll feel loved. 🖤

SnowAngel: can u believe it's only a little over a month until we graduate?!

SnowAngel: omg, that means we have GOT to figure out our senior quotes. when are we supposed to turn them in? the end of april?

SnowAngel: aside from that, get this: i saw glendy last night. the girl is internet-obsessed. she made me look at her facebook profile with her, where she now has—yes, it's true—4,987 friends. ridiculosity!

SnowAngel: k, off to get a latte. hope yr having fun with the grands!

Sat, Mar 25, 3:21 PM E.D.T.

zoegirl: hello to my ladies from I-75!

zoegirl: either of y'all there?

zoegirl: just inhaled delish dairy queen blizzard, as per driving-back-from-TN tradition. one of those full-service dairy queens with hot dogs and hamburgers and everything.

zoegirl: i find it a little freaky, to tell the truth. mads, you would have loved. i know, i know.

zoegirl: next up: obligatory stop in chatanooga so mom can revel in the outlet stores. oh, and then that horrible bridge across the mountain where i always think i'm going to die. joy!

Sat, Mar 25, 5:55 PM E.D.T.

zoegirl: i'm back! i'm back! i am no longer trapped in the car with my parents, nor did i plunge to my death off the twisty turny mountain road!!!!

mad maddie: welcome, dudette!

zoegirl: they would not shut up about princeton the

entire trip, i'm not kidding. they were bragging about it to my tennessee relatives—and i haven't even gotten in! "well, when zoe's at princeton . . . ," as if my aunts and uncles are these big hicks who are going to be impressed by an ivy league school. aaaargh!

mad maddie: what are they gonna say if you DON'T get in?

zoegirl: i don't know, and i don't care. and it's WHEN i don't get in, not if. i should get my rejection in a week, and then it'll all be over.

mad maddie: maybe they'll feel sorry for you. pity could work to your advantage, cuz then you can win them over to kenyon more easily.

zoegirl: that's the plan

zoegirl: how'd pelt-woman do with the squishies?

mad maddie: pelt-woman is in 7th heaven. pelt-woman is fulfilling her destiny as earth-goddess-chicken-lover, making the squishies homemade chicken feed and letting them run loose around their apartment. she loves them so much she wants to keep them fo-evah.

zoegirl: seriously?

mad maddie: i think they're good for her image—it makes her seem authentically eccentric. one of her friends has a ferret . . . but what's a ferret compared to 11 squawking chicks?

zoegirl: true

mad maddie: i brought ian over to see the chicks, and he let them walk on his tummy, it was cute.

zoegirl: so you hung out with ian over break, did you? verrrrry interesting. does this mean . . . ?

mad maddie: that he has nerves of steel? yes it does. he put one of the chicks on my stomach, and it was like some

	terrible tickle torture. pokey scratchy chicken feet, trip-trip-tripping along.
zoegirl:	nooooo. does it mean that things r moving forward with you and ian?
mad maddie:	hmmm
mad maddie:	i don't know how to answer that question. i am confused in my own head about that question.
zoegirl:	why?
mad maddie:	cuz think about it! we're graduating in may!
mad maddie:	when i broke up with ian last year, it was awful. i was just so stupid about it. and i never told you or angela, but part of me really regretted it.
zoegirl:	we knew that. you didn't have to tell us.
mad maddie:	well . . . i've always thought that if i ever DID get back together with ian, it would have to be for real. for the long haul, you know?
mad maddie:	but even tho i tell myself and tell myself that neither of us is ready for that, i DO like him. a lot. and he told me he . . . oh god. please don't make a big deal of this, ok?
zoegirl:	he told you what???
mad maddie:	we were outside my house, just leaning against his car and talking, and suddenly he got all solemn. he said, "i can't believe this. after last year . . . i never thought we'd be doing this again."
zoegirl:	oh my gosh
mad maddie:	and he took my hand, and we just . . . looked at each other for a really long time.
zoegirl:	oh, maddie
zoegirl:	i'm getting the chills!
mad maddie:	but i can't talk about it anymore. too scary.
mad maddie:	what about you and doug? have you planned a date for the big wonka wonka love-fest?
zoegirl:	this friday. eeeek, talk about scary!

zoegirl:	i'm telling my parents i'm going to the senior daze campout, but really doug's going to get us a hotel room.
mad maddie:	👍
zoegirl:	i'm nervous
zoegirl:	it's all so big. everything about this year is big.
mad maddie:	and there's nothing we can do about it, is there? we just have to hang on and enjoy the ride.

Sun, Mar 26, 2:20 PM E.D.T.

SnowAngel:	hiya, madikins. yes, pelt-woman can keep the chicks—as long as i get visitation rights.
mad maddie:	hey hey! u back on atlanta soil?
SnowAngel:	just flew in an hour ago, and boy my arms r tired. (hardy-har-har . . .)
mad maddie:	that's great about the chicks—pelt-woman will be so happy.
mad maddie:	and now, time to report the results of a very scientific experiment. ready?
SnowAngel:	uh, sure
mad maddie:	the tacky gold glitter polish you made me put on my toes is finally gone.
SnowAngel:	what gold glitter polish?
mad maddie:	from last summer. remember?
SnowAngel:	from last . . . ?
SnowAngel:	hold on. you mean that time you borrowed my sandals and your toes looked like little crabs, so i gave you a pedicure? THAT gold polish???
mad maddie:	i was too lazy to ever use nail polish remover, so i just clipped off little moons of glitter as virgin growth inched up my toes. and today i clipped off the very last bit! my toenails are pure once more!
SnowAngel:	are you telling me you left that nail polish on for . . . omg . . . 8 months???

mad maddie:	that's the scientific experiment part! now we know that it takes 8 months for toenails to completely cycle thru!
SnowAngel:	no, now we know that yr an unhygienic slob!
mad maddie:	didn't we already know that?
SnowAngel:	wow. i'm both disgusted and impressed.
mad maddie:	why thank u
SnowAngel:	and now i'm outta here. i'm biking over to logan's to do the deed. wish me luck!

Sun, Mar 26, 9:31 PM E.D.T.

SnowAngel:	hey again. and before you ask: NO, i didn't break up with logan. but it's not my fault! it's like, where is he? he's not at home and he's not answering his cell. what's up with that???
mad maddie:	i told you he was acting weird that day i saw him at the drugstore. maybe he's avoiding you.
SnowAngel:	why would he be avoiding me? i've been gone for a week—you'd think he'd be DYING to see me.
SnowAngel:	oh well. can't say i didn't try!

Mon, Mar 27, 10:04 AM E.D.T.

SnowAngel:	logan is acting WAY odd. almost rude!!!
mad maddie:	did you break up with him?
SnowAngel:	not here at school. gonna meet to talk this afternoon.
mad maddie:	maybe he knows it's coming?
SnowAngel:	maybe, i dunno. strange, that's all!

Mon, Mar 27, 8:15 PM E.D.T.

SnowAngel:	well, i did it. i broke up with logan.
zoegirl:	oh, a. how'd he take it?
SnowAngel:	not so great. hold on just a sec—i don't wanna have to tell you and maddie separately. i'm gonna start a new thread with both of y'all.

SnowAngel: hey, mads. already told zo, but the deed is done. I broke up with logan.

mad maddie: ah. finally.

mad maddie: so how's the ol' guy doing? is he suicidal?

SnowAngel: gee, mads, how sympathetic

SnowAngel: no, he's not suicidal, unless by suicidal you mean uncharacteristically antagonistic.

zoegirl: what do you mean?

SnowAngel: remember how i told y'all he was acting strange in the hall? well, that's how he acted when we talked after class, 2. like . . . i dunno. pissy. like he'd forgotten my b-day and knew he was gonna get reamed for it, so he was trying to head me off by being mad 1st. does that make sense?

mad maddie: but your b-day's in july

SnowAngel: uh, yeah. that was me giving an example.

zoegirl: i know what you mean, i think. like, 1 time doug forgot to call when he said he would, and i was upset, but he didn't think i *should* be, so he acted defensive rather than just apologizing. like that?

SnowAngel: but what did logan forget to do? meet me at the airport? call me when i was in el cerrito? what does he have to be defensive about?

mad maddie: give us the play-by-play, maybe that'll shed some light

SnowAngel: SIGH

SnowAngel: i waited till we were alone, and then i told him i needed to tell him something. in this hostile voice he goes, "yeah? what?" and i said i thought we should break up, cuz things hadn't been good b/w us for a while and we both knew it.

mad maddie: and?

SnowAngel:	and there was a super-long silence—a BAD silence—and then he just said, "fine." i reached out to touch his arm, and he jerked away.
SnowAngel:	i feel awful. did i do the right thing?
zoegirl:	yes, angela, you did the right thing. you've just got to give him time.
mad maddie:	**and if you find yourself having a moment of weakness (cuz you will, i guarantee it), just remind yourself: plump bottom. got it?**
SnowAngel:	plump bottom, right. *smiles wanly*
SnowAngel:	it just didn't go the way i expected. but maybe that's part of the hardness of it? maybe break-ups aren't supposed to go the way you expect?
zoegirl:	did you bring up the jeep?
SnowAngel:	he said, "keep it," and i said, "no, no, that wouldn't be right. once it gets out of the shop, YOU keep it." and he said, "fine."
mad maddie:	**oh man, that's harsh**
zoegirl:	shop? why's it in the shop?
SnowAngel:	i can't believe the jeep is gone! poof, just like that!
mad maddie:	**but your conscience is clear—that's the thing to remember.**
zoegirl:	i'm still not getting the "shop" bit. would somebody please explain?
mad maddie:	**teeny repair work, ok? now stop talking about the jeep. yr not exactly being Miss Sensitive.**
zoegirl:	right, right. sorry.
SnowAngel:	don't worry, zo. there's nothing you could say to make things worse than they already r.
zoegirl:	oh. um, okay.
zoegirl:	but in that case . . . can i ask you something else? although it might be on the insensitive side too, so i'll wait if you want.
SnowAngel:	go ahead, i don't care

zoegirl:	what about senior prom? who are you going to go with now that you and logan have broken up?
mad maddie:	zoe! wtf?!
zoegirl:	i'm not trying to be a jerk. just . . . it's 2 weeks away!
SnowAngel:	oh god. what have i done?
mad maddie:	zoe, yr not only Miss Insensitive, yr Miss Complete and Utter Idiot.
mad maddie:	angela, I'LL take you to prom. you can go with me and ian.
SnowAngel:	you asked ian to prom? YOU ASKED IAN TO PROM?
mad maddie:	er . . . guess i did. but you can come with us, and i swear you won't be a 3rd wheel.
zoegirl:	oh, now that's reassuring
mad maddie:	shuddup, you started this!
zoegirl:	i deliberately didn't mention it BEFORE she broke up with him, okay?
zoegirl:	angela, i don't wanna make things more complicated. i just didn't know if you had considered this 1 particular aspect, and i thought maybe you'd wanna figure something out before it's too late. you've been looking forward to prom your whole life!
SnowAngel:	omg
SnowAngel:	i think everyone's gonna have to go away now. i think my brain has had enough.
mad maddie:	nice work, zo

Tues, Mar 28, 5:14 PM E.D.T.

zoegirl:	maddie, i have something big to say, and it's not about angela—although i did feel sorry for her today wandering around all mopey.
mad maddie:	yeah, me too. but she's tough. she'll be ok.
mad maddie:	wassup?
zoegirl:	my mom just got a call from ms. kelley.

mad maddie:	ms. kelley, the college counselor? pourquoi?
zoegirl:	i got into princeton. i got into *princeton*, mads.
mad maddie:	whoa! for real?
zoegirl:	i'm, like, stunned. i'm technically not supposed to know yet, but ms. kelley heard from princeton's admissions office and she was so excited she let the secret slip.
mad maddie:	what happened to the sabotage?
zoegirl:	that's the ironic part. they LOVED my essay on nat'l pigtails day—they thought it was "indicative of an independent thinker" and that it was a refreshing change of pace from the essays they usually get!!!
mad maddie:	holy shit
zoegirl:	i know!
mad maddie:	so how do you feel?
mad maddie:	i mean, crap, zo, you got into PRINCETON. that's gotta make you a little happy?
zoegirl:	that's what's so confusing! it *does* make me happy. or proud, or whatever. especially because my mom is so happy and proud.
zoegirl:	but even though princeton is a great school—it's not where i want to go! it's not me, maddie. it's stodgy and elitist and pretentious. they have "drinking clubs," if that gives you any idea.
mad maddie:	drinking clubs? i'm liking that idea. what's wrong with drinking clubs?
zoegirl:	you're imagining some rowdy, casual, bar scene kind of deal. it's not like that. it's more of an old boys network, where you sit around a polished oak table and make witty literary references while drinking beer from a stein. sooo not my cup of tea, especially because i don't even like beer.
mad maddie:	have you told that to your mom?

zoegirl: no

zoegirl: yes

zoegirl: i don't know. she thinks once i go there i'll love it, just like she did. and when i bring up kenyon and how that's where i really want to go, she blows it off like i'm a little kid who doesn't know what she's saying.

mad maddie: **so just say, "no, i'm not going."**

zoegirl: ugggggggghhhhhh

zoegirl: you don't understand. you've known since day one that you want to go to santa cruz, and even though your parents aren't thrilled, they're not psycho about it. for you everything's simple.

mad maddie: **yeah? what if it's not?**

zoegirl: what's not simple about going to your dream school? what's not so simple about, and i quote, "getting the hell out of this dump"?

mad maddie: **nothing, yr right. what was i thinking?**

zoegirl: i've got to go, my mom and dad want to take me out for a celebratory dinner.

mad maddie: **the irony. i get into a school i want to go to, and my parents do nada. you get into a school you don't want to go to, and your parents lavish you with fine cuisine. so sad!**

Wed, Mar 29, 4:50 PM E.D.T.

SnowAngel: i passed jana in the hall today, and she thoroughly laughed in my face. she whispered something to terri that i KNOW was about logan, and then she smirked like she knows something i don't.

mad maddie: **she just wants you to THINK she does. anywayz, why do you care? you've risen above the whole jana malarkey, remember?**

SnowAngel: i know, i know. but when i saw logan in the hall—not at the same time as jana, but later—he didn't even look at me—and not in a "i am hurting so i will ignore you" kinda way. it was just . . . stone-cold nothing.

mad maddie: **well, you broke up with him. not to be harsh, but that's just the way of it.**

SnowAngel: it's not that i want him to be devastated . . . but maybe i do? at least a little?

SnowAngel: it's so out of character for him to be totally "whatever" about it.

mad maddie: **let it go, that's my advice. think about something else.**

SnowAngel: like what?

mad maddie: **like . . . the fact that ian got accepted into georgia's honors program! i knew he would, but i'm still happy for him.**

SnowAngel: which means we'll prolly hear soon ourselves. eeeek, that makes it feel so real! you and zoe have already gotten your 1st acceptance, but not me!

mad maddie: **i was thinking that instead of the senior daze campout, we should drive to athens to visit your soon-to-be-home. wanna?**

SnowAngel: yeah!

mad maddie: **do you mind if ian comes too?**

SnowAngel: the more the merrier. and i promise i'll be in a better mood!!!

Thu, Mar 30, 8:12 PM E.D.T.

SnowAngel: hey, zo. i just got off the phone with mary kate— we were going over all the end-of-the-year senior activities—and she says mr. pittner authorized the bonfire for the campout tomorrow night. he said they can do it in the faculty parking lot as long as they have an adult chaperone present at all times.

zoegirl:	that's awesome. too bad we're all gonna miss it!
SnowAngel:	i know, it almost makes me wish i was going. they're gonna make s'mores and tell ghost stories and sing songs, and practically the entire senior class is planning to be there. it'll be so corny!
SnowAngel:	but athens'll be fun too . . . and i do need a break from the whole school scene. did i tell you my secret plan to show maddie such a good time that she decides to go to UGA after all?
zoegirl:	omg, i will be sooo jealous if you two end up at the same school.
SnowAngel:	well we can't all go to princeton, ya big stud. *winks*
zoegirl:	all day long, people have been congratulating me. it's so weird. ms. aiken pulled me over during french and told me how pleased she was for me, and then she goes, "but don't let it define you, zoe. we all like positive strokes, but what's important is who we are inside."
SnowAngel:	that's random
zoegirl:	random, but true. sometimes, even if i work really hard for something, i don't feel good about it unless i get praised for it. that's stupid, isn't it?
SnowAngel:	praised, like getting good grades?
zoegirl:	and having people be impressed that i got into princeton. having my parents be so proud. like that.
SnowAngel:	that's a pretty high-class problem, as aunt sadie would say.
SnowAngel:	let's talk about something juicier, like your big night with doug. while the rest of the seniors are warming their bods by the campfire, you'll be warming yours in a cozy hotel room. are you ready???

zoegirl:	i'm excited, but antsy. and no, i'm not ready. how *could* i be??
zoegirl:	what i hope is that i get swept away by the moment. i want to be . . . seduced, if that makes sense. that would be the greatest thing, just to be carried away by the passion so that i don't have to THINK about anything.
SnowAngel:	just relax and enjoy it—and don't put too much pressure on yourself. OR doug. this is a once-in-a-lifetime thing. you don't wanna screw it up.
zoegirl:	angela!!! "relax and enjoy it—but don't screw up because it's a once-in-a-lifetime thing"?!!
SnowAngel:	oops—guess that's not so helpful?
SnowAngel:	anyway, it's not like i have a clue what i'm talking about! i'm the perpetual virgin, and apparently will be for the rest of my life.
zoegirl:	about that. you know how you said logan seems totally fine with y'all's break-up? i think he's less fine than you think. it's like he's trying to be all frat-boy-tough and punch-'em-in-the-shoulder, but at lunch, even when he was joking around with his buds, there was something that made it seem like an act.
SnowAngel:	that actually makes me feel better—isn't that sick?
SnowAngel:	when you really think about it, he's being WONDERFUL. i mean, he could be being super-snotty, you know?
zoegirl:	he's a good guy. just not the guy for you.
SnowAngel:	you think i should call him? just to tell him i appreciate how cool he's being?
zoegirl:	no!
zoegirl:	you should *not* call him. NO.
SnowAngel:	i think i will . . . and i'll tell him i'm not planning on going to the bonfire. that way he won't feel

strange about going, if it's true what you said and he's just trying to be strong whenever he's around me.

zoegirl: angela, you're just gonna make it harder for him. don't do it!

SnowAngel: he's still an important person in my life. i don't wanna NOT call him when i feel like calling him, cuz then i'm like, validating the weirdness. anyway, he deserves a nice fun night. bye!

Thu, Mar 30, 8:49 PM E.D.T.

SnowAngel: zoe, i called logan . . . AND JANA PICKED UP!!!

SnowAngel: zoe? plz be there. PLZ be there.

SnowAngel: are you not? nooooo!

SnowAngel: omg, i'm hyperventilating. JANA is at logan's house. JANA picked up the phone. WHAT THE HELL IS GOING ON?!!

SnowAngel: all she said when she picked up was, "yeah?" i didn't recognize her voice, so i said, "uh, is logan there?" and she started LAUGHING. well, first she said, "is this angela?" THEN she started laughing, cuz that is evidently the theme with her these days, to laugh her butt off about anything concerning me.

SnowAngel: and then she goes, "sorry, we're a little busy right now." and hangs up!

SnowAngel: oh screw it. i'm calling maddie!!!!!!!

Fri, Mar 31, 9:58 AM E.D.T.

mad maddie: hiyas, a. you've been hiding out in the media center all morning. you surviving in there?

SnowAngel: i'm hiding cuz i keep worrying that i'm gonna run into jana. ever since last night i've been feeling very insecure, even more than when she spread that rumor about me hitting on doug!

mad maddie:	**you know this is what she wants, right? you've got to fight it.**
SnowAngel:	do you think she's fooling around with logan? for real?
mad maddie:	**as i said before, that's what she WANTS you to think.**
SnowAngel:	i'm having serious flashbacks to that time in 10th grade when i caught rob tyler kissing tonnie wyndham. remember?
SnowAngel:	what is WRONG with me? why am i the girl who everyone screws around on?!!
mad maddie:	**point 1: logan is not rob tyler. point 2: dude, sweetie, YOU broke up with HIM. he's hardly screwing around on you if yr not going out. and point 3: we don't know that he's screwing around at all!**
mad maddie:	**why would he even WANNA mess around with jana??? is he that desperate?**
SnowAngel:	she's pretty, even if she's a bitch. she's never had any trouble finding guys to mess around with before.
mad maddie:	**obnoxious guys. skurvy guys.**
SnowAngel:	i can't believe i called him to tell him how wonderful he was being, and that's how i caught him with jana!
mad maddie:	**you didn't CATCH him with jana, you just . . .**
mad maddie:	**ack. could we talk about something else?**
mad maddie:	**like this: our very own zoe is gonna have her cherry popped tonight!!!**
SnowAngel:	don't say "cherry." that reminds me of the jeep, which reminds me of logan. *stomps around feeling like a weenie*
mad maddie:	**ok, forget zoe. let's discuss our lurvely trip to athens. when do you want me to pick you up?**

SnowAngel: you and ian go on without me. i'm gonna make a surprise appearance at the senior campout and spy on logan and jana. *makes slitty eyes to show she means business*

mad maddie: oh, man, angela. not a good idea.

SnowAngel: tough, i don't care

mad maddie: all right, it's your grave. call me when you need me to pick up the pieces!

Fri, Mar 31, 7:25 PM E.D.T.

mad maddie: has the cherry popping commenced?

zoegirl: maddie! no, but we're at the hotel.

mad maddie: which one? ian and i will come visit.

zoegirl: as if!

mad maddie: in that case, off to athens. have big fun!

Sat, Apr 1, 11:01 AM E.D.T.

mad maddie: i have been extraordinarily patient, zoe, and i have NOT called for over 12 hours, even tho i wanted to many times.

mad maddie: SO?!!!

zoegirl: omigosh, still processing. but i'll tell you everything once i'm home, you and angela both. can't text now—in car and about to drive.

mad maddie: well, drive quickly, then. i'm giving you 10 minutes or i'm calling the nat'l guard! and, ok, i don't know what the nat'l guard will DO, exactly ... but i'll tell ya this: u don't wanna find out!

Sat, Apr 1, 11:18 AM E.D.T.

zoegirl: hey, girls

mad maddie: hey, zo. guess what? angela has news too ... only she's not gonna tell us till after you.

zoegirl: you have news, angela? about what?

mad maddie:	she wldn't tell me over the phone, but i assume it's about logan and the j-word. she blew off our athens trip and went to spy on them at the senior campout.
zoegirl:	what?!
zoegirl:	omg, tell us!
SnowAngel:	NO *glares at maddie*
SnowAngel:	after you, zo. cuz mine is bad.
zoegirl:	then you should go 1st!
SnowAngel:	i'm not going 1st. will you plz just tell us?
mad maddie:	yeah, you non-virgin, we're DYING for details!!!
zoegirl:	well, it was a *wonderful* night. wonderful, wonderful, wonderful.
zoegirl:	but actually . . . i'm still a virgin.
mad maddie:	pardon?
zoegirl:	we didn't . . . make it to completion. well, *he* did, but it was before he . . . you know.
mad maddie:	squeezed it in you?
zoegirl:	maddie!
zoegirl:	afterward, he was all, "ah, crap. zo, i'm sorry!"
mad maddie:	well, yeah! nice way to blow your wad, doug!
zoegirl:	i didn't care. afterward we just held each other. it was nice.
mad maddie:	did he at least finish you off? return the favor, as it were?
zoegirl:	he offered, but i just wanted to cuddle. we watched HBO and snuggled and made each other laugh. it was perfect.
zoegirl:	i felt good that i made *him* feel so good. that's all that mattered.
mad maddie:	but it's supposed to be MUTUAL, little miss fifties housewife.
zoegirl:	i'm not allowed to want to please doug?
mad maddie:	oh good lord. angela? a little help here!

zoegirl:	yeah, you've been awfully quiet. i've told y'all enough about my night. tell us what's going on with you, angela.
SnowAngel:	i say, so what if doug couldn't go the distance? at least he really loves you, zo, and at least he wasn't humping the 1st available female just to get his cheap thrills. at least he's not a total asshole fuckwad.
mad maddie:	whoaaaaa. what r you saying here, a?
SnowAngel:	i'm sorry. i'm such a loser. but i DID wait, you have to give me credit!
zoegirl:	sweetie, what's going on?
SnowAngel:	i'm just a little wrecked right now, that's all. i'm trying to hold it together, but . . . but . . .
mad maddie:	angela, i think you better explain what happened at the senior campout.
SnowAngel:	i don't know if i can! it's too horrible!
mad maddie:	we're right here. we're not going to let anything bad happen.
zoegirl:	unless the bad thing already *did* happen. were logan and jana . . . together?
SnowAngel:	they were sitting in the parking lot by the bonfire, and logan had his arm around her!!! i was so shocked, i just stood there looking like an idiot. and then logan's friend dan came up and was like, "dude, i've gotta give you props. most girls would be flipping."
zoegirl:	what did you say?
SnowAngel:	i was in a fog. i said something like, "why? he's allowed to go out with other girls if he wants."
mad maddie:	other whore-sluts, you mean
SnowAngel:	dan made this expression like i was being too nice for my own good, so i said, "dan, logan and i broke up. didn't you hear?"

SnowAngel:	and he goes, "sure, but wasn't that AFTER spring break?"
zoegirl:	uh oh
SnowAngel:	i said, "yeah, so?" and he said, "dude—they hooked up when you were out of town. i thought you knew."
mad maddie:	**NO!**
SnowAngel:	i felt like i was having a panic attack. i swear to god. so dan pulled me over to the curb and sat me down, and i made him tell me everything.
zoegirl:	which was . . . ?
SnowAngel:	well, dan says that jana and logan "happened" to run into each other at a party the first weekend of break, and jana flirted with logan all night. like basically threw herself at him, that's what dan said. apparently they talked about ME, about that night at ethan's when i was such a jerk.
mad maddie:	**and lemme guess: jana was a VERY sympathetic listener.**
SnowAngel:	uh huh, so sympathetic that she led him to an empty bedroom so they could be alone. AND THEY SLEPT TOGETHER!!! as maddie would say, he squeezed it in her, and who knows how many times they've had sex since then. now do you understand why i'm such a mess?!!
mad maddie:	**that lying scheming skanky bitch!**
zoegirl:	oh, angela, i am sooooo sorry!
SnowAngel:	and YES, i wasn't in love with him, and YES, i wanted to break up with him, but that is so not the point. he fucking screwed me over for JANA!
zoegirl:	how could he do something like that? how could she?!!
SnowAngel:	it hurts so bad. i feel so STUPID. i told you jana's been laughing at me!

mad maddie:	the two of them won't last, angela. you know they won't.
SnowAngel:	no, i don't know that, cuz i don't know anything anymore.
SnowAngel:	all i know is that jana fucking won. that's what it comes down to, doesn't it?
zoegirl:	what do you mean?
SnowAngel:	don't you get it? i called jana a slut in that stupid health center letter, so she was like, "fine, i'll show you a slut."
SnowAngel:	jana. fucking. won.
mad maddie:	we're coming to get you, angela. right, zo?
zoegirl:	we're on our way!!!

Sun, Apr 2, 11:01 AM E.D.T.

mad maddie:	man, angela's really shattered, isn't she?
zoegirl:	it kills me that she's going to end her senior year feeling like our archenemy stomped all over us. it's just wrong!
mad maddie:	so what are we gonna do about it?
zoegirl:	i don't know. i just don't know.
zoegirl:	what i *do* know is that it puts things in perspective. on friday night—when doug and i went to the hotel? there's a little more to the story than i told you guys, because of the angela stuff.
mad maddie:	that's funny—because there's more to my athens story too. but the timing wasn't right to tell it once angela shared her news.
mad maddie:	you wanna go first, or should i?
zoegirl:	i will, because i need to get it out. it's making me feel icky.
mad maddie:	???
mad maddie:	i thought you said the nite was wonderful, wonderful, wonderful.

zoegirl:	it was! but then . . . oh god.
mad maddie:	**what?**
zoegirl:	it was *so* wonderful that as i was lying there on doug's chest, i found myself thinking, "how am i going to live without him? seriously, how am i gonna survive next year when we're not together?" and then i had the thought that i'd rather die than be without him, which i know is ridiculous. but it wasn't like i CHOSE to think it. it just crept in!
mad maddie:	**zoe, that IS ridiculous. completely and absolutely ridiculous.**
zoegirl:	i know! but i was thinking that, and listening to doug's heart and feeling how warm he was, and the next thing i found myself wondering was, does he care as much as i do? what would he do if i actually did die?
zoegirl:	so i pretended i *was* dead. i stopped breathing and let my eyes go vacant and went limp in his arms, right there in the hotel bed.
mad maddie:	**no**
zoegirl:	yes
mad maddie:	**yr more messed up than i realized, girl! i mean, i love ya, don't get me wrong . . . but sheesh!**
zoegirl:	doug said, "zoe? zoe?!" he shook me by the shoulders, and i *kept* playing dead. in my head i was like, "why are you doing this?" but i did it anyway. doug's breathing got fast and he was like, "zoe, oh my god!"
zoegirl:	finally i came back alive and giggled. he was REALLY mad.
mad maddie:	**you must have scared the piss out of him!**
zoegirl:	i know—and i know that giggling was the wrong

move. i knew it even then. but what else could i do? pretend i'd had an epileptic fit?

mad maddie: holy crap

mad maddie: you do realize that you need to chill out on the whole doug front, right? yr not gonna die without him. you shouldn't WANT to die without him. good lord.

zoegirl: duh, that's my whole point

zoegirl: angela legitimately has something to be upset about. but me? i've got a boyfriend i love and who loves me. what do i have to complain about?

mad maddie: nothing

zoegirl: but sometimes i can't help it. i feel this huge gaping hole at the thought of not being with him. i don't want to, i just do.

mad maddie: what did doug say, after he got over being scared?

zoegirl: he made me promise not to ever do that again, and i said i was so so sorry. we hugged, and eventually things got good again. after that, we just didn't bring it up.

mad maddie: you've gone over the deep end with this codependency shit.

zoegirl: i know

mad maddie: it's not the zoe i'm used to.

zoegirl: i know

mad maddie: so snap out of it, will ya?

zoegirl: i'll try, i swear

zoegirl: um, what about you and ian and your night in athens? what's *your* news?

mad maddie: i don't know if i wanna tell you anymore, cuz if i do, it'll make it official that ian and i are a couple. and then I'LL lose my head and fall into couple-land and the next thing you know, I'LL be playing dead!

zoegirl:	don't be cruel
zoegirl:	you and ian are a couple????? does this mean . . . ?
mad maddie:	this means that if you hush, i'll tell you. we drove to athens, right? and on the way we had a really fun convo, as we always do. i was bummed angela wasn't there, but not TOO bummed, if ya catch my drift. we took ian's car, and it was weird sitting there in the front seat and remembering all the times we'd fooled around on that very mock-leather upholstery.
zoegirl:	good weird?
mad maddie:	good weird. it was . . . relaxed. that was the best part. like, neither of us was trying to impress the other or prove anything. none of that 1st date shit. we just talked about music and movies and ian's recent trip to the dentist.
mad maddie:	he called his teeth his "pearly whites." i love that.
zoegirl:	ian does have a great smile
mad maddie:	doesn't he?
mad maddie:	so then we got to the uptown lounge, and there was a huge crowd. i got out to put our name on the list while he parked, but ian, genius boy with his 4.0 average, has zero ability when it comes to a sense of direction.
zoegirl:	oh no. did he get lost?
mad maddie:	yes! he frickin got lost 2 blocks from the club! he texted me, cuz there was a super-loud frat party going on, and i was like, "ok, take a left on lumpkin!" then he'd text back and say, "i'm in front of a florist. is this right?" and i'd be, "nooo! your OTHER left, fool!"
mad maddie:	i'm standing in front of the restaurant, craning my head looking for him, and i get a text that says, "uh . . . should i be seeing fireworks?" so i type, "what?!

	NO, you shouldn't be seeing fireworks! there r no fireworks anywhere NEAR here!" he texts, "you sure? turn around!"
zoegirl:	oh my gosh! omigosh omigosh omigosh!!!
mad maddie:	so i turned around, and there he was. and he kissed me.
zoegirl:	ohhhhhh!
zoegirl:	and were there fireworks?
mad maddie:	bright crazy sparkling fireworks, boom boom boom. and for the whole rest of the night we didn't let go of each other. we just kept grinning and kissing and laughing all goofily.
zoegirl:	aw, mads!!!
mad maddie:	but now comes the part of the story that reveals my own pathetic-ness.
zoegirl:	oh yeah? please tell—it'll make me feel better!
mad maddie:	i can't stop wondering if maybe, just MAYBE, i should go to georgia instead of santa cruz. assuming i get in, that is.
zoegirl:	omigosh. cuz of ian?
mad maddie:	AND angela. it's not just ian.
mad maddie:	i'm not gonna actually DO it, obviously.
zoegirl:	are you not excited about santa cruz anymore? santa cruz has been your dream forever!
mad maddie:	not forever, just since last summer. and yes, i'm still excited. i mean, when i think about living in california . . . and being near the ocean . . . and going to a super-liberal school . . .
zoegirl:	that all sounds perfect for you
mad maddie:	but then i also think about everything i'd be giving up.
mad maddie:	it's like, why do i wanna start over at someplace new when i've got so many great things going on here?

zoegirl:	that's true
zoegirl:	sometimes i think it's good that doug and i *didn't* apply to any of the same schools, because if we did, and we both got in, i'm not sure i'd be able to say no.
mad maddie:	**grrrr. why do i have to think about having to say "goodbye" to ian when we just re-said "hello"?**
zoegirl:	would you regret it, later in life? if you didn't go to santa cruz?
mad maddie:	**yes. no. i dunno!**
zoegirl:	oh, maddie, it's so hard!!!
zoegirl:	tomorrow's the day i can check on-line to see if i got into kenyon. after that—well, depending on the answer—i'll have to have the big discussion with my parents.
mad maddie:	**i wish we all didn't have to be split apart. i know this is supposed to be a time filled with excitement—but sometimes it feels like a time of sadness instead.**
zoegirl:	which makes me want to cry
mad maddie:	**and add to that the angela suckiness . . .**
zoegirl:	we're just a barrel of laughs, aren't we?
zoegirl:	but i am awfully glad about you and ian. that's awesome.
mad maddie:	**thanx, zo. i'm glad, too.**

Mon, Apr 3, 1:05 PM E.D.T.

mad maddie:	**dude! i just checked my application status—i got into UGA!**
zoegirl:	yikes! i mean, congrats congrats congrats! but . . . yikes! what does this mean?!!
mad maddie:	**i called the moms. she's soooo much more excited than she was about santa cruz.**
zoegirl:	did angela get in 2?

mad maddie: she doesn't wanna check till she gets home, but i'm sure she did.

mad maddie: what about kenyon?

zoegirl: site is "experiencing delays," so i have to wait. letters have been mailed out using snail mail, but . . . aaargh!

Mon, Apr 3, 5:52 PM E.D.T.

zoegirl: hey girl. did you check your UGA status?

SnowAngel: i got in. blah. who cares?

zoegirl: angela! i care, and i know you do too. you can't let jana and logan take that away.

SnowAngel: whoop-di-do! *makes expressionless face while dixieland band marches thru bedroom*

SnowAngel: wanna know what i did after i found out? i took a bath, cuz that's how exciting my life is. and cuz i feel so SORDID knowing that jana and i are grotesquely connected by logan's spit.

zoegirl: angela . . .

SnowAngel: his tongue touched my tongue, and that same tongue has now touched HER tongue. i dated a jana-licker! i can't stop thinking about it!

zoegirl: but logan is nothing to you, remember?

SnowAngel: what do you mean, logan is nothing to me?! i might have broken up with him, but he's still someone i care about. or DID.

zoegirl: i didn't mean "nothing" like that. i'm sorry.

SnowAngel: but now jana has tainted everything. in the future when i think back on logan, SHE'S what i'll remember. and when i think back on senior year, SHE'S what i'll remember! 😊

zoegirl: i'm so sorry!

SnowAngel: in the bath, when i was trying to cleanse myself of her evil spirit, i looked thru the water at my body, and it's like i was this pasty disconnected FLESH thing. especially my fingers, which were floating there looking flat and weird.

SnowAngel: i thought to myself, "i am a piece of fruit, suspended in Jell-O." that is what my life has come to.

zoegirl: uh . . . ok. well, let's think about the positives: fruit is good. Jell-O is good.

SnowAngel: oh WHATEVER. i'm gonna go eat all of aunt sadie's chocolate truffles and get fat. bye!

Tues, Apr 4, 7:27 PM E.D.T.

mad maddie: hey, zo. what r we gonna do about angela???

zoegirl: and prom, you mean?

mad maddie: prom, sure, and EVERYTHING. watching her mope around is making ME depressed!

zoegirl: i felt so bad for her at lunch. she was sitting with me and mary kate and kristin, and we were all talking about our prom dresses.

zoegirl: mine came back from the alterations lady, by the way. i love it so much. now the hem hits about four inches above my knees, and i am tres sexy. well, for me.

mad maddie: ooo la la

zoegirl: when am i gonna get to see yours?!! you're not going to make me wait until saturday night, are you?

mad maddie: yep, sorry. it's cool, tho. it's black and long and the entire back is cut away in a diamond shape. i'm gonna have to go bra-less.

zoegirl: ian's going to love that

zoegirl: have y'all decided which pre-party you're going to?

mad maddie: macee mcgovern's—she's having it catered by piebar.

mad maddie: you?

zoegirl:	if you're going to macee's, we probably will too. unless doug has other plans. i don't really care, just as long as we don't end up at some hotel afterward to have sex. i am *not* gonna be that girl!
mad maddie:	**er . . . aren't you already that girl?**
zoegirl:	that was different. our first real time isn't going to be in a post-prom hotel room with three other couples and everyone (except me) drunk on cheap champagne.
zoegirl:	and to make sure, i have a plan.
mad maddie:	**which is?**
zoegirl:	i told doug that i want to spend the night *before* prom with just him. he's got the key to his church's basement, so i'm going to suggest we go there. it's not perfect, but it's better than prom night insanity!
mad maddie:	**very nice. and i think it IS perfect that yr gonna lose your maidenhood in the house of the lord. you'll be like a nun!**
zoegirl:	uh, no, i'll be the opposite of a nun
mad maddie:	**an anti-nun! yeah!**
mad maddie:	**but back to angela: WHAT R WE GONNA DO???**
zoegirl:	well . . . i do have 1 idea
zoegirl:	i think she should go to the prom with andre.
mad maddie:	**omg, that's brilliant! i'm gonna call her right now and suggest it. unless you want to?**
zoegirl:	that's ok, i've got to finish my homework.
mad maddie:	**but . . . why?**
zoegirl:	silly maddie. some of us still care about our final grades!

Tues, Apr 4, 8:19 PM E.D.T.

SnowAngel:	well . . . guess i've got a date. *smiles bravely in face of adversity*

mad maddie: way to go, you!

SnowAngel: andre said there's no one he'd rather go with except a lusty sea captain, but since atlanta has a shortage of sea captains, he's my man. 😊

SnowAngel: he also said—and i thought this was interesting—that when it comes to affairs of the heart, it's even harder being gay than it is being, well, me. which kinda put me in my place, you know?

mad maddie: i think that's terrific. (not that it's hard being gay, but that you'll be joining us at prom.)

mad maddie: whatcha gonna wear?

SnowAngel: WELL. aunt sadie has a silver sequined cocktail dress that i've been salivating over, and i'm gonna ask very nicely if i can borrow it, along with her kate spade slingbacks. and her diamond studs.

mad maddie: that's the way to get back on that horse.

mad maddie: ya glad you asked him?

SnowAngel: yeah

mad maddie: and do you attribute it all to ME, your angela-lovin' friend?

SnowAngel: yeah *huggy hug hug*

mad maddie: then my job here is done. cheers!

Wed, Apr 5, 5:55 PM E.D.T.

zoegirl: i got accepted to kenyon!!!

mad maddie: wh-hoo! yr such a stud muffin!

zoegirl: i can't believe it. i mean, i *can* believe it, but it's just so HUGE. i got accepted to my first choice college!

zoegirl: i have to tell you how i found out, okay? cuz it's, like, full of cosmic unconsciousness.

mad maddie: cosmic unconsciousness, nice. tell away.

zoegirl: well, i'd just finished watching big bunny #4, which was as disturbing as all the others.

mad maddie:	disturbing? i dare say you mean DELIGHTFUL.
mad maddie:	didn't you love the story about the bluebird that rose from the dead and preyed on the flesh of the living?
zoegirl:	no. that bluebird ate a girl's eyeball!
mad maddie:	a girl who looked an awful lot like susie, did you notice? cuz big bunny knows that susie's onto him. lulu and the round-headed boy, they're all, "la la la, we'll do whatever you tell us to do." but susie thinks for herself.
zoegirl:	good ol' susie
mad maddie:	but, ok. you'd just finished big bunny, when all of a sudden . . .
zoegirl:	the doorbell rang, and it was the jehovah's witnesses. tina and arlene.
mad maddie:	oh joy. did you invite THEM in to watch big bunny?
zoegirl:	uh . . . no
mad maddie:	pity
zoegirl:	we were at the door talking about how god has a plan for all of us—that's the cosmic unconsciousness part, that we would be talking about that very thing in terms of the future and what we're supposed to do with our lives and all that—when the postman pulled up. i was like, "tina, arlene, i've got to go. i'm expecting something really important."
zoegirl:	and there it was in the mailbox! my kenyon acceptance!!!
mad maddie:	that rocks!!! have you told the rents?
zoegirl:	not home yet. ack.
mad maddie:	they can't MAKE you go to princeton. just remember that. when it comes down to it, they'll want you to go where YOU wanna go, right?
zoegirl:	you don't know my parents.

zoegirl:	well, actually you do . . . so you know what i'm up against.
mad maddie:	i can see the headlines: GIRL FORCED AT GUNPOINT TO ATTEND ELITE IVY LEAGUE UNIVERSITY. PARENTS CHARGED WITH GROSS ABUSE.
zoegirl:	no, not at gunpoint. they'd have a psychiatrist prescribe zoloft and analyze me into submission.
mad maddie:	now see, that's good humor
zoegirl:	but i'm not going to give in, so there.
zoegirl:	what about you—have you figured your own stuff out in terms of georgia versus santa cruz?
mad maddie:	i think about it all the time
zoegirl:	and?
mad maddie:	and as much as i might want to, i can't pick georgia over santa cruz. i just can't.
zoegirl:	yeah. i kind of figured that's what it would come down to.
mad maddie:	i can't NOT do something cuz i'm afraid of change, you know?
zoegirl:	i think that's good, maddie. i think you're making the right decision.
zoegirl:	have you told ian?
mad maddie:	not yet
zoegirl:	have you told angela?
mad maddie:	are u kidding?
mad maddie:	1st i'm gonna give myself time to get my own head around it and really make sure this is what i want. then, once i've officially mailed my acceptance in, i'll deal with telling ian and angela.
zoegirl:	well, i'm proud of you. and i'm proud of me, too, for my good news. and now i wanna call and tell doug, k?
mad maddie:	whoa. you told me before you told him?!

zoegirl: erm . . . he had track practice, so i couldn't reach him. but that doesn't change the fact that yr the 1st to know!!!

Wed, Apr 5, 9:12 PM E.D.T.

SnowAngel: maddie told me about your acceptance—that's awesome! what did your parents say?

zoegirl: oh, they were sooo supportive. my mom said, "if kenyon's your top choice, we won't stop you from going. but you'll have to pay for it yourself."

SnowAngel: *winces*

SnowAngel: well . . . can u? like with financial aid?

zoegirl: the deadline for financial aid has already passed, which i'm sure my mom knew.

zoegirl: i feel like such a dumb little rich girl! i didn't even *think* to apply for financial aid!

SnowAngel: your parents never gave you any reason to think you shld, that's why.

zoegirl: i'm tempted to not go to college at all. i'm tempted to get a job and live on my own and save up the tuition money myself, even though it would take a zillion years. people our age DO do that, you know!

SnowAngel: your parents will freak if u don't go to college.

zoegirl: so?

SnowAngel: YOU will freak if you don't go to college. you were born for college, zo.

zoegirl: it just sucks, that's all

SnowAngel: you got that right. the world sucks in general, that's what i'm sadly coming to realize.

SnowAngel: life sucks and then you die. THAT'S gonna be my senior quote!

SnowAngel: hey, mads. wassup?

mad maddie: nmjc. u?

SnowAngel: feeling sorry for myself. i keep thinking about how tomorrow zoe and doug are going to make love for the first time.

mad maddie: and this makes you feel sorry for yourself becuz . . . ?

SnowAngel: YOU know. cuz yay for them, it'll be this wonderful moment cuz they'll be sharing it with someone they love. UNLIKE SOME WEAK AND SHALLOW PPL I HAPPEN TO KNOW.

mad maddie: uh oh

SnowAngel: i called logan tonight—can we say "masochist"?

mad maddie: masochist!

SnowAngel: i asked him outright how he could have slept with jana while we were still going out. i was like, "that REALLY hurt, you know? like stabbed-me-in-the-heart-with-an-icepick kind of hurt."

mad maddie: what did he say?

SnowAngel: NOTHING. nada, zilch. didn't deny it, didn't fight back, didn't do anything but sit like a lump on the other end of the line. i could hear him breathing, that's it.

mad maddie: so lame. he should at least be a man about it and apologize.

SnowAngel: yeah, but he didn't. and that's why he sucks!

mad maddie: oooo! doug and zo must be going at it in the church basement by now!

mad maddie: think he's gonna blow his wad again? prematurely, i mean?

SnowAngel: that's not nice. this is a big and tender moment for zoe.

175

mad maddie: i know, but it's still funny to think of doug blowing his wad . . .

SnowAngel: i hope he doesn't. after all the stress she's been dealing with, she deserves something that's just plain good.

SnowAngel: i had an idea for her about that, btw. her college stress. i told her even tho she didn't apply to UGA she should write a letter and tell them how cool she is . . . and of course throw in who her mom is and how she's buds with the president of the university.

mad maddie: her mom's not gonna help her get into georgia

SnowAngel: she wouldn't have to TELL her mom. she'd just mention it as background info. plus, what university wouldn't want zoe???

mad maddie: how would she pay for the tuition? georgia's cheaper than kenyon, but there's still a lot of money to be forked over.

SnowAngel: duh! the Hope Scholarship!

mad maddie: oh yeah!

SnowAngel: zoe didn't even KNOW about the Hope Scholarship. i was like, "girl, there is free money just waiting for smart chickies like you!"

madmaddie: you have to have a B average and your tuition is paid for, right?

SnowAngel: as long as yr a georgia resident, which she is. and btw, i happen to know someone else who's a georgia resident . . . *looks meaningfully at friend*

mad maddie: a free ride, that's pretty amazing

SnowAngel: you can thank the state lottery for that 1

mad maddie: what did zoe think of yr idea?

SnowAngel: she said something very zoe-ish about how it was sweet of me to try and help, but that it would never work. what she DIDN'T say, but what i know she was thinking, was that georgia's not good enuff.

SnowAngel:	sometimes she's waaaaay more like her parents than she realizes.
mad maddie:	**interesting theory**
mad maddie:	**but you don't want her to end up somewhere she doesn't want to go, do you?**
SnowAngel:	if it's b/w 2 schools she doesn't wanna go to, then heck yeah, i'd rather her come to georgia!
mad maddie:	**i want us all to go to our dream schools and be the super-cool studs we are.**
SnowAngel:	whatEVer. what *i* want is for us all to be together.
SnowAngel:	so i'm gonna keep working on her. AND you.
mad maddie:	**well, don't hold your breath**
SnowAngel:	i AM gonna hold my breath.

Fri, Apr 7, 10:09 PM E.D.T.

zoegirl:	well . . . i did it!
SnowAngel:	OMG!!! for real? all the way???
zoegirl:	yeah, but not going to tell all unless maddie's here, too. maddie? you here?
mad maddie:	**yes'm!**
zoegirl:	hey, girls. yes, it's true: i'm a woman now.
mad maddie:	**way to go, you sexy beast!**
SnowAngel:	*squeals!!!*
mad maddie:	**just to be clear, we're talking full insertion?**
zoegirl:	we made love. it was amazing. and now all i can think is, "holy cow, i'm no longer a virgin! i will never be a virgin again!"
SnowAngel:	what was it like???
zoegirl:	hmm, where to start?
zoegirl:	it was more complicated than i thought it would be, for one thing. i'm sooo glad it was doug i was with, cuz i can't imagine doing that with some stranger. it's so incredibly intimate!
SnowAngel:	in what way was it complicated? and don't leave

anything out, cuz as you know i am going to be a virgin-for-life. my only solace is to live thru you.

zoegirl: i'll tell you, but first you both have to promise that you'll keep it to yourselves and not tell a single soul. and that you'll be respectful of doug in your minds and not make any crass jokes, MADDIE.

SnowAngel: i promise

mad maddie: yeah, yeah, whatevs. of course!

zoegirl: because it really is a big deal. it's something i'll remember forever, and it's something doug will remember forever. we will always be each other's firsts.

SnowAngel: we get it! now spill!

zoegirl: the complicated part was . . . getting it in. it wasn't effortless like in the movies. i *knew* it wasn't gonna be like in the movies, i'm not clueless, but part of me still expected that it would happen naturally, you know? (the getting it in part)

mad maddie: it DIDN'T happen naturally? what are you saying, that you used a

mad maddie: nvm, i'll be good

SnowAngel: what were you gonna say, a forklift?

mad maddie: no, a crowbar. but a forklift's even better, more complimentary to doug.

zoegirl: you guys! no jokes!!!

SnowAngel: ok, so how DID you get it in? *sits attentively with pen and paper*

zoegirl: he kind of guided it in. with his hand. i tried to help, but i felt pretty fumbly.

SnowAngel: did it hurt, when it finally happened?

zoegirl:	a little. and i think i bled some, but doug had brought a quilt which we'd spread on the floor. he also brought candles and roses, and afterward he held me tight and told me he's never loved anyone as much as me.
SnowAngel:	awwwww!
mad maddie:	**did you have the Big O?**
zoegirl:	what's the big o?
mad maddie:	**don't play coy with me, missy! YOU know!**
zoegirl:	no, i really don't! what are you
zoegirl:	ohhhhhhh
mad maddie:	**yeah, OOOOOOOO**
zoegirl:	erm . . . not exactly. at least, i don't think so . . . ?
zoegirl:	but lots of girls don't their first time. that's what i've read.
SnowAngel:	did HE have the Big O?
zoegirl:	well, yeah!
mad maddie:	**guys always do! der!**
zoegirl:	we'll get better with practice, that's what i think
zoegirl:	plus doug wore a condom, which i've read can inhibit the woman's pleasure. he's going to look into different brands for next time.
SnowAngel:	doug wore a condom? but you're on the pill!
zoegirl:	he wanted to be doubly safe.
mad maddie:	**oh my god**
zoegirl:	what?
mad maddie:	**that is so doug, that's all. *and* so you. you've found your soul mate, haven't you?**
zoegirl:	i know you're saying that to tease me—but yes, i have.
zoegirl:	i love him so much. i already *did* love him so much, and now i love him even more. it's SO intense. it makes me understand "Need You Now" in a whole new way.

SnowAngel:	Lady Antebellum?
zoegirl:	"i need you now, and i don't know how i can do without." that's seriously how i feel.
mad maddie:	you're saying you wldn't know how to, like, keep going if you had to go without him???
mad maddie:	zoe . . . PLEASE tell me you didn't play dead again
SnowAngel:	huh?
zoegirl:	no! and of course i WOULD keep going without doug . . . i just don't want to. ever!
SnowAngel:	when did you play dead? you guys aren't . . . yr not into kinky stuff, r you?
mad maddie:	oh man, i am enjoying this so much
zoegirl:	no, angela, we're not into kinky stuff. (maddie BE QUIET)
zoegirl:	when you're in love, all you need is each other.
SnowAngel:	AND your friendz!
zoegirl:	of course, and your friends
mad maddie:	but not in bed with you. that WOULD be kinky!
zoegirl:	you know what the strange thing is?
zoegirl:	this gigantic tremendous life-changing event happened, and now here i am back in my bedroom like a good girl, doing my (cough cough) homework.
SnowAngel:	and your parents have no idea
mad maddie:	neither does the minister of doug's church. or all the little old church ladies! if they did, they'd have brought you pineapple upside-down cake.
SnowAngel:	"here you go, sweetie. what a fine young woman you've grown up to be. and you too, dougie! my, my!"
zoegirl:	very funny
mad maddie:	well, zo, that's awesome. like you said, yr a woman now.
mad maddie:	quick change of subject—unless there's more you wanna tell?

zoegirl:	i'm good, go on
mad maddie:	i just wanna know: are we getting ready for prom together tomorrow?
SnowAngel:	spa day! spa day! just for us girls!
mad maddie:	excellent
SnowAngel:	come over around 3:00, and we can raid aunt sadie's makeup cabinet. she's got this new bobbi brown cheek-sparkle stuff that's supra-cool, plus 5,000 shades of lipstick. 😊
mad maddie:	good by me
zoegirl:	good by me, too. and now i've *got* to go to bed.
SnowAngel:	nighty-night, non-virgin!

Sat, Apr 8, 1:12 PM E.D.T.

mad maddie:	prepare thyself: my UCSC accep. has been mailed!
zoegirl:	omg! way to go!!!!
mad maddie:	gonna tell ian tonite. might as well get it out in the open.
zoegirl:	he'll be thrilled for you, mads. are you going to tell angela too?
mad maddie:	um, i'm thinking no, not at the prom. but i'll def tell her tomorrow
mad maddie:	hold on, incoming call
mad maddie:	crap!
zoegirl:	?
mad maddie:	we can't go to macee's pre-prom—just heard from vincent that jana & logan are gonna be there.
zoegirl:	together?
mad maddie:	uh, yeah! will doug care if we go to jocelyn's instead?
zoegirl:	ugh. jocelyn lives sooooo far out. will our limo take us that far?
mad maddie:	if we pay them, they will. aargh, guess i better call

angela. she's not gonna be happy, but better for her to find out now than l8r!

Sat, Apr 8, 2:02 PM E.D.T.

SnowAngel: zoe, why aren't you here?! we're supposed to be getting ready for PROM!!!

zoegirl: i thought we were meeting at 3

SnowAngel: change of plans—i need you now. (like Lady Antebellum! ha!)

SnowAngel: but seriously. if i'm gonna have to face jana and logan, i need to be smokin' hot. 🔥

zoegirl: you're already smokin' hot

SnowAngel: AND i need a drink. i really really need a drink to calm my nerves. should i raid aunt sadie's liquor cabinet?

zoegirl: NO! not a good plan!

SnowAngel: no time for arguing. just get your booty over here!!!

Sat, Apr 8, 9:15 PM E.D.T.

404-555-1787: hahaha! aren't i clever? i'm txting you from Mr. Limo Driver's blackberry cuz he is soooo nice. thank u, Mr. Limo Driver!

mad maddie: angela, i'm sitting right next to you. i can see that you're txting.

404-555-1787: hiiiiii! 😊💨

mad maddie: oh good god. we took your phone for a reason! you kept threatening to call logan!!!

404-555-1787: well, i'm over that idea, and stop whispering to zoe, and no i have NOT had too much peppermint schnapps. i'm offended you'd even

404-555-1787: whoops, sorry! is ian's foot ok?

mad maddie: foot's fine. will you stop with the damn txting? yr pissing off the limo driver.

404-555-1787: no i'm not. he thinks i'm cute. because i *am* cute!

404-555-1787: yr pissing ME off by not giving me logan's number. just hand me yr phone and i'll look it up myself.

404-555-1787: isn't it weird how few telephone numbers we memorize anymore? i know yours, and zoe's . . . and my parents' cell numbers AND land line . . .

404-555-1787: hey. mads.

mad maddie: 🙂

404-555-1787: ian's looking verrrrrry yummy. and what's this BIG THING you need to tell him? i heard you say you've got some BIG THING to tell him. it better not be that yr pregnant with his child!

mad maddie: good grief

404-555-1787: i wonder what logan's wearing, tux or suit. prolly something stupid to match stupid jana. i'm NERVOUS to see them, maddie. why am i nervous?

mad maddie: you have no reason to be. can we quit txting & talk like normal ppl, plz? plus it's weird to keep seeing this unknown number show up on my screen.

404-555-1787: not unknown. it's . . .

404-555-1787: hold on . . .

404-555-1787: it's peter hoyt! i'm peter hoyt, hahahaha! You can enter me as a contact now and call me Mr. Hoyt instead of Mr. Limo Driver!!!

404-555-1787: HEY! yr whispering again! you said something about jana, i heard you!

404-555-1787: she's WHAT?

404-555-1787: tell zoe to stop trying to grab peter's phone. stop it, zoe, you are being very disrespectful of peter hoyt's possessions.

404-555-1787: oh look! u think u got me, but i can still type with oboe hand!

mad maddie: oboe hand? that so?

mad maddie: yr done, babe. cutting you off. say yr good-byes!

mad maddie: **zo, where r you? did you & doug have a fight?**

zoegirl: this is the worst prom ever!

mad maddie: **come back—I'LL dance with you!**

zoegirl: thanks but no thanks. i'll just stay here in the parking lot where i can't be too "needy."

mad maddie: **don't be that way. just come back and we'll**

mad maddie: **ah shit, g2g. angela trouble!**

SnowAngel: oh. my. god.

mad maddie: **you can say that again**

SnowAngel: i am MORTIFIED. was i as drunk last nite as i think i was?

mad maddie: **drunker. i'm surprised yr even conscious. how ya feeling?**

SnowAngel: like crap 😣

SnowAngel: my mouth is soooo dry, and i've got a killer headache. and i smell like barf. did i barf, mads?

mad maddie: **yes, all over logan. this was after your whole "no touching allowed" speech. do you remember?**

SnowAngel: i threw up on logan? *cringe*

SnowAngel: i remember him coming up to me all hang-dog, and i very clearly remember jana storming up after him. she looked SPOOKY, didn't she? all glittery-hard, but with her words coming out slurry and wrong.

mad maddie: **cuz she'd had even more to drink than you, that's why. altho she's also had way more practice.**

SnowAngel: did something happen b/w me and her? i have this vague itchy thought that it did.

mad maddie: **you don't remember?**

SnowAngel: der, that's why i'm asking

mad maddie: **well, logan wants you back—do you remember that? he kept trying to apologize, and you kept**

pushing him away and telling him he wasn't allowed to touch you anymore. and jana snorted and said, "that's for sure," meaning the "no touching" rule was what drove logan away in the 1st place.

mad maddie: and then she laughed, and that's when you threw up.

SnowAngel: on logan?

mad maddie: on logan.

SnowAngel: christ

mad maddie: no, not on christ. wld have been nice if you'd thrown up on jana, tho

SnowAngel: *conks head on desk and wants to die*

SnowAngel: why did SHE have to be there to c me do that? why???

mad maddie: she wasn't especially supportive, i'll give you that. i believe her exact words, after she jerked back to avoid the splatter, were, "what a fucking loser."

SnowAngel: oh, how original

mad maddie: yep, that's jana

SnowAngel: it's still humiliating. it'S BEYOND humiliating.

SnowAngel: did you say anything back, when she said that?

mad maddie: i was too busy cleaning you up

SnowAngel: so you didn't stand up for me?

mad maddie: i didn't UNstand up for u

mad maddie: but what good would yelling at jana have done?

SnowAngel: fine, whatever

mad maddie: r you mad???

SnowAngel: no, i'm not mad

SnowAngel: i'm just depressed. and bitter. and pretty much disillusioned with life in general.

mad maddie: cuz i didn't stoop to jana's level?

SnowAngel: yes, cuz it makes me lose faith.

mad maddie: in what? in ME?

SnowAngel:	in all of us
mad maddie:	**angela, it was PROM. i needed to get you out of there before a chaperone noticed!**
SnowAngel:	i'm not trying to argue, i'm just stating the hard cold facts. i spent my senior prom puking my guts out while jana stood there and sneered. once again she had the final laugh.
mad maddie:	**sheesh, angela**
SnowAngel:	*shrugs*
SnowAngel:	it's how i feel
mad maddie:	**then i'll do something to get back at her. again. whatever you want me to do, i'll do it.**
SnowAngel:	don't bother. if anyone was gonna do something, it would need to be zoe. but she won't . . . so there it is.
mad maddie:	**why would it need to be zoe?**
SnowAngel:	don't give me that. cuz i already have and you already have, but she hasn't. and that's why the power of 3 is no more.
mad maddie:	**so tell her**
SnowAngel:	what's the point? she'd go all doe-eyed and whimper-y, but she still wouldn't DO anything.
mad maddie:	**yr being pretty melodramatic, even for you. you sure yr not just looking for a reason to be hopeless?**
SnowAngel:	why wasn't she there when jana was calling me a fucking loser, huh? cuz she was with doug, that's why. doug's more important to her than we are!
mad maddie:	**that's crap, angela. anywayz, she and doug had a fight.**
SnowAngel:	they did?
mad maddie:	**she was hiding in the parking lot for the whole last half of the nite. THAT'S why she wasn't there to see you puke your guts out.**

SnowAngel:	what was the fight about?
mad maddie:	**i dunno, he said something that made her feel bad. something about how she's too codependent.**
SnowAngel:	well . . . it's true. she IS codependent. she cares *way* too much about what he
SnowAngel:	omg—another horrible memory is intruding. no, no, no!
mad maddie:	**sweetie?**
SnowAngel:	it has to do with you NOT being codependent, and something you said to ian in the limo. not on the way to the prom, but after, when we were going home.
mad maddie:	**oh. that.**
SnowAngel:	is it true??? did you really send in your acceptance to santa cruz???
mad maddie:	**maybe this isn't the best time to be talking about this**
SnowAngel:	nooooo! *puts hands over ears*
mad maddie:	**see? i didn't wanna tell you, cuz i knew you'd take it badly.**
SnowAngel:	but you told ian?
mad maddie:	**well, yeah, but just cuz i couldn't NOT tell him, once i'd actually done it and sealed the envelope and put it in the mailbox. it would be too big a thing b/w us.**
mad maddie:	**and for the record, i thought you were too out of it to hear**
SnowAngel:	why DID you do it and seal the envelope and put it in the mailbox? why?!!
mad maddie:	**angela . . . you know it was the right thing for me to do. and so does ian, who was great about it, btw.**
SnowAngel:	of course he was. he's perfect. but i'm not perfect—i just want my world back!

mad maddie:	it would be nice if you could be happy for me, you know.
SnowAngel:	i'm sorry, but i can't
mad maddie:	yr being impossible. you come down on zoe for being codependent, and you come down on me for NOT being codependent. does that seem fair to you?
SnowAngel:	logan cheated on me with jana, i made a fool of myself at prom, and in three months my 2 best friends r leaving me forever. does THAT seem fair to YOU?
mad maddie:	ok, like i said, maybe we should talk about this l8r.
SnowAngel:	whatever
SnowAngel:	oh look, zoe just posted a pic on instagram.
SnowAngel:	what IS it? oh. it's a high heel. her high heel from last night, but just one of them, all by itself looking lonely.
SnowAngel:	SHE understands sadness, so maybe i should stop being "impossible" with you and be "impossible" with her instead
mad maddie:	maybe you shld
SnowAngel:	fine, i will. misery loves company!!!

Sun, Apr 9, 12:59 PM E.D.T.

SnowAngel:	hey, zo. maddie's going to santa cruz, i barfed on logan, and jana is prolly STILL laughing at me. life sucks. oh, and i hear you and doug had a fight?
zoegirl:	i don't want to talk about it.
zoegirl:	crap, he's texting me. what should i do?
SnowAngel:	tell him yr too busy txting ME
zoegirl:	i can't say that!
SnowAngel:	why not?
zoegirl:	he wants to know how i'm feeling, but i'm not in the mood to get into it. aaargh.

SnowAngel:	tell him yr fine, but super-tired, and that yr gonna go take a nap. then put yr phone in stealth mode so if he calls it'll go straight to voicemail and he'll think u really are napping. then come back and keep txting.
zoegirl:	i can do that?
SnowAngel:	yeah—it's under "settings"
zoegirl:	okay, hold on
zoegirl:	done. that's kind of cool, because now i can ignore him without him totally knowing i'm ignoring him. thanks, angela.
SnowAngel:	any time. now tell me about the fight!
zoegirl:	i'm just . . . i'm having bad feelings toward him and i really don't want 2, cuz i love him.
SnowAngel:	what r the bad feelings about?
zoegirl:	about him being a weiner, that's what.
zoegirl:	NOOOOO, not really. but kinda.
SnowAngel:	tell me what happened
zoegirl:	at first everything was great. jocelyn's pre-party was a blast, and i didn't mind that he was hanging out with tilman and those guys because i knew i had all night to spend with him. plus that meant i got to hang out with you and andre and maddie and ian, and that was awesome.
SnowAngel:	jocelyn's party, imho, was the only good part of the whole night.
SnowAngel:	god, i feel sorry for andre. he got stuck with such a loser date.
zoegirl:	you don't think he had fun?
SnowAngel:	not once i was covered in barf, i don't. but whatevs, go on.
zoegirl:	so we got to the actual prom and i thought, "at last, now we get to be romantic." i asked doug if he wanted to dance, and he was like, "sure, sure,

in a sec." and then he *kept* talking to tilman. i mean, he had his arm around me and he kept rubbing my shoulder, but still.

zoegirl: a slow song came on, and i said, "doug? let's dance."

SnowAngel: i saw you guys out there. you looked cute.

zoegirl: except for the fact that even though he was pretending to be into it, i could tell that he wasn't. i asked and asked and asked what was wrong, and finally he said he didn't really feel like dancing after all. i said, "fine! let's not, then!" i told him i really didn't care what we did, and that if he had a preference one way or another, then we should do that.

SnowAngel: i thought you DID wanna dance.

zoegirl: i didn't care *that* much

SnowAngel: so then what?

zoegirl: so we walked over to where tilman and pete had been, but they were gone. i asked if he wanted to go find them, and he shrugged. he was still acting all gloomy, and when i asked why, he was like, "now i feel bad that we're *not* dancing."

SnowAngel: oh good grief

zoegirl: he said, "i feel like you're too dependent on me, and even though i like that sometimes, sometimes i don't. if you wanted to dance, we should have danced."

SnowAngel: sounds like a no-win situation

zoegirl: it kills me to think that he thinks i'm so weak i wouldn't stand up for myself. that i'd change what i felt to suit his needs, even if that meant giving up something i wanted to do.

SnowAngel: erm . . .

zoegirl: but at the same time, maybe i'm afraid i *am* that

way a little. i know i let him be too important to me sometimes, but that's normal, right?

SnowAngel: well . . .

zoegirl: whenever we hang out with tilman and pete, i turn into the biggest blob. i just sit there with a smile pasted on and feel so boring. have you ever had that experience?

SnowAngel: do you mean boring or bored?

zoegirl: both! i'm bored by them *and* i, myself, am boring. and now to find out that doug feels the same exact way—that i *am* a big codependent blob—it just sucks!

SnowAngel: so yr gonna punish him by not talking to him?

zoegirl: do you have a better plan?

SnowAngel: no. only . . .

zoegirl: only what?

SnowAngel: nothing, just that sometimes—like in life in general— yr so passive. and i just wondered, i suppose, if that was working for you.

zoegirl: i'm "passive"?

SnowAngel: i don't mean to offend you. i just . . . i dunno. i don't even know what i'm talking about.

zoegirl: i'm not passive, angela. name one time (other than prom) that i've ever been passive!

SnowAngel: you don't wanna go there, zo. trust me.

zoegirl: ???

SnowAngel: i'm gonna stop talking before i get myself into trouble!!!

Sun, Apr 9, 1:45 PM E.D.T.

zoegirl: angela says i'm passive. can you believe that?

zoegirl: i told her to give me an example, just one, and she couldn't. that says it all, don't you think?

mad maddie: the whole jana deal—that's what she was talking

191

	about. i mean, if yr curious. but she didn't wanna get into it because she thinks there's no point.
zoegirl:	i don't understand
mad maddie:	plus she's mad at me for going to santa cruz, which is ridiculous. the two things are totally not related.
zoegirl:	what two things?
mad maddie:	well . . . i'm not supposed to tell you, but i will.
mad maddie:	angela thinks jana stole our power cuz we haven't been a united front. cuz even tho she and i fought back against her, you never did.
zoegirl:	oh
mad maddie:	and add to that the fact that i'm leaving for california . . . and you'll be leaving for either princeton or kenyon . . .
mad maddie:	she thinks her whole world is crashing down.
zoegirl:	because we're going to different colleges? she's always known we'd be going to different colleges!
mad maddie:	if everything else was going well, maybe she could handle it. but as it is, it's just 1 more thing that's out of her control.
zoegirl:	and the other thing that's out of her control . . .
mad maddie:	. . . is jana. so she's turned it into this passion play, with us on one side and jana on the other. and in her mind, jana came out on top.
zoegirl:	let me see if i've got this straight. angela thinks jana robbed us of our power because in her mind i haven't stood up for the three of us. and doug thinks i'm needy and weak because i wouldn't stand up for myself.
mad maddie:	wow. when you put it that way . . .
zoegirl:	i'm feeling even more depressed than i already was.

mad maddie:	i wanted you to know what was going on, that's all.
zoegirl:	and now i do
mad maddie:	just don't tell angela i told you!!!

zoegirl:	i've spent all afternoon thinking, and you know what? angela's right.
mad maddie:	ah, zo. i felt really bad after that last text. you didn't need that shit on top of your whole fight with doug.
mad maddie:	how r things with him, btw? have you talked?
zoegirl:	i set my cell to voicemail, and i turned the ringer off our landline. that way, even if he does call, i won't know.
mad maddie:	yr still pissed?
zoegirl:	more like embarrassed that he would see me as so . . . spineless.
mad maddie:	all he made was that 1 comment. he still loves you, zo.
zoegirl:	don't try to downplay it when you know there's truth to it. you personally have told me 5,000 times that i'm under doug's thumb.
mad maddie:	i never said under his thumb
zoegirl:	the worst part is, i don't know how it happened. i was gutsy last year, wasn't i? when you made me parade thru the mall with marshmallows on my nipples?
zoegirl:	what happened to that girl?!
mad maddie:	two words: doug came back
mad maddie:	wait, that's three. lemme try again: doug returned.
zoegirl:	no, because doug was still in town when i did the marshmallow dare. remember?
mad maddie:	yeah, but then he did his Sea the World thing,

	and when he came back it was a whole new ball game.
zoegirl:	???
mad maddie:	you became pod girl. maybe you didn't mean to, but you did.
zoegirl:	no i didn't
zoegirl:	i did?
mad maddie:	before he left, the power b/w you guys was equal. maybe even in your favor, since he was head-over-heels for you and you were kinda resisting. but then he came back, and he was so much more wordly and confident, and for some reason you let that matter. you fell into the role of letting him call the shots.
zoegirl:	but that's pathetic
mad maddie:	you were all, "oh doug, what is life w/o you? yr soooo important to me!"
zoegirl:	okay, i get the picture
mad maddie:	angela and i wished you'd snap out of it, but you didn't.
zoegirl:	okay! i get the picture!
mad maddie:	it actually helped me when it came to going to santa cruz, tho. cuz in my head i was like, "i love zoe, but i refuse to BE zoe," in terms of the whole neediness thing.
zoegirl:	great, i'm glad i could be of service
mad maddie:	as for the jana thing, it's more of the same. more of you saying, "i'll just study and be stressed and hang out with doug, and nothing else matters."
mad maddie:	that's what angela meant by you being passive.
zoegirl:	well that's why i'm texting. if i'm going to stop being passive—if i'm going to get jana back once and for all—then i need your help.
mad maddie:	ha! yr cute.

zoegirl:	i'm serious, mads
mad maddie:	**for real?**
zoegirl:	what do you mean, "for real"? of course for real!
mad maddie:	**it's just that**
zoegirl:	just that what?
zoegirl:	i can't believe i'm finally willing to do something and you're telling me not to!
mad maddie:	**i'm not telling you NOT to . . . i just don't know if it's worth it, frankly.**
zoegirl:	why???
mad maddie:	**jana didn't "steal" our power. it's not your job to steal it back.**
zoegirl:	except that it is!
zoegirl:	look at the facts: JANA SLEPT WITH LOGAN. jana had SEX with angela's ex-boyfriend, who at the time *wasn't* her ex, for the sole sake of messing with her. you know it's true!
mad maddie:	**well . . . yes**
zoegirl:	and she planted rumors about me and angela . . . and put sex ads about you on craigslist . . . and put a dead bird in angela's jeep! a dead bird—how sick is that?
mad maddie:	**pretty frickin sick**
zoegirl:	and throughout it all i sat there and did nothing, because that's me, do-nothing-girl. BUT NO MORE.
mad maddie:	**ok, fine**
mad maddie:	**so what r you gonna do?**
zoegirl:	well, that part i don't know yet. but i'll think of something!
mad maddie:	**yes ma'am, non-passive zoe**
zoegirl:	don't be sarcastic
mad maddie:	**me???**
mad maddie:	**hey, i'm outta here. i'm meeting ian at starbucks.**

zoegirl: oh good—ian needs some quality maddie-time. i feel so bad for him, spending prom alone while you babysat angela!

mad maddie: **yeah, wasn't that lovely?**

zoegirl: and see? that's just one more example of my being a lame friend. i should have been there. i should have been helping out.

zoegirl: did you tell angela about how ian got the DJ to play "my girl" for you?

mad maddie: **why? it would just make her feel bad.**

zoegirl: it breaks my heart to think of you sitting there, wiping away angela's vomit, when the song came on. and ian looking everywhere but not finding you!

mad maddie: **and—don't forget—he'd found out only two hours earlier that i for sure wouldn't be going to UGA with him.**

zoegirl: that is *so* sad

mad maddie: **do you know why he requested that song? he told me later that it was to say, "it's gonna be ok, let's just enjoy this night, you'll always be mine regardless of where we end up."**

zoegirl: oh, mads!

mad maddie: **yeah. well.**

mad maddie: **i don't wanna keep him waiting, so i'm gonna go!**

Mon, Apr 10, 10:12 AM E.D.T.

SnowAngel: there's a new sheriff in town, and her name is zoe barrett. 😈

mad maddie: **she's on a mission, man. i tried to talk her out of it, but no go.**

SnowAngel: what?!

SnowAngel: i'm loving the fact that she has finally grown a spine. LOVING it. don't you dare talk her out of it!

mad maddie:	she was not to be dissuaded, so chill.
SnowAngel:	i feel bad about doug, tho
SnowAngel:	a while ago she told me that she really really needs praise, and i think the opposite is true, too. if someone tells her she's "bad" in some way—like doug suggesting that she depends on him too much—she takes it waaaaay hard.
mad maddie:	i know. she obsesses over it.
mad maddie:	ack—ms. hathoway's coming over. i'm supposed to be entering quiz grades for her. sayonaras!

Tues, Apr 11, 5:15 PM E.D.T.

mad maddie:	hiya, zo. get your history assignment done?
zoegirl:	hold on, just have to type the very last . . .
zoegirl:	done.
zoegirl:	what's up?
mad maddie:	saw you talking to doug today. you guys all mended?
zoegirl:	i don't know. he knows he hurt my feelings, and he's being very sweet to try and make up for it. like leaving notes in my locker and meeting me after class.
zoegirl:	but even though he's being so nice, i feel like i have to keep a wall up between us . . . otherwise he's gonna think i'm too "dependent" on him again.
mad maddie:	a LITTLE dependent's ok. just not whole hog.
zoegirl:	his side of things is that it was prom, it was a party, he wanted to hang with his friends *and* be with me. i'm like, yeah, i get that. but at the same time i'm thinking, "we made love for the first time 24 hours earlier. LESS than 24 hours earlier! shouldn't that count for something?"
zoegirl:	but i can't SAY that, because . . . you know.

mad maddie: too dependent

zoegirl: yeah

mad maddie: have you made any progress with your jana plan?

zoegirl: yes, actually! 👍 because when i work on that i *don't* feel loserish. in my head i'm like, "see? i can be brave. i can take action."

mad maddie: and what form has that action taken?

zoegirl: to be honest, no actual action yet. but here is my brilliant idea: steal jana's car!

mad maddie: pardonay moi?

zoegirl: not STEAL it steal it. just borrow it . . . and then leave it at a sex addicts anonymous meeting!

mad maddie: oh, zoe, yr priceless

zoegirl: i know! it's perfect! sex addicts anonymous, that's *so* jana. she'll be humiliated just like angela!

mad maddie: sigh. must i always be the lone sage in the wilderness?

zoegirl: huh?

mad maddie: how are you gonna "borrow" her car, zo? and say you do manage to get your paws on the heapmobile. do you actually have a sex addicts meeting in mind to drop it off at?

zoegirl: well . . .

mad maddie: and how is jana gonna know that's where it is, so that she can go retrieve it and be humiliated?

zoegirl: i guess i would

zoegirl: somebody could just

mad maddie: mmm-hmm

zoegirl: don't say that! it's a great plan!

mad maddie: your instincts are great, your plan is horrible

mad maddie: back to the drawing board, dude!

mad maddie: check this out: vincent told me that things are NOT going well with jana and logan. good news, eh?

SnowAngel: do i care?

SnowAngel: no. yes. but don't give me any details. i don't wanna hear about it.

mad maddie: pourquoi?

SnowAngel: cuz i don't WANT to care.

SnowAngel: when i think about logan and how much mental energy i've wasted on him . . . it's ridiculous!

mad maddie: yes. yes, it really is, so let's move on.

mad maddie: altho i *will* tell you one thing. well, two things.

mad maddie: thing one: logan still wants to get back together with you. that's what vincent heard from jana.

SnowAngel:

mad maddie: thing two: vincent also said that jana found out who her stepmonster's doing the nasty with. it's some guy who works at a liquor store.

SnowAngel: do I care? I do not.

mad maddie: she found the guy's work shirt in her stepmonster's car. it smelled like her stepmonster's perfume.

SnowAngel: did you get glendy's latest spam offering? about the bad guys who go around with fake perfume samples, only really it's ether?

mad maddie: u read it? i thought u automatically deleted her emails.

SnowAngel: well, i've been showing a little more caution recently, after she called me all giddy to tell me her spiffy new trick. get this: she's learned how to dump some bug on ppl's computers which makes them shut down and reboot automatically. and when they reboot, they relay the owners' log-on names and passwords straight to glendy.

mad maddie: dude, that's some serious hacking. why???

SnowAngel: cuz apparently some ppl have had the audacity to block her (incroyable!), and this way she can go to twitter or tumblr or whatever and UNblock herself. can you imagine? *pretending to be glendy: hi!!!! i'm baaaack!*

mad maddie: jesus

mad maddie: doesn't the fact that she's been blocked in the 1st place tell her anything?

SnowAngel: so you better stay on her good side . . . or else!!!

Thu, Apr 13, 8:13 PM E.D.T.

mad maddie: hey, babe. wanna hear about my healthy dinner? a reese's big cup and a glass of nestle quik.

zoegirl: mmmm. nutritious *and* delicious.

mad maddie: the rents r playing bridge with their buddies, so i'm on my own. you should come over!

zoegirl: sorry, charlie. gotta finish my physics so i can keep my A. i do NOT want to take the final exam!

mad maddie: are you gonna have to take any finals at all?

zoegirl: i don't think so. straight As all the way . . . yeah!

zoegirl: i did, however, take a study break to watch big bunny episodes 5 & 6. big bunny finally ate the kitty!

mad maddie: au contraire—the kitty went away on a business trip! the kitty has a very good head for figures, remember?

zoegirl: do you have every episode memorized? yr freaking me out.

mad maddie: heh heh heh

zoegirl: what freaked me out even more were those psychotic squirrels who hacked up the other forest creatures and turned them into pie . . .

mad maddie: "chop chop chop went the squirrel. slice slice slice went his associates!"

zoegirl: so guess what? i heard back from UGA, about my late application.

mad maddie: WHAT?

mad maddie: wait a sec—you actually did that? used angela's idea about writing the prez of the university?

zoegirl: uh huh. i used my mom's letterhead.

mad maddie: holy frickin shit, zo. you ARE taking a stand!

mad maddie: what did they say?

zoegirl: that i've got a spot if i want it. what do you think of that?

mad maddie: what about the Hope Scholarship?

zoegirl: they said my transcript demonstrates "the academic excellence the Hope Scholarship is in place to support." so i could do it, if i want. i could honestly and truly go to georgia.

mad maddie: free ride, baby! tell your mom to put THAT in her pipe and smoke it!

zoegirl: i know. it's incredible. i can't wait to see her face when i tell her.

zoegirl: well, no, that's not true. i'm totally nervous about telling her, because it'll be me fighting back in a real way. me saying, "are you *sure* you're not willing to pay for kenyon?"

mad maddie: ahhhh, a power-play

mad maddie: smart smart smart, little zoe

zoegirl: we'll see. i've got to play it just right if it's going to work.

mad maddie: SHOW NO FEAR

zoegirl: but i'm not going to tell angela till it's done, because she'd just latch onto the UGA part and refuse to let go. you know.

mad maddie: uh, yeah. been there, done that.

mad maddie: what about your jana revenge plot? making any progress?

zoegirl:	i'm tossing some ideas around, but i'm not telling what they are because you'd just tell me they wouldn't work. for now i'm just . . . letting her get her confidence up.
mad maddie:	**uh, i think her confidence IS up**
zoegirl:	i'm just waiting for the right opportunity. and for a chance to talk privately with vincent.
mad maddie:	**vincent?!**
zoegirl:	g'night!

Fri, Apr 14, 4:02 PM E.D.T.

SnowAngel:	my graduation announcements came today! they're so beautiful!
zoegirl:	yay!
SnowAngel:	now i just have to address them and stamp them and trudge off with them to the post office. *slumps shoulders*
SnowAngel:	but they're so beautiful! *perks back up*
zoegirl:	mine aren't here yet, because my mom made a last-minute decision that they should be ivory instead of cream. did i have any say in this? no. so now they're like on a rush job.
SnowAngel:	zoe! you have gotta learn to stand up to that woman!
zoegirl:	i know, i know. and actually, she and i are supposed to have "a chat" this evening. i have something i want to tell her.
SnowAngel:	that yr gonna blow off princeton altogether and come live with me in athens? *smiles charmingly* that yr gonna get a job as a waitress and learn how the other half lives?
zoegirl:	er . . . not exactly. i'll tell you after we talk, okay?
SnowAngel:	okey-dokey, smokey
SnowAngel:	off to address envelopes!

SnowAngel: waaaah! waaaah! why does everybody have to be so frickin *independent* all the time?!!

mad maddie: independent? the horror!

SnowAngel: zoe just called and told me about georgia, which i know you already know, so don't rub it in. i can't believe she got accepted and yet she's not going to go!!!

mad maddie: hold on, i actually *don't* know this part. did she talk to her mom???

SnowAngel: yes *sniffs*

mad maddie: and her mom caved? omfg!

SnowAngel: apparently there were tears and yelling and a big fat scene, which as we know is not zoe's strong point.

SnowAngel: but zoe stayed strong, and her stupid mom finally gave in. she decided she'd rather c zoe go to kenyon than UGA—how snobby and hypocritical is that? she won't pay for kenyon, and now all of a sudden she will, just so her daughter doesn't have to go to a state university?

mad maddie: angela . . . zoe was never going to go to georgia.

SnowAngel: i think mrs. barrett should have held her ground and refused to pony up. then zoe would have HAD to go to georgia!!!!

mad maddie: i hope you didn't act like this when she told you. i hope you were supportive, even if you had to fake it.

SnowAngel: *turns up nose* hmmph

mad maddie: dude, i'm gonna call and congratulate her.

SnowAngel: yeah, u do that. and don't worry about me! just leave me in the dust!

SnowAngel: maddie?

SnowAngel: don't i need support? i'm the one who's gonna be all alone in athens! alone and lonely! all by myself!

Sat, Apr 15, 6:13 PM E.D.T.

zoegirl: hey, mads. you think angela's going to be okay?

mad maddie: about what?

zoegirl: you know, about my going to kenyon.

mad maddie: she HAS to be. she has no choice.

zoegirl: i kind of felt like i was kicking her when she was down, when i told her the news last night.

mad maddie: listen. you can't base your life around angela, any more than you can around doug.

zoegirl: i know, i know

mad maddie: it's AWESOME that you get to go to kenyon. YOU made it happen, you know? i'm so incredibly proud of you.

zoegirl: thanks, mads. i'm proud of me too.

zoegirl: and to my mom's credit, she's being cooler about it than she could have been.

mad maddie: oh yeah?

zoegirl: this morning, when we were both a little calmer, she told me that even tho kenyon's not the school she would have chosen for me, she admired my spirit. like, it surprised her what i'd done.

mad maddie: i bet it did!

zoegirl: she admitted that *maybe* she'd been too controlling, and that *maybe* my own desires should factor into the equation. novel concept, huh?

mad maddie: well, blow me down. maybe she's growing up as well.

zoegirl: doug's excited for me too. angela was all, "yr picking him over me," and i had to remind her that no, actually, he's still gonna be 2 hours away. we'll be apart no matter what. but we'll just take it as it comes.

mad maddie: tell me about it. it's so hard, with ian, knowing that the time is ticking down. tick tick tick.

zoegirl: doug and i have a "hot date" tonight. i'm assuming he wants to have sex.

mad maddie: does this mean things are back to normal?

zoegirl: i suppose. i just have to be careful about what i say and how i act, that's all.

mad maddie: oh, well in that case, no prob . . . you just have to totally change your personality.

zoegirl: it's sad, because i feel like i can no longer open my soul and let my true feelings out. but too bad— he's the one who made it happen.

mad maddie: and yet yr still gonna have sex with him

zoegirl: well, yeah. maybe it'll bring us closer.

mad maddie: i just hope you have the Big O this time. i'm rooting for ya, girl!

Sat, Apr 15, 11:23 PM E.D.T.

mad maddie: Big O? ian & i wanna know!!!

Sun, Apr 16, 12:02 AM E.D.T.

zoegirl: *just* got in. my mom was sitting at the door with a clock.

mad maddie: honest?

zoegirl: no, but i had to go check in with her and let her know i'd arrived home safely. groan groan groan. you'd think things would be different now that she knows i'm an actual mature individual, but no.

zoegirl: doesn't it seem silly to have a curfew when we're about to graduate and be on our own?

mad maddie: yes

zoegirl: you didn't really tell ian about me and doug, did you?

mad maddie: no, u goof

mad maddie: but did u? have an orgasm?

zoegirl: well . . . no

mad maddie: damn!

zoegirl: but i'm fine with it, i really am. it's about more than just physical pleasure.

zoegirl: anyway, you talking about it kinda makes me feel loser-ish.

mad maddie: oh, zoe! that's not what i meant.

mad maddie: listen. yr having sex—making love—with someone you truly care about. yr not having one-night stands or being a slut machine, like some ppl we know. of course it's about more than whether you got off or not!

zoegirl: could you please not be so graphic?

mad maddie: oopsy-daisy

zoegirl: i *wish* i was someone sex came easily to . . . but i'm just not.

mad maddie: that doesn't mean you never WILL be. you just gotta keep practicing.

zoegirl: it's still fun, don't get me wrong. and doug's skin is so incredibly smooth . . . and warm . . . and there's this one spot, right below his hip bone . . . it's like, wow. just to be so close to another human being—that's worth it, right?

mad maddie: u bet

mad maddie: i truly didn't mean to make you feel bad, zo. i was just being my normal obnoxious self.

zoegirl: no worries.

zoegirl: i love your normal obnoxious self!

Mon, Apr 17, 11:43 AM E.D.T.

SnowAngel: it's happening, our 2nd to last week of school! aaaaahhhhhh!

SnowAngel:	i STILL don't have my senior quote. do you?
mad maddie:	**i've been using class time to think about it, since it's not as if anybody's doing any actual work. but everything i come up with sounds too corny or too cliche.**
SnowAngel:	i'm in the same exact boat. grrrr . . .
SnowAngel:	did you hear what jana did today? she swiped megan's hw during mr. bradley's class, right off her desk, and threw it out the window!
mad maddie:	**what?!**
SnowAngel:	for no reason at all! cuz megan made one small comment about jana's handwriting or something.
SnowAngel:	so megan yelled at her, and then MEGAN got yelled at by mr. bradley.
mad maddie:	**dude, that is just ridiculous**
SnowAngel:	i don't understand how jana can be such a bitch and get away with it. i truly don't.
mad maddie:	**well, yeah. i guess no one wants to take her on cuz they've seen how futile it is.**
SnowAngel:	i s'pose
SnowAngel:	zoe's not gonna beat her up for me after all, is she?
mad maddie:	**she WANTS to, but she hasn't worked out the details. i keep telling her to forget the details and just go for it, but you know zoe.**
SnowAngel:	😕
mad maddie:	**but don't give up on her completely. sometimes ol' zo can pull one out of her butt at the last minute!**

Tues, Apr 18, 9:19 AM E.D.T.

zoegirl:	our graduation gowns are in! come to the main office if you want to see!
SnowAngel:	omg. and those square hats? w/ tassles?
zoegirl:	mortar boards, that's what they're called.

SnowAngel:	can we try them on?
zoegirl:	that's what everybody's doing. get over here!!!

Wed, Apr 19, 10:45 PM E.D.T.

mad maddie:	yr not gonna believe this.
SnowAngel:	what?
mad maddie:	my laptop got stolen! ian and i were at starbucks, and when ian got up to get some sugar, this guy came over and grabbed my laptop right off the table. and then he ran out the door!
SnowAngel:	nooooooo!
mad maddie:	yesssss!
SnowAngel:	that's awful! what did you do?
mad maddie:	i just sat there, flabbergasted. ian, on the other hand, went all noble and tried to rescue it. it totally cracked me up.
SnowAngel:	did he get it back?
mad maddie:	he chased the guy into the parking lot, but the guy made it to his car and started the engine. so ian flung himself onto the guy's hood!!! the guy starts swerving, and ian's spread-eagled on the hood, and i'm like, "omfg!!!"
SnowAngel:	jesus, maddie!
mad maddie:	finally the guy turned on his windshield wipers, and ian bounced onto the pavement. all that for my crappy laptop which doesn't even turn on half the time!
SnowAngel:	i can't BELIEVE ian jumped onto the car. i'm so glad he's ok!
mad maddie:	he's more than ok. he's wonderful. after we stopped laughing, he took my hands and looked at me with his sweet brown eyes. and you know what he said? he said, "yr the one, maddie."
SnowAngel:	ohhhhh! *melts into warm gooey puddle*

mad maddie: i knew you'd get mushy

mad maddie: it made me pretty mushy, 2

SnowAngel: ian is wonderful, maddie. yaaaaaaay! 😍

zoegirl: hey, angela. i just wanted you to know that i haven't forgotten about you.

SnowAngel: as if! how could u ever possibly forget about ME?

zoegirl: the jana thing, i mean. i saw how she was throwing her arm over logan's shoulder on the senior patio. she was totally doing it to taunt you.

SnowAngel: logan texted me in 6th period to tell me they're no longer going out, on the off chance that i cared.

but megan heard from carrie that they still hook up, so whatever.

zoegirl: i *do* feel bad for logan. i can't help it.

zoegirl: do you see yourself ever being buds with him again?

SnowAngel: no, i really don't

zoegirl: so sad. but i understand.

SnowAngel: maybe i'll feel differently one day in the very distant future.

SnowAngel: but i'm not there yet. not even close.

zoegirl: well if it helps, i'm almost there in terms of my plot against jana. i met with vincent about it this afternoon, although it didn't exactly go as planned.

SnowAngel: i'm so intrigued! explain!

zoegirl: i wanted him to hotwire jana's car for me, so that i could drive it onto the school's front lawn. i had this great idea of strewing it with beer cans and condoms. well, maybe condoms. wouldn't that have been awesome?

zoegirl: but vincent wouldn't do it

SnowAngel:	aw, man! why not?
zoegirl:	first he acted indignant that i assumed he knew how to hotwire a car. except then he admitted he *does* know how, so it's not like he had a leg to stand on.
SnowAngel:	busted!
zoegirl:	huh? who's busted?
SnowAngel:	both of you! you for assuming that cuz he's puerto rican he'd be a car thief, and him for being able to steal a car if he had to.
zoegirl:	i never called him a car thief!
SnowAngel:	racist! racist! zoe's a closet racist!
zoegirl:	oh god, now i feel terrible. i didn't mean it like that i swear! you know i'm not racist!
SnowAngel:	so why wouldn't he do it? is it cuz he's friends with jana?
zoegirl:	i didn't see him as the type to get hung up on morals since all along he's been amused by the jana war. and he's never taken sides one way or another. but when i brought that up, he gave me this pointed stare and was like, "yeah, that's right. i never took sides."
zoegirl:	then he put his hand on my knee and said, "you guys are funny and all that . . . but, amiga, eventually you've got to let it go."
SnowAngel:	oh god help me. maturity lessons? from vincent???
zoegirl:	he said, "you want to know what the best revenge is? happiness. *that's* the best revenge."
SnowAngel:	easy for HIM to say
zoegirl:	i know, i know. i mean, he's got a point . . . but you're *not* happy. and how can i be happy if my angela's not happy?
SnowAngel:	yeah!

zoegirl: he invited us to come over saturday, by the way. he's having a party.

SnowAngel: r jana and her minions gonna be there?

zoegirl: terri and margaret: yes. jana: no. apparently terri and jana are in a snit again, and jana refuses to be in the same room as her until terri grovels at her feet.

SnowAngel: that is so pathetic

zoegirl: truly

zoegirl: wanna go? could be fun.

SnowAngel: not with terri and margaret there, it wouldn't. not for me.

zoegirl: oh

zoegirl: i was hoping you'd, you know, not let that get in the way of your good time.

SnowAngel: wouldn't that be nice *tilts head and considers alternate-reality version of enlightened and transcendent self*

SnowAngel: but, nope

zoegirl: well, then i won't go either. you and maddie and i can rent a movie instead, whatever you want.

SnowAngel: no, no, you go on. just cuz i'm a big huge loser doesn't mean y'all have to be too.

zoegirl: like we'd really wanna go to a party without you. give me a break.

SnowAngel: god, i'm pathetic

zoegirl: oh, angela

zoegirl: just . . . hold on, k? i'm *this* close to the absolute perfect plan, better than all the others combined. because finally i thought to myself, "what does jana care about? what would hurt her the most?"

SnowAngel: and . . . ?

zoegirl: i just have to work out one last kink. i can't do it in the school parking lot, because the only time she parks there is in broad daylight. and i can't do it at her house, because if her car's there, then obviously she'd be there too.

SnowAngel: can't do WHAT?

SnowAngel: no, nvm, i know yr not going to tell me. i believe you when you say yr trying, but i'll believe it MORE when i actually see results!

Fri, Apr 21, 6:30 PM E.D.T.

mad maddie: why did my coffee drink fizz all over when i opened it? WHY?

SnowAngel: ???

mad maddie: it's a starbucks double shot in a can. but espresso really shouldn't fizz.

SnowAngel: *le shrug*

mad maddie: it's scary how much money i spend at starbucks.

mad maddie: omg, they should buy me a new computer! with all the money i've given them, they totally should.

SnowAngel: yeah, good luck with that

mad maddie: so wanna come hang with ian and me tonight?

SnowAngel: what r u doing?

mad maddie: er . . .

SnowAngel: lemme guess. *starts cracking up* going to starbucks!

mad maddie: fine, make fun. wanna come or not?

SnowAngel: nah, i'd just be the sad tag-along. i'm already making y'all miss vincent's party to babysit me tomorrow night—i refuse to burden you twice in a row.

mad maddie: oh, plz

SnowAngel: one day i need to get up off my butt and take MYSELF out. no one but me. only it always seems easier to just stay put.

mad maddie: if you change your mind, you know where to find us!

SnowAngel: i just played a trick on aunt sadie, tee hee. remember that sex toy party her friend wanted to have?

zoegirl: vaguely. i remember the pole-dancing party.

SnowAngel: well, the sex toy party is part of that whole lineup, and aunt sadie finally agreed to host it, and it's set for next thursday!

SnowAngel: anyway, emma, she's the sex toy woman, has been calling endlessly to pester aunt sadie about details. would aunt sadie be willing to pose in lingerie? how many pairs of handcuffs should she bring? what about s&m, is that going too far?

zoegirl: good god. are they actually going to try the stuff out at the party?

SnowAngel: the idea is to "normalize" the sex toys so that the women wanna take them home to spice up their sex lives. but aunt sadie's insisting that emma only bring the catalogue. she can do a pole dance for her innocent niece, but she's too embarrassed to pass around a vibrator!

zoegirl: oh, wow. this is *so* not my mother's pampered chef party!

SnowAngel: so a few minutes ago aunt sadie was in the shower, and her celly beeped. i picked it up and it was a text message from someone named "dilemma." dilEMMA, get it? and the msg was "sadie, 5pm good?"

SnowAngel: so i typed back, "5pm great, but changed mind about dildos. bring lots—all sizes!" 😃

zoegirl: angela!

SnowAngel: so now emma's gonna show up next thursday with a humongous box of dildos! i love it!

zoegirl:	i don't understand the point of a dildo. doesn't it just sound gross, a fake penis that flops around in your hand?
SnowAngel:	i don't get it either. altho i don't think it "flops."
SnowAngel:	do you think they make fake vaginas for men to use?
zoegirl:	ewwwww!
zoegirl:	i don't like the thought of any of that stuff. can you imagine what doug would say if i whipped out a pair of handcuffs the next time we were fooling around?
SnowAngel:	THAT would prove yr not submissive! zoe the dominatrix, yeah!
SnowAngel:	*cracks whip* sshwing!
zoegirl:	nice whip noise
SnowAngel:	thanks! 😊
SnowAngel:	are you and maddie still coming over to watch "pride & prejudice"?
zoegirl:	you bet
SnowAngel:	i DO appreciate it, even if i don't always show it.
zoegirl:	angela, it's our pleasure. i'll be over in about an hour!

Sat, Apr 22, 6:58 PM E.D.T.

SnowAngel:	uh oh *giggles uncontrollably*
zoegirl:	what?
SnowAngel:	that woman who called? turns out it wasn't emma-the-sex-toy-guru. it was emma, aunt sadie's personal banker!
zoegirl:	oh no!
SnowAngel:	they've got a late meeting tomorrow. THAT'S what she was referring to!
zoegirl:	and you told her to bring dildos! lots—all sizes!
SnowAngel:	why would a personal banker be entered into my

aunt sadie's phone as "dilemma"?! would you trust a banker called "dilemma"?

zoegirl: maybe the point is that she *solves* dilemmas

zoegirl: also, this emma person didn't enter herself into your aunt's phone as "dilemma." your aunt sadie did, so you can't blame the banker lady.

SnowAngel: i can if i want to!

SnowAngel: she gave aunt sadie this huge lecture on identity theft after aunt sadie explained the dildo comment. *rolls eyes* like i'm gonna use aunt sadie's celly to do something evil—yeah right!

zoegirl: except you did. you used her celly to

zoegirl: omg . . . that's it!

SnowAngel: i could maybe pretend to be aunt sadie and order a pizza, but i'd still have to come up with the cash to pay for it, you know? i'm thinking emma-dilemma needs to take a chill pill.

zoegirl: no, about jana! that's totally how to make it work!

SnowAngel: by ordering a pizza on aunt sadie's cell?

zoegirl: got to go. i have to catch maddie and tell her the movie's off—she needs to go to vincent's party instead.

SnowAngel: the movie's off? why????

zoegirl: um, because i'm seizing the moment, and it's all due to brilliant you!

zoegirl: i'll call you after i kidnap Boo Boo Bear!!!

Sat, Apr 22, 10:33 PM E.D.T.

zoegirl: are you at vincent's yet? are you, are you, are you?

mad maddie: zo! be a little more obvious, will ya?

zoegirl: well that's why i'm texting! duh!

zoegirl: do you have terri's cell???

mad maddie: no, but just saw her put it down on pool table. about to make my move.

zoegirl:	remember, keep the message you send short and sweet. something like, "jana, this is your biyatch here. i'm prepared to grovel."
mad maddie:	**ok, uh, zo? on a scale of 1 to not-cool, that is SO not cool. "biyatch"???**
zoegirl:	fine, just make it sound like terri
zoegirl:	tell her to go to the buckhead barnes & noble. say that you'll be INSIDE. inside, got it? so that jana has to physically get out of her car.
mad maddie:	**I WILL**
zoegirl:	and afterward, be sure to delete jana's number from terri's call list. and put her phone back right where you found it!
mad maddie:	**i can't till you quit yer yammering!**
zoegirl:	right. very good.
zoegirl:	call me when you have news!!!

Sat, Apr 22, 10:46 PM E.D.T.

zoegirl:	just talked to maddie—she's at vincent's right this very second! she's setting up the sting!
SnowAngel:	eeek!
zoegirl:	i'm SO nervous . . . and nothing's even *happened* yet!
SnowAngel:	except for the fact that you used the word "sting." you've been watching too many episodes of "breaking bad"!
zoegirl:	this is not the time to make fun of me. i'm about to steal her most cherished possession, don't you get it?
SnowAngel:	isn't it kinda mean to trick her into thinking terri wants to make up, tho?
zoegirl:	um . . . well . . .
SnowAngel:	oh, what am i saying??? *throws conscience to the wind* trick away, you tricky girl!

zoegirl:	omigod, maddie's calling! be right back!
SnowAngel:	zoe!
SnowAngel:	can't you type AND talk?
SnowAngel:	you can't leave me hanging like this!!!!
zoegirl:	maddie texted jana from terri's phone, and jana went for it! only jana nixed barnes & noble and said to meet at a coffee house in little five points called aurora. as in *now*!!!
SnowAngel:	then go! go go go go go!

Sat, Apr 22, 11:15 PM E.D.T.

SnowAngel:	zo, where r you? why aren't you answering your phone???

Sat, Apr 22, 11:17 PM E.D.T.

mad maddie:	**hey, a, got your message. what's going on?**
SnowAngel:	it's been half an hour and zoe hasn't checked in. all she was gonna do was get to the coffee place, get the bear, and get out. where IS she?
mad maddie:	**have you called her?**
SnowAngel:	200 times, plus i sent a text. no reply.
mad maddie:	**maybe she's somewhere where she can't talk**
SnowAngel:	but where? and why couldn't she at least respond to my text???
mad maddie:	**hmmm, good question . . .**
SnowAngel:	listen, your job at vincent's is done, so i think you should say g-bye and come be with me. i can't handle being on my own and not knowing what's going on!
mad maddie:	**you got it. see ya in 5!**

Sat, Apr 22, 11:20 PM E.D.T.

SnowAngel:	zoe, plz answer! yr scaring me!!!
zoegirl:	i'm ok. don't worry.

SnowAngel: oh thank GOD. i've been imagining all these awful scenarios, like that jana caught you and stabbed you to death with her eyeliner.
SnowAngel: did you get the bear? did she c you?
SnowAngel: zoe, yr not answering again!
SnowAngel: zoeeeeee!

Sat, Apr 22, 11:31 PM E.D.T.
zoegirl: mads, i need you to come get me. call me!

Sat, Apr 22, 11:35 PM E.D.T.
SnowAngel: oh great, maddie. now UR not answering. it's been way longer than 5 minutes since you left vincent's . . . WHERE R YOU????

Sat, Apr 22, 11:50 PM E.D.T.
zoegirl: angela—we're here. we're safe. *please* don't be mad!
SnowAngel: don't tell me not to be mad! i AM mad!
SnowAngel: and who's the "we"? you and Boo Boo Bear?!
zoegirl: no, not Boo Boo Bear. maddie. she had to drive me home so i'd make curfew.
SnowAngel: drive you home from where? why didn't you drive yourself home?
zoegirl: hold on, maddie's saying something . . .
zoegirl: she's gonna head out. she says she'll call you tomorrow. and if you calm down, i'll tell you everything.
SnowAngel: *taps foot verrrrrrry impatiently*
zoegirl: ok, let's see. the last time we talked was when i was leaving for the coffee house, right?
SnowAngel: yes, and what i wanna know is how you got from there to going incommunicado. why didn't you call or text or something?!!

zoegirl:	well . . . because i was trapped in the back of jana's station wagon.
SnowAngel:	WHAT?!!
zoegirl:	i sent you that one message because i didn't want you flipping out, but even with the sound turned off, i didn't want to risk sending any more.
SnowAngel:	fyi, the not-flipping-out thing? totally ineffective! i was flipping out then, and i'm doubly flipping out now!
zoegirl:	you can stop. like i said, i'm fine!
SnowAngel:	how in the world did you end up in the back of jana's station wagon???
zoegirl:	i drove to that coffee house called aurora, and there was jana, just that second heading inside. i was like, "all right, zoe, GO."
SnowAngel:	*bites nails nervously* aye-yai-yai!
zoegirl:	she had NOT locked her car, just as we expected, because who'd wanna steal anything out of that heap?
zoegirl:	well, other than me
zoegirl:	but, whatever. i got into the backseat to look for Boo Boo Bear, and i pulled the door shut behind me so that anyone in the parking lot wouldn't wonder what was going on.
SnowAngel:	oh no. oh no!
zoegirl:	except jana came back a lot sooner than i thought. i didn't even hear her until she was opening the front door.
SnowAngel:	holy shit!
SnowAngel:	i'm like totally having an insane nervous-laughter attack as i'm reading this, i want you to know. aunt sadie prolly thinks i'm possessed!
zoegirl:	so i dove under a ratty army blanket she has and covered myself up as best i could . . . and by the

	way, i *did* find Boo Boo Bear. he smelled like spit, just like terri said.
SnowAngel:	ok, zo? soooo not interested in Boo Boo Bear. far more interested in what the hell happened next!!!
zoegirl:	well, jana cursed and slammed the car into reverse. it was obvious she was in a huge hurry, which i understood later, but right then all i could think was, "oh CRAP."
SnowAngel:	keep telling! keep telling!
zoegirl:	she drove down peachtree and turned left on some side street, and the whole time she was muttering "that bitch" over and over. i thought she was talking about maddie. i was like, "yikes, she found out maddie set her up, and now she's going to hunt her down."
zoegirl:	but it *wasn't* maddie she was talking about. it was her stepmom.
SnowAngel:	???
zoegirl:	have you ever seen the liquor store that's a couple stores down from aurora?
SnowAngel:	no
zoegirl:	turns out that's where that guy works, the guy jana's stepmom is having an affair with. and what i've pieced together, now that it's all over, is that jana must have spotted him from inside the coffee house. maybe he was getting off work, maybe that's why jana picked aurora in the first place, maybe she's been trying to catch him with her stepmom for a while.
SnowAngel:	and did she?
zoegirl:	uh huh. jana's stepmom was waiting in his car— that's why jana tailed them.
SnowAngel:	you saw them with your own two eyes? 👀 jana's stepmom with the liquor store guy?

zoegirl: she followed them to an apartment parking lot, then killed her engine. all this time i was absolutely frozen, trying not to breathe and watching as more and more frantic messages popped up from you.

zoegirl: finally jana said "f***" under her breath and got out of the car. i waited a few seconds, then peered over the seat and saw her striding to the guy's truck.

SnowAngel: omg

zoegirl: she yanked open the passenger side door, and her stepmom and the liquor store guy jerked up like deer in headlights. and . . . well . . . there was pretty much no question what they'd been doing.

SnowAngel: oh my GOD

zoegirl: and then it was awful, because jana was yelling and her stepmom was yelling and the liquor store guy was holding his hands out and going, "whoa, whoa, whoa!"

SnowAngel: geez louise, this is like a jerry springer episode

SnowAngel: can you imagine something like this happening to one of us?

SnowAngel: i mean, seriously. can you imagine one of our moms having an affair with some random liquor store guy?

zoegirl: i can't. it made me feel very . . . lucky.

zoegirl: it also made me feel like i better get the hell out of there. i tried, i almost made it, but then liquor store guy's truck roared off and jana screamed "f*** you" at the taillights. then she stormed back and kicked her tire. she was literally shaking, angela.

SnowAngel: oh man. and then . . . ?

zoegirl:	and then she saw me. i was crouched by the car and wearing the world's most shell-shocked expression, i'm sure.
zoegirl:	it was one of those out-of-body experiences where we were both like, "oh shit," and at the same time, "is this real? is this really and truly happening?"
SnowAngel:	of all the ppl in the world to be stuck with in that situation . . .
zoegirl:	i know! and with Boo Boo Bear watching it all!
zoegirl:	it was a crazy stretched-out moment, and neither of us knew what to do. then time snapped back to normal and jana lunged for me and i tripped on a beer bottle and fell on my butt. i was like, "wait! i can explain!"
SnowAngel:	yeah sure. "i can explain why i was hiding in your car when you caught your stepmonster doing it with the liquor store guy."
SnowAngel:	that's gonna go over real well!
zoegirl:	i was so far gone, i didn't care. i mean, i *cared*, i didn't want to be the horrible and-then-she-killed-her-fellow-student ending of the jerry springer show. but i also knew i was screwed no matter how i played it.
SnowAngel:	so what did you say???
zoegirl:	i told her the truth—that i was trying to get her back for everything she did to us. she was like, "the shit you were." so i explained about the kidnapping plot, which didn't come out making the slightest bit of sense, and in fact the whole convo seemed out-of-place and wrong.
SnowAngel:	if she hadn't slept with logan and done all that other stuff, you wouldn't have been there. it's her own fault.

zoegirl:	i brought that up, actually. and angela, you're not gonna like this next part.
SnowAngel:	what?
zoegirl:	i came to the part about the dead bird, and she was like, "what dead bird?"
zoegirl:	"the dead bird you put in angela's jeep," i said. "if you hadn't done that, the whole revenge thing would have been over. we would have let it go. but you did, which is why angela mailed you the baby chicks. which led to that comment you made about angela not putting out, which led to the fake health service letter, which led to you proving you're a slut by sleeping with angela's boyfriend."
SnowAngel:	damn. you go, girl!
SnowAngel:	what did jana say to that?
zoegirl:	she said, "you're f***ing pathetic, all three of you. i never put a dead bird in angela's jeep."
SnowAngel:	what?! she's such a liar!
zoegirl:	she didn't deny any of the rest of it, just that.
SnowAngel:	but . . .
SnowAngel:	if she didn't put the dead bird in there, then . . .
SnowAngel:	ohhhh *turns very tiny*
zoegirl:	maddie was in hysterics when i told her this part, just so you know
SnowAngel:	oh yeah, i bet she was. *crawls into hole*
zoegirl:	you left the window down. the bird must have flown in and rammed into the dashboard. then it died.
SnowAngel:	jana had nothing to do with it?
zoegirl:	jana had nothing to do with it.
SnowAngel:	*slinks away . . . then turns around and comes back*
SnowAngel:	jana's still evil
zoegirl:	yep, she is

SnowAngel:	she still slept with logan!
zoegirl:	she did, it's true.
SnowAngel:	r you sorry you went after her?
zoegirl:	it didn't end the way i thought it would, that's for sure. but it *did* end, i think.
zoegirl:	i saw her stepmother cheating on her dad. it made kidnapping Boo Boo Bear seem pretty meaningless.
SnowAngel:	so what was the final scene b/w you? what happened after the dead bird remark?
zoegirl:	jana looked at me like i was dirt, and then she got in her car and left. and then i called maddie . . . and you know the rest.
SnowAngel:	yr not dirt, zoe
zoegirl:	i know, neither are you. but i *am* completely worn out. i'm like a thumb-typing zombie.
zoegirl:	we'll talk more in the morning, okay?
SnowAngel:	you better believe it. we'll be rehashing this for days and months and years!
SnowAngel:	i love you, zo! YR MY HERO!!!

Sun, Apr 23, 10:02 AM E.D.T.

mad maddie:	**hey, a. found any dead birds recently?**
SnowAngel:	ha ha
mad maddie:	**just messing with ya. so can you graduate in peace, now that zoe finally went to bat for you?**
SnowAngel:	why yes, i can. *smiles radiantly*
SnowAngel:	i woke up this morning thinking, "something good happened—what was it?" and then i was like, "right! zoe caught jana's stepmom going at it with the liquor store guy!"
mad maddie:	**kind of a terrible thing to be glad about, but what is it they say? one person's pain is another's pleasure?**

mad maddie:	what do you think jana's stepmonster is gonna do, now that jana knows?
SnowAngel:	make jana's life a living hell?
mad maddie:	i wonder if jana's gonna tell her dad. what do you think he'll do?
SnowAngel:	ya got me
mad maddie:	talk about an awkward conversation. can you imagine having to tell your dad that his wife's been whacking the liquor store guy's salami?
SnowAngel:	STOP! it's possible i feel a tiny bit sorry for jana's dad, but not for jana and certainly not for her stepmom.
SnowAngel:	if i feel sorry for anyone, it's zoe. she's the one who went thru it all.
mad maddie:	when i showed up at the parking lot, her face totally collapsed in relief. and then she burst into tears. like she'd been holding it together and holding it together, and could finally let go.
SnowAngel:	i'm so glad you were there for her. if i still had the jeep . . .
SnowAngel:	grrrr!
mad maddie:	she said something really smart when i was driving her home, tho. she was like, "being there in such an awful situation DID make me realize something. that no matter what i'm feeling, i get to choose how to act."
SnowAngel:	meaning what?
mad maddie:	she said that when she was in the back of jana's car, her heart was pounding so hard she thought she might die. but she thought, "what would maddie do? what would angela do?"
SnowAngel:	hey now—why do YOU get to be 1st? does she think yr braver than i am?!
mad maddie:	yes, cuz i am
mad maddie:	and it was like a revelation to her that SHE'S the

	one who gets to define what kind of person she is, despite being scared or anxious or whatever.
SnowAngel:	ohhhh! like last year when i decided i'd had enuff of california, so i just took off. it was so liberating to realize that i could make such a bold move and not be struck down by lightning.
mad maddie:	it sounds dumb when i write it down in words, cuz of course we're the ones who get to decide how to live our lives.
mad maddie:	but still. it seems important.
SnowAngel:	it IS important. it's not dumb at all.
SnowAngel:	so should we call zo and tell her how great she is? i tried her once, but she wasn't awake.
mad maddie:	ah, let her rest. she deserves it. but tonite let's take her to din-din.
SnowAngel:	thumbs up, big buddy!

Mon, Apr 24, 8:45 AM E.D.T.

SnowAngel:	OMG, it's officially our last wk of skool! 4evah!!!!
zoegirl:	and mad's sleeping in. go figure.
SnowAngel:	lame x 100. cya at grad rehearsal!

Mon, Apr 24, 9:01 AM E.D.T.

SnowAngel:	wake up, you lazy bum!!! i'm calling you over & over till you do!!!

Mon, Apr 24, 3:55 PM E.D.T.

zoegirl:	did you see jana at graduation practice?
mad maddie:	yeah. so?
zoegirl:	she was smirking at me. snidely. she was snidely smirking at me.
mad maddie:	and again i say . . . so?
mad maddie:	you didn't expect things to change b/w you, did you?

zoegirl: well . . .

mad maddie: she snidely smirked at me and angela 2. AND she whispered something to terri about my tevas, which i ignored.

zoegirl: i think it was something about how you weren't as dressed up as everyone else. i couldn't quite hear, but i *think* that's what it was.

mad maddie: whatevs, i'm just glad my fashion statement could bring jana and terri back together again. nothing like a catty remark to mend a friendship, that's what i say.

zoegirl: i told jana it wasn't really terri who called, by the way. that night in the parking lot.

mad maddie: well aren't you sweet

zoegirl: i didn't want her thinking terri had stood her up, that's all.

mad maddie: listen, jana and terri will do their dysfunctional dance till the end of time. and if one day they realize they've wasted their lives being nasty? tuff tootle birds for them.

zoegirl: "tuff tootle birds"?

zoegirl: maddie, i'm going to miss you soooo much.

mad maddie: oh god, here we go. 1st angela with her waterworks . . . now UR getting mushy?

zoegirl: it was the graduation music that got me. otherwise i would have been fine!

mad maddie: curse marching in 2 by 2! curse "pomp and circumstance"!

zoegirl: you got teary too, don't try to deny it. and i *am* going to miss you. and angela, of course. and mary kate and kristin and DOUG . . . i'm going to miss everybody so much!

mad maddie: ian and i had another talk about next fall

zoegirl: and?

mad maddie:	he said we'll make it work no matter what. that we just have to be honest with each other and tell each other what we're feeling.
zoegirl:	awww
zoegirl:	i hope you guys *do* make it. and doug and me, too. do you think we will?
mad maddie:	i don't know. but at the same time, i don't see why not.
zoegirl:	yeah. i like that way of thinking about it.
mad maddie:	what did doug say about your jana adventure?
zoegirl:	he was shocked. and he told me how stupid it was, which was oddly gratifying. he was being mr. protective.
mad maddie:	a little too late for that, bucko
zoegirl:	it changed the way he looked at me, i think. in a good way.
mad maddie:	that's awesome

Tues, Apr 25, 5:45 PM E.D.T.

SnowAngel:	heya, zo. i'm txting on this beautiful day to tell you that even if you super-duper want to, you can't ask me out for dinner tonight.
zoegirl:	uh . . . okay. only i never was planning on asking you to dinner. was i?
SnowAngel:	i'm just saying that if you got a wild urge for burritos, you'd have to call mads. not me. k?
zoegirl:	right. well. that was out of nowhere, but sure.
zoegirl:	anything else going on? did mrs. evangelista decide whether your exam's gonna be take-home?
SnowAngel:	*huffs in indignation* i can't believe yr talking about exams instead of asking me to dinner. do you not WANT to ask me to dinner?
zoegirl:	you just told me NOT to!
SnowAngel:	so?

SnowAngel:	i make this big deal out of telling you and maddie that i'm not available for dinner, and do either of you even fight it? nooooooo, yr both just like, "sure, whatevs, is your exam gonna be a take-home?"
zoegirl:	sweetie. r we having an angela moment?
SnowAngel:	it's like yr not even aware that we only have 3 more days of school. THREE MORE DAYS to enjoy just being us, and then come exams, followed by graduation, followed by 5 billion zillion graduation parties. and the parties will be fun, but they won't exactly be winsome-threesome intimate. i'm just SAYING.
zoegirl:	oh good heavens
zoegirl:	angela . . . would you like to go to dinner tonight?
SnowAngel:	oh, thank you so much for asking! that is so thoughtful! *hugs zoe and smothers her with smooches*
SnowAngel:	but no, i can't. sorry.
zoegirl:	!!!!!!!!!!!!!!!!!!!
SnowAngel:	i'm taking *myself* out, that's why. this is STAND TALL FOR ANGELA DAY, and in my brain i will be saying "hahahaha" to logan and every other boy on the planet, cuz i do not need a boy to be complete.
SnowAngel:	i'm going to have a lovely time if it kills me, and that's why i can't drag you or maddie along. make sense?
zoegirl:	yes, altho you could have just said that.
SnowAngel:	g2g. gotta go primp for my hot date—with myself!!!

Wed, Apr 26, 4:45 PM E.D.T.

zoegirl:	hola, madikins. big bunny is gone 4ever, squeezed out by the Crusty Pines Executive Housing Complex, Phase III.

mad maddie: ah, the end of an era. and with big bunny gone, susie, lulu, and round-headed boy r safe and sound.

zoegirl: they wouldn't be if it wasn't for susie

mad maddie: so true. we can learn a lot from susie, can't we?

zoegirl: like what?

mad maddie: like . . .

mad maddie: like that the forest is out there whether we like it or not, and we can't just stay in our pretty houses and lock the doors. we have to make the bold move. but what we CAN do, when we venture bravely forth, is be aware of giant pink bunnies. that's the lesson we all should heed!

zoegirl: ohhhhh. i thought it was that only a few people like bunnies and trees, but everybody likes executive housing complexes.

mad maddie: look at you, quoting the bunny! nice!

zoegirl: tina and arlene came by today. the jehovah's witnesses. i think we've reached the end of an ear there, 2.

zoegirl: oops—end of an ERA.

mad maddie: if it was the end of an ear, they'd be like vincent van gogh, who cut off his own ear. did you know that?

zoegirl: as a matter of fact i did

mad maddie: can you imagine cutting off your own ear? and then afterward holding it in your hand and being like, "huh. not so sure why i did that . . ."

zoegirl: not something i see myself doing

mad maddie: no, i suppose not

mad maddie: so why was it the end of an era with tina and arlene?

zoegirl: i think they've had enough of me and my heathen ways, that's all. even though in reality i'm so *not* a heathen.

mad maddie: let's consider. you lied to your parents about your princeton application. you had (and are continuing to have) pre-marital sex—and in a CHURCH, no less! you hitched an illegal ride in the back of jana's car . . .

mad maddie: yr sure yr not a heathen?

zoegirl: God is bigger than all that—what's important is that we try to be good people. that's what i told tina and arlene.

mad maddie: did you tell them about the pre-marital sex part?

zoegirl: yes. bet you thought i didn't, huh? but i'm not ashamed of it.

mad maddie: what did they say?

zoegirl: arlene looked extremely disapproving, and tina—she's the young one—looked shocked. arlene said something like, "well, everything happens for a reason," implying that i could learn from my mistakes. but i was like, "i don't believe that."

mad maddie: you don't believe we can learn from our mistakes?

zoegirl: no, i don't believe everything happens for a reason. people who say that are imagining God up in the sky, making things happen. but in reality, WE'RE the ones who make things happen. and when crappy things happen anyway, WE choose how to respond. that's what i meant.

mad maddie: tell that to glendy, will ya? she's definitely a "hand in the sky" kind of gal, altho for her it's more superstition than God.

zoegirl: she sent you another chain letter?

mad maddie: yeah, but this one's FOR REAL!!! (note ironic use of all caps)

mad maddie: i'm supposed to tell everyone i love how much they mean to me, and if i don't, i'll have bad luck for the rest of my lifelong days. oh, and i was supposed to do it within the hour. whoops.

zoegirl: i can't believe you didn't. don't you love me???

mad maddie: of course i do, i just don't need any stupid email telling me to proclaim it.

zoegirl: awwww

zoegirl: you honestly can block her name from your account, you know.

mad maddie: she'd just hack her way back in.

mad maddie: anywayz, it'd be a shame to let such drivel go to waste. one of these days i'm gonna come up with a genius use for glendy's crapmails, just wait and see! 1 of these days i'm gonna

zoegirl: yr gonna what?

mad maddie: ooo, baby, i gots to go—i's been inspired!

Thu, Apr 27, 6:08 PM E.D.T.

SnowAngel: tomorrow's senior mudslide! yeahhhhhhh! *takes flying jump onto oozing hill of mud*

mad maddie: what a great way to go—last day of classes and an oozing hill of mud.

mad maddie: you gonna try to pull anybody in?

SnowAngel: heck yeah! mrs. evangelista, if she's foolish enuff to come near me. that'll be her payment for sticking us with our sucky take-home exam!

mad maddie: i'm so jealous of zo. after tomorrow, she's DONE. as in, kaput, finito, no more classes and not a single exam. so unfair!

SnowAngel: quit complaining. at this point, final exams r just a formality. it's all about closure, baby. 😁

mad maddie: so. dude. you said something in the parking lot about an idea you had—then zoe came up and the convo somehow veered off. what's the scoop?

232

SnowAngel: right, i'm so glad you remembered!

SnowAngel: friggers, i just spilled my coffee all over my frickin
               shirt. one sec.

SnowAngel: k sorry, i'm back

mad maddie: i once spilled an entire dr pepper on the keyboard
               of my laptop. totally ruined it.

SnowAngel: ooo, sux for you

mad maddie: so, yer idea?

SnowAngel: well . . . i think we should all wear our hair in pigtails
               tomorrow! for National Pigtails Day! 🎎

mad maddie: i'm drawing a blank. nat'l pigtails day?

SnowAngel: from zoe's princeton essay! when we say "screw it"
               to being a grown-up and wear our hair in pigtails
               and slide down the mud hill and just have fun!!!

mad maddie: ohhh

SnowAngel: plus we would look so cute. plus it would be a way of
               saying "yay for us," cuz sure, we're graduating from
               high school, but that doesn't mean we're letting go
               of our carefree youth.

SnowAngel: you in?

mad maddie: YEAH!

mad maddie: should i be pumping my hand wildly in the air?
               somehow that seems appropriate.

SnowAngel: pump away, babycakes. and then call zo and tell
               her our plan, now that we've both agreed. i can't,
               cuz i've gotta help aunt sadie get ready for her SEX
               TOY PARTY which is tonite. ahhhhhh!

mad maddie: buy me some fudge-flavored body icing? plz plz
               plz?

SnowAngel: to use with ian? ooh-la-la!

SnowAngel: OH, and don't forget to turn in your senior quote!
               tomorrow's the last day to get it in if you want it
               included in the graduation program!!!

SnowAngel: you outta the shower?

mad maddie: **yeb'm, altho that mud took some serious scrubbing.**

mad maddie: **shall i come get you for our supa-dupa celebration?**

SnowAngel: first let's enjoy the moment . . . altho we can't w/o zoe, now can we?

mad maddie: **do-over, and include zoe too**

SnowAngel: friends! 'ello!

zoegirl: hi!!! i was hoping y'all wld text!

mad maddie: **heya, zo. were you able to salvage your sneaks?**

zoegirl: no, they're goners. oh well.

SnowAngel: you should have gone barefoot *wags finger in zoe's face*

SnowAngel: you looked adorable in your pigtails, tho

mad maddie: **ahem. and me?**

SnowAngel: yes, maddie, you looked adorable 2. we ALL did. *preens happily*

zoegirl: you guys, i can't tell you how much i loved it that we did that. i'll print up my phone pics tomorrow and make copies.

mad maddie: **i got a good shot of when doug pulled you in from the side, heh heh heh**

SnowAngel: omg, that was so funny!

zoegirl: to you, maybe! you weren't the one tumbling headfirst into the slime!

SnowAngel: you know you loved it 😊

SnowAngel: .seems like things r better than ever with you guys, yeah?

zoegirl: i guess so. i hope so!

zoegirl: i still get worried about next year—sometimes to the point of hyperventilating—but then i just slow down and *breathe*. it is what it is, you know?

SnowAngel: and what it IS is fabulous, schweetheart.

SnowAngel: think about it: for all intents and purposes we r DONE WITH HIGH SCHOOL 4-EVAH!!!

mad maddie: and tonite we're celebrating with just us 3, right?

SnowAngel: correctamundo

mad maddie: no ian

zoegirl: no doug

SnowAngel: and NO JANA. i have washed my hair of that girl once and for all!

zoegirl: altho i DO have something to say about her, real quick

SnowAngel: nooooo *covers ears*

zoegirl: no, this is good

zoegirl: i couldn't help but notice her today, since she was totally showing off and playing to the crowd, and you know what i realized?

mad maddie: that her thong was tracking mud into her woo-woo?

SnowAngel: ewww!

zoegirl: no, what i realized was that jana never won, even when we thought she did.

mad maddie: how do you figure?

zoegirl: think about it. maddie's back with ian, and they're like the couple of the century. i've gotten over (or at least am in the process of getting over) my codependency issues. and yes, jana slept with logan, but angela, you took yourself out for a solo date to houston's, cuz that's how strong you are!

SnowAngel:	hate to point it out, but i didn't take myself to houston's until AFTER you and jana had your showdown.
zoegirl:	the key elements were already there. you DID break up with logan before the showdown, after all. which was also before you knew he and jana had slept together.
mad maddie:	it's true. jana was beaten before she even began. and speaking of . . .
SnowAngel:	yessssss?
mad maddie:	well, even tho zoe is absolutely right, i decided jana needed a touch more winsome-threesome love to take with her after graduation. so i put in a little email to our friend the glendinizer.
SnowAngel:	no!
mad maddie:	i told her hi, and that i sure have appreciated her chain letters over the months. i mentioned that as a matter of fact, i knew a girl who could really benefit from said chain letters. i told her all about jana's tortured past, and suggested that deep down what jana needs is to be showered with love.
SnowAngel:	maddie!!!! *shrieks and has a coronary*
mad maddie:	i passed along all of jana's deets, and here's the real stroke of genius. i told glendy not to ever EVER give up, and that if anyone knows how to connect with others, it's her. think that pushed the right buttons?
SnowAngel:	jana's gonna have glendy latched on for life! 😊
zoegirl:	you're awesome!
mad maddie:	aren't i?
SnowAngel:	*flings self to ground and hugs maddie's knees* i love you so much!
SnowAngel:	*hugs zoe's knees too* and you, of course! i have the two bestest friends in the universe, and we will

	ALWAYS be there for each other . . . even if you guys r stupid idiots who feel compelled to go far far away to college, you naughty children!
mad maddie:	**yr not gonna start guilt-tripping us again, r you? cuz angela, yr gonna have to get over it one day. you know that, don't you?**
SnowAngel:	actually . . . i do
zoegirl:	you do?
SnowAngel:	just lemme explain something, something i've been thinking a lot about. when i lived in el cerrito last year—i have never been that lonely in my life. i missed you guys sooooo much.
mad maddie:	**we missed you too**
SnowAngel:	yeah, but you guys had each other. i was all alone. and it made me feel . . . un-whole. and i'm so afraid that's gonna happen again this fall.
zoegirl:	oh, angela!!!
SnowAngel:	but like i said, i've been thinking a lot about it, and— *gulp*—i'm gonna try really hard to stop being such a baby about it.
mad maddie:	**you haven't been a baby about it, you've just . . .**
SnowAngel:	been a baby about it. yeah.
SnowAngel:	but just cuz we're splitting up doesn't mean we're "splitting up." i mean, we can visit each other, right?
zoegirl:	of course
SnowAngel:	and we have to text and call and skype every single day!!!
mad maddie:	**DUH!**
mad maddie:	**(except maybe not skype *every* day. mark says that the freshmen who do that kinda get ragged on. like, cuz it makes it seem like they can't let go of home.)**
SnowAngel:	can we still skype sometimes?
mad maddie:	**of course**

SnowAngel: well ok then *straightens spine in a queenly fashion*
               maddie, you may go to santa cruz. and you, zoe,
               may go to kenyon. i give you my permission.

zoegirl: thanks, angela. your support means the world to
               me.

mad maddie: ah, dudes. life is good. in fact i had a zen moment
               about this very thong, when i was driving home
               from school all muddy and disgusting.

SnowAngel: this very "thong"?

mad maddie: *THING*, u freak

mad maddie: the window was down and my music was blasting
               and i was like, i am the sun on my skin. i am the
               clouds in the sky. i'm everything i've ever seen or
               done or felt or heard, and one day i will be gone.

SnowAngel: now THAT'S cheerful

mad maddie: no, just . . . we're our own destiny, that's all. and
               one day we WILL be gone, so we better appreciate
               life while we can.

SnowAngel: i get it. it's like my senior quote, from that beetles
               song: "blackbird singing in the dead of night, take
               these broken wings and learn to fly. all your life, you
               were only waiting for this moment to arise."

zoegirl: i love it! that's a *great* quote, angela!

mad maddie: but it's BEATLES, you doof. not scurrying little
               insects.

zoegirl: mads, what'd you put for your quote?

mad maddie: after much deliberation, i went with a classic that
               perfectly captures my life philosophy.

zoegirl: which is?

mad maddie: "there's something strange about that giant pink
               rabbit . . ."

zoegirl: HA!

SnowAngel: huh?

zoegirl: i can't believe you . . . but then again, i totally can.

SnowAngel: i don't get it. will someone plz explain?

mad maddie: they're words of wisdom from my role model, the great and wonderful susie.

zoegirl: who dared to enter the forest, and who triumphed despite all odds.

SnowAngel: what forest? what odds?

mad maddie: go to big-bunny.com and all will be revealed.

mad maddie: what's yours, zo?

zoegirl: originally i was gonna use that quote from shakespeare. "this above all, to thine own self be true."

SnowAngel: aw, that's nice

mad maddie: gross, barf, vomit. and the character who said it, that polonius dude? total windbag! you can't use something from him!

zoegirl: well, i didn't. i ended up going with something from dr. seuss: "don't cry because it's over. smile because it happened."

SnowAngel: oh, zoe!!! *blinks back tears unsuccessfully*

mad maddie: it's absolutely perfect . . . even tho thanks a lot, now you've got ME all weepy!

zoegirl: me 3. i can't help it!

mad maddie: NO! STOP! the point is to REJOICE, not fall to pieces.

SnowAngel: omg, yr so right *lifts chin and sniffs in snot bubble*

zoegirl: i'll try if y'all will

mad maddie: damn straight we will

mad maddie: so what r we waiting for? it's time to party!!!!!

SnowAngel: *flings mortar board jubilantly into sky*

SnowAngel: come pick me up, ya big softie!

zoegirl: and then me! i'll be waiting at the door!

mad maddie: u sure as heck better be

mad maddie: l8r, g8rs!!!

THE WINSOME THREESOME
ARE BACK!
TURN THE PAGE FOR
A SNEAK PEEK OF

yolo

THE LATEST
INTERNET GIRLS BOOK,
COMING AUGUST 2014!

mad maddie: omg, i'm finally here! I'VE FINALLY JOINED THE COLLEGE GIRL RANKS!

mad maddie: do i get my special beret now?

SnowAngel: maddie! wh-hoo! 💣 and wh-hoo, UC santa cruz! sooo smexy, babe!

mad maddie: not smexy, and wld u plz delete that word from yr vocab?

mad maddie: but it *is* SO FRICKIN GORGEOUS HERE, i can't even tell u.

mad maddie: i'm outside the dorm we're staying in for orientation, and the sky is so blue and the forest is everywhere and there are no cars and tons of sunshine and I LOVE IT.

SnowAngel: we have the sky and the sun in athens, too, dumb-dumb. and! omg! we also have 🌲🌲🌲

mad maddie: is different. is stunning. and so are the students, as apparently it is the law that all california kids must have good genes. i might have to dye my hair blond.

SnowAngel: yr hair is already blond

mad maddie: eh, fair enough

SnowAngel: it's still weird to me that yr just now starting the semester. u *do* realize that i've been at UGA for over a month, and that zoe's been at kenyon for almost as long?

mad maddie: yes, angela. yes, i do. do *u* think i've lived in a time bubble for the last four weeks? do u think i wanted to stay in atlanta—IN MY PARENTS' HOUSE, WITH MY PARENTS WHO STILL USE TV TRAYS SO THEY CAN EAT TOTINO'S FROZEN PIZZA WHILE WATCHING "THE FAMILY GUY"—after everyone else in our class sailed away into their new lives?

SnowAngel: first of all, i'm sure yr parents heat up the pizza
               before eating it, silly.

mad maddie: u'd be surprised

SnowAngel: and second of all, it's just that . . .

SnowAngel: it's like zoe and i have graduated, practically, while
               you're still a wee freshman. *pats wee maddie on
               her blondie head* *uses teensy voice* look at you,
               all grown up wearing yr big girl college beret!

mad maddie: yeah, that's lovely, angela. thx, babe.

**mad maddie: but i did a lot of thinking on the five-hour flight
               from atlanta to san jose.**

SnowAngel: but UCSC is in santa cruz. uh-oh, i think u went to the
               wrong college, mads.

**mad maddie: haha. and btw, can we rewind to make sure u
               heard what i just said? my FIVE-HOUR flight??**

**mad maddie: FIVE HOURS, girlie! and for the whole five hours,
               i was in airplane bondage next to a man who
               watched episode after episode of "House Hunters"
               on his iPad WITHOUT WEARING HEADPHONES.
               what was wrong with that dude?**

SnowAngel: "House Hunters" normal or "House Hunters
               International"?

**mad maddie: he was on a plane full of other ppl. how cld he
               not know to wear headphones? i kept wanting to
               say something to him, but i didn't. and then i kept
               hoping that one of the flight attendants wld say
               something to him, but none of them did! ever!!!**

SnowAngel: i like "House Hunters," even tho it's fake. the couple
               already knows which house they're going to buy
               before the show is filmed—did u know that?

SnowAngel: at first i felt a little disillusioned. *single tear*

SnowAngel: then i said, "ah, wtf."

mad maddie: ok, great, thx for sharing.

mad maddie: now back to what i was saying, which is that i did some thinking on my long-ass flight, as i believe i mentioned.

SnowAngel: *nods* you did

mad maddie: then i did even MORE thinking on the shuttle from san jose to santa cruz.

SnowAngel: ah, a shuttle! clever girl, u! 🚅

mad maddie: and all that thinking led to a brilliant idea. 💡

SnowAngel: awesome. let's hear it.

mad maddie: you know the expression "you only live once," right?

SnowAngel: as in yolo? *lifts eyebrows*

SnowAngel: um, yes, maddie, i know the term yolo. the ten-year-old my sister babysits knows the term yolo. my *grandmother* knows the term yolo. a bit overused, but still fun to say.

SnowAngel: *pretends to be girl from ricola commercial* *throws back head atop a snow-capped mountain*

SnowAngel: RI-CO-LA!

SnowAngel: oops. i mean . . . YO-OH-LO!

mad maddie: uh huh. well, "yolo" has to do with you and me and zoe and how we've all—corniness alert—gone our own ways. we're growing up and shit.

SnowAngel: mmm. corn. num num num.

mad maddie: but . . . (more corn is about to come, deal with it) . . . just cuz we're growing up doesn't mean we have to grow apart.

SnowAngel: aw, little sweetie. that IS corny. 🌽

SnowAngel: i'm all about making the best of life since we only get one chance at it, absolutely. but before we go any further, can we agree that if we keep using "yolo," we'll have an implied understanding that we know it's on the 🌽-y side?

mad maddie: omg. being in a sorority has made u way too concerned about what other ppl think, hasn't it?

SnowAngel: no! *huffs indignantly*

mad maddie: yr right. my bad. you've always cared too much about what other ppl think.

SnowAngel: maddie!

mad maddie: kidding! 😊

SnowAngel: 😊

SnowAngel: so what's yr brilliant idea?

mad maddie: oh! yes!

mad maddie: it's more of a plan than an idea.

SnowAngel: mmm-kay, a plan. and the plan is . . . ?

mad maddie: well, it's pretty simple. simple but important.

SnowAngel: okay, and . . . ?

mad maddie: it's just that i think we shld all—

mad maddie: shit, my orientation leader is calling everyone over for a group activity. i better go.

SnowAngel: *deadpan stare of disbelief*

mad maddie: SWEAR TO GOD i'm not messing with u. i'll call or text as soon as i can, i promise.

SnowAngel: don't use drugs! drugs make you stoopid! that's what the orientation person's going to tell you!

mad maddie: kk, i won't—and don't u, either!

Why were your books banned and do you personally believe that they should have been?

Lots of my books have teen girls in them. Teen girls sometimes talk about sex. Teen girls sometimes have sex. Lots of grown-ups would like to believe that this is not true. I am not one of those grown-ups, and I think it's important and meaningful to give readers stories that reflect reality—in a respectful way. Like, not salaciously, but with the intent of saying, "Let's look at how this story played out. How'd it seem to work out for so-and-so?" And then the readers—who are SMART, damn it—can grapple with those issues themselves. And no, I do not believe my books should have been banned. I do not believe that any author should be banned, ever. Freedom of speech, dude. :)

What's your response when you are censored? Are you ever frustrated, or do you take pride in it?

At first I cried. And called my editor and apologized, because I felt so terrible about it. Now I take pride . . . but it requires a bit of emotional effort, because it still hurts to have people say, out loud and with venom, "Your books suck. YOU suck."

What was your favorite part of writing the Internet Girls series?

My fave part of writing this series was NOT HAVING TO WRITE SETTING. I hate setting. In other books that aren't purely written in text/IMs, my annoying (awesome) editor makes me include setting, and it is hard.

Which of your characters is most like you, and which character do you wish you were more like?

I'm most like Winnie from the Winnie Years series. She's a good girl, funny, tries to do the right thing. Often gets into embarrassing situations. I once ran over a squirrel on my bike.

Whom do I wish I were more like? I'm going to go with Cat from *Shine*, because she has courage in spades. She doesn't let the haters get to her. Sometimes I do.

How do you come up with your characters?

I follow my children around as they go through their lives and I spy on them. I wear a trench coat and carry a notepad. I am vair vair subtle.

Except, really, I do.

As an author, what's your average day like?

Oh, an average day of writing means MAKING MYSELF WRITE. And then thinking, "Oh, this is fun." And then writing some more.

What do you think books offer that other forms of entertainment don't?

Books engage readers in a more intimate way than other forms of entertainment/media, I think. They encourage critical thinking.

What is your very best life advice?

Best advice? Sheesh. Imagine life is like this: You're waiting at a red light. You're stuck there. You didn't choose to be, but there you are. How are you going to spend your time? Bitching and moaning and looking at your watch, or thinking INTERESTING thoughts? Looking at the beautiful sky? Laughing at a joke? So, use this life WISELY—we're dead a lot longer than we're alive—and leave the universe a better place than when you got here.

ACKNOWLEDGMENTS

Oh, bless my stars—so many people to thank! Which is lovely, yeah? Because it just confirms that the world is a big bundle of goodness, with people helping one another all around. So first and foremost: Thank you, world! (I'm cheesy, what can I say? But I totally mean it!)

Smilies galore to the hundreds (omg, thousands?) of girls who have contacted me through MySpace or my Web site. You all keep me real and give me soooo many fab ideas. And, of course, smilies to those sweet guy readers who e-mail me, too. Be proud! There are more of you than you think!

Thanks to Amy Winfrey for being the genius behind Big Bunny, thanks to Amber Kelley and her friend Cherie for helping me figure out my Boo Boo Bear problem, thanks to Brittany Lesser for her insights into the "evil girl" psyche, and thanks to the amazing and talented Melanie Dearman for her incredibly helpful feedback on the first draft of the novel. Thanks to Sarah Burnett for her naughtiness regarding the chicks. And thanks most emphatically to my friends and family, just because.

Thanks to my agent, Barry Goldblatt, for fearlessly embracing the bizarre culture of teenage girls as seen through the eyes of an oldhead (that would be me) who can't quite seem to grow up.

Thanks to everyone at Abrams for making the book so spifftacular, especially: Scott Auerbach, who is so good with details; Celina Carvalho, the gal responsible for the adorable cover art; Jason Wells, publicist and cutie-pie extraordinaire; Erica Finkel, goddess of cool and slave-driver of scary fierceness; and the ever brilliant Susan Van Metre, who makes these books what they are. I'm not kidding. Any good things, give credit to Susan. Any crappy parts, blame on me!

Finally, all the thanks and love in the world to Jack, Al, Jamie, and Mirabelle. You guys make my life so sunny, and that's why I'm able to spread some of that sunlight in my books. I love you!!!

ABOUT THE AUTHOR

LAUREN MYRACLE is the author of many books for teens and young people, including the *New York Times* bestselling Internet Girls series, *Shine*, *Rhymes with Witches*, *Bliss*, *The Infinite Moment of Us*, and the Flower Power series. She lives with her family in Fort Collins, Colorado. Visit her online at laurenmyracle.com.